THE YOUNG RUNAWAY COWBOY

BY RICH MANN

Proverbs 3: 5-8

Rich Mann

DEDICATION

I would like to dedicate this book to the memory of the first man that encouraged me as I started my adventure in writing many years ago.   He believed I could write and gave me very kind but helpful criticism. He was a lover of the many stories and books of the old west. I am sorry that he did not live to see the completion of this work. That great man of God was Pastor Mark Malles.

ACKNOWLEDGEMENTS

I must give a great note of thanks to Eunice Holbert who corrected my manuscripts and encouraged me significantly. Her patience and encouragement were priceless. Not least, I truly appreciate my wife, Kathy, who gave me continual encouragement. Lastly, thanks to all my students who had to listen to me read my story to them, sometimes, before it was finished. It was so nice of you to say you liked it!

CHAPTER ONE

"Tom! Tom! Thomas! Git out here and help us git these birds out of the corn! I already let ya oversleep an hour now, and if we don't keep the birds off the fields, we ain't gonna have any crop left! Tom! Tom! Git yourself out here!" Tom's pa hollered through the window.

Tom Fleming rolled over on his narrow cot and sat up, rubbed his eyes and scratched his tousled red hair. *Poor ole Pa,* thought Tom. *Here he goes and lets me sleep in 'cuz we was up late last night since I let the cow get out the far gate.*

As the eleven-year-old boy raced to put his worn work clothes on, his mother came in red faced and out of breath. "I ain't never seen the likes of it before!" she exclaimed between gasps of breath. "I ain't never seen the likes of it before!" she repeated herself. "I ain't never seen so many birds on one man's place in my whole life! Those birds are almos' fearless. Why, they don't hardly fear man or beast, much less those ole scarecrows we put up. I think I know how the Egyptians felt now when God sent them plagues."

With that outburst, Ma Fleming suddenly got a gleam in her eye, and jumped up almost like something had just struck her for the first time in her life. Falling to her knees before her tattered-looking bed, she cried out, "Oh, God! Why are you doin' this to us? We ain't done nothin' wrong! We ain't bothered your people! Why, God? Why? Oh, please make them birds go away!"

As Tom finished buttoning his shirt, he leaned over to look out the small frame window of the one-room shack his family called home. Now he realized why his mother was so out of breath and upset. Crows, ravens and blackbirds seemed to be coming in like a dark storm for his pa's cornfields. Tom knew that his father was depending on these crops for the future winter food supplies and the little money that was necessary to see them through the long, cold winter that lay ahead.

Pa Fleming had worked from sunup until sundown constantly for almost five months now. Often he would come in overly tired, eat whatever Ma could scrape together, and then lie down and fall right off to sleep, mumbling something about weeds, rain or fences.

Tom remembered all too well last winter when they almost froze to death and food supplies were so scarce that they had to make do with one meager meal a day for almost a month. Tom remembered, too, how his pa had labored day after day plowing row upon row of the prairie sod in early spring only to get barely enough rain to produce just enough to survive on. Now the second crop had been planted, fenced and cared for much like a mother would care for a newborn baby.

There was one particular night that Tom could remember well. That was the night he had come in from milking the cow in the barn just in time to see his pa kneel down by the bed rather slowly and humbly. Tom had tiptoed on bare feet over to the kitchen counter and set the milk pail down just in time to hear his pa say, "Lord, you know that we need help. This here is the second crop; the first didn't do no good, and now this here second crop is dryin' up again."

Tom stood motionless by the sink not knowing what to do. He had never heard his father pray so intensely. Gradually Pa's voice changed and then began to tremble. It was the kind of awesome sound almost never heard except from a widow at the funeral of her wonderful husband.

"Oh, God!" Pa continued with quick gasps of breath between sobs. "Please send some rain to us and let these here crops grow and produce and save our poor souls!"

Tom had never heard his pa pray that way before, and now he was not sure what his reaction was to be. Almost without knowing it he began to cry, and at the same time he heard his mother starting to cry somewhere in the room. Tom looked to see his mother but could not because his eyes were so wet that everything looked as if he were trying to wear an old man's glasses.

Pa Fleming had straightened himself up shortly thereafter, called his son and middle-aged wife to him and hugged them both. He patted Tom on the head and back and motioned him to go to bed.

Tom had lain in bed for a little time thinking about things. He tried to pray but found that he could not. Then somewhere, something out of the black awakened Tom. He sat up and listened. It was rain! Tom hollered at the top of his lungs, "Rain!"

Tom's parents bounced out of bed almost at once, and without bothering to put other clothes on, they all ran out into the downpour. The night was so black that absolutely nothing could be seen, but the Flemings knew what they felt streaming down their faces. They ran, they jumped, they hollered, they laughed, they shouted, and they squealed until they ran out of breath and fell down together in the mud with the rain continuing to pour all around them in the pitch black.

Then, right there in the slush and all, Pa had got on his knees and prayed, "Lord, we give Thee thanks!" In fact, to young Tom it seemed that Pa prayed that one sentence about fifty times. Ma had started crying again, and that was something Tom had not been able to understand.

All these thoughts of the events of the last five months had flashed through Tom's head before his feet left the creaky wooden stairs of the front porch. *And now the birds!* thought Tom. *Why the birds?*

As Tom ran toward the fields, he felt a heavy sinking feeling within him. Pa was in the middle of one beautiful tall cornfield, with stalks some two feet above his head, and he was hollering, yelling and probably waving his arms. Tom could not see his pa yet, but he could hear him. It was easy to tell where Pa was because the birds would fly up momentarily as Pa moved, but then circle and fly right back down.

Tom felt helpless! What could he do? What could his pa do? Tom knew that nothing could be done. The birds were upon the cornfields like grasshoppers, and their ability to destroy the fields was much greater.

Tom ran down the narrow trench between the corn stalks toward his pa and felt tears of grief and anger form in his eyes as the leaves swatted him in the face. The birds swarmed in and out around him. Finally, after heading back down the next row, Tom saw his pa.

The anguished look on Pa's tear-streaked face must have been much like the look on Tom's face; Pa was an adult, though, so at least a part of the tears were not there. Pa's face was red, redder than Tom had imagined possible. He was yelling at the birds with all the ability God had given any one human being.

"It's no use, Pa! It's no use!" Tom hollered.

Pa turned and looked at Tom. "No use, you say?" Pa screamed. "What do you mean no use? Did anybody say 'no use' when I plowed, when I sweated, when I hurt, when I worked, when I tried to feed the mouths of the likes of my poor family last winter? Well, did they? Huh? Did they?"

Tom did not know what to say. He knew that if he said anything, it would probably be wrong, so he just stood speechless and shook his head back and forth. Big tears were rolling down his tanned cheeks.

"Okay then," Pa said with his voice only slightly toned down. "Run and holler and scream and shout and don't quit 'til these birds leave here!"

Pa turned and started running, hollering and waving his arms with renewed vigor. Tom did likewise but was not sure his Pa knew what he was doing.

One long hour later, Tom felt his voice giving away, his arms tiring, and his entire body starting to ache. He slumped down out of breath between some green stalks of corn. It felt so good to sit still and rest although the birds overhead continued their noise and the devouring of the crop. It was then that he noticed a strange quietness. Yes, the birds were still flapping their wings, the crows were cawing, and all the other varieties were still chattering, but Pa was not to be heard.

Alarm flashed through Tom as he remembered the red face his Pa had and the strange glint in his eyes. He felt scared.

Forgetting his aching body, the boy ran back toward where he had seen Pa last, but he could not find him. Then he ran to the shack to find his mother. As he went into the room, he found her lying exhausted and asleep on the colorful old quilt bedspread. Tom tried to speak but found that he had lost his voice. Instead, he grabbed his mother's arm and tugged on her until she woke with a start.

"Huh? What? What is it, Tom?" she asked. "Tell me!"

Tom repeatedly pointed to his mouth and tried to speak. His mother finally understood that he had lost his voice. Then Tom pointed toward the fields. Ma was still puzzled, so Tom went and grabbed an old handkerchief that belonged to Pa, looked at it, and shrugged his shoulders.

When Ma understood, she lifted her skirt as high as her knees and ran out the door. One leap later she was off the porch and into the fields. Ma speedily looked down the end of each row of corn while Tom hurried off in the opposite direction toward a different field.

Thoughts raced into Tom's head. *What if we can't find Pa? What if I can't find Ma?* That thought caused Tom to look back over his shoulder to reassure himself that Ma was in sight. In a moment, he stopped and retreated. His ma had motioned to him to come. He knew that she had found Pa.

Before Tom reached his mother, she hollered for him to draw a pail of water and bring some rags. Quickly, Tom ran to the well and dropped the rope and bucket in until he heard the familiar splash, and then started turning the crank with all the ability an eleven-year-old boy can muster.

Tom did not think about the fiery pain in his weary arms as he ran to the house, picked up some rags, and hurried to his mother with the bucket of water. He found her sitting on the ground between crowded rows of corn with Pa's head in her lap. Pa was holding completely still. Tom wondered if his Pa was dead, but he could not ask because he still could not speak.

Ma soaked the rags, placed them on Pa's forehead and bathed his red face with water. Ma had loosed Pa's shirt and was now bathing his red chest. She sat doing this for quite some time, then said in an unbelievably calm tone, "Take yourself a drink of this water, Tom."

The drink was very refreshing to Tom. It was the first time he had thought about himself since he first noticed his father was not yelling. The water helped his throat a little, and Tom croaked out the question that had been haunting him: "Is he dead?"

"Naw, he ain't dead, Tom. He's just overdid it and is a-restin'. He got himself too hot," explained Ma.

Tom and Ma sat quietly for quite some time. The birds overhead were as busy as ever. Tom felt anger inside himself that he could not quite understand. He had the urge to run and catch a bird and squeeze the very life out of it, and then yell to the rest of the birds that the same would happen to them if they did not leave. Tom knew, however, it was no use; and with that thought in mind, and seeing his pa there on the ground like he was, he started to cry in a rather babyish, blubbering way.

Something smarted across Tom's face. For an instant, Tom was startled. Then he realized that his mother had slapped him and was saying, "Ain't no use for you to start goin' and actin' like that! You're gonna have to be strong, Tom Fleming; you're gonna have to be strong! Our next move is to git your pa into the house, and it ain't a-gonna be easy."

Ma did not say anymore. She just sat there looking frustrated. She really did not know how to get Pa to the house, which was perhaps a quarter of a mile away. It seemed it would be impossible for her and Tom to get Pa there. Tom thought about the carriage they used to have. Pa had gone to town last winter and traded it for food for the family; however, they still had their mare and two plow horses.

"Shall I go get Blackie?" Tom asked in a quiet voice.

"Yes, Tom, get Blackie–and bring a saddle blanket," Ma replied thoughtfully.

When Tom had brought the big black mare near the row of corn Pa was in, he took the saddle blanket to his ma. She rolled Pa on his side and slipped the blanket under him, rolled him the other direction, and unfolded the blanket so that Pa was lying on the blanket. "Now, Tom, let's see if we can drag your pa to Blackie," Ma said with a strained tone in her voice.

In about fifteen minutes, the two had managed to drag Pa to where Blackie was patiently standing at the edge of the cornfield. Ma stopped and rested. The late summer sun was bearing down upon them. "Gotta hurry; this sun isn't good fer yer pa, Tom!" she exclaimed out of breath.

Straining hard, Ma and Tom managed to stand Pa straight up and balance him next to Blackie. Tom could not understand why his pa was so limp. Carefully, but with much effort, Ma was able to lean Pa stomach down on the side of the mare. "Try and hold yer pa right there!" she said to Tom as she ran around

Blackie and grabbed the arms of her husband. "Now push, Tom! Really, really push!"

Slowly Pa fell into place over the mare's back, and the two headed straight for the house. Blackie seemed to understand the importance of her mission, and it seemed to Tom that she stepped extra carefully as she hurried along.

Ma led Blackie right up onto the porch and stopped in front of the open door so that when they slid Pa off Blackie's back, he sat right down in the doorway and leaned backwards into the house. The same kind of effort that it had taken to get Pa onto Blackie's back finally got Pa onto his bed.

Ma started to work over her husband like a mother hen over her little chicks. She had no thought for her own tiredness, but managed to tell Tom that there was some bread in the breadbox, and to help himself to some milk out of the cobbler. Tom sat down at the small, homemade wooden table, eating quietly, watching his mother bathe his pa with cool water. She opened the windows just right in order to blow any breeze that was to be had onto his pa.

The next thing that Tom knew, his ma was shaking him to wake up. Startled, Tom looked up and over to where Pa lay.

"Ma, how is he?" Tom asked.

"No change, Tom. Do you think that you could ride into town an' see if you can git Doc Jordan to come out an' take a look? You've gone into town several times with yer pa; you should know the way," said Ma.

As Tom stood up, he found that his legs and arms felt like the creaky door on the barn from all the running he had done. His mother noticed, and as he headed toward the door, she stopped him with a hand on his shoulder and said in a very motherly way, "Thank you, Tom; be careful."

Tom went out and found Blackie not far from the barn, saddled her up, and stepped into the stirrups and headed toward the farm gate. As he stooped to unlatch the gate, his ma hollered,

"Tell Doc Jordan that if he needs more than one dollar that we kin give him Pa's old shotgun."

The seriousness of the situation hit Tom as he rode past the bird-deluged cornfields. Apparently Blackie felt the urgency; and without Tom nudging her, she started into a gallop and soon settled into a nice lope which she kept most of the fifteen miles to Dale Town.

As they approached town, they slowed to a walk and Tom hopped off and walked next to Blackie. Tom knew where to go to find the doctor. He headed straight for the Golden Wheel Saloon. He had heard his pa say several times that Doc Jordan would be a great doctor if he could just leave the bottle alone.

The sun started to cast its setting rays on the town as Tom stepped into the saloon. The lamps were dim inside and already the local ranchers and range hands were starting their usual rough play and wild jesting.

"Hey, boy! Wha'cha want? We don't serve no milk in here!" Tom was not sure, but he thought the voice came from a table in the corner on his left.

He turned and said, "Lookin' for Doc Jordon!"

"Over here!" said another voice, but it was not Doc Jordon's.

Tom walked to where the second voice had come. A range hand sitting next to a man with his head on the table motioned that the man was Doc.

"Doc! Doctor Jordon! Wake up!" shouted the boy. "You have to come and help my pa! He had somethin' go wrong with him! He won't move or anything!" Although Tom yelled, the doctor did not move.

The man next to him just looked rather sorry and said, "In about two hours you can probably talk to him. By then he'll sober up."

Tom walked dejectedly toward the saloon's swinging doors. Outside he found Blackie drinking from the trough in front of the saloon. Automatically Tom grabbed the reins of Blackie and forced her from the water. He knew that if the sweat-covered mare over drank she would get bloat, and he did not need any more problems right then.

Tom slowly walked Blackie around the town while he was waiting for the doctor to sober up. The mare cooled down, and Tom tied her and walked down toward the sheriff's office. Inside, Tom met a man that both Tom and his pa had been very fond.

"Well, hello, Tom," a familiar voice said. "What do you be a-doin' here?"

Before Sheriff Roy Cunningham could understand it all very well, Tom blurted out all the problems that they had on the farm, how his father had fainted as if he was dead, and how he could not get the doctor to wake up.

The sheriff did not say anything, but he walked over to the Golden Wheel Saloon with a determined look on his face. Tom stayed outside and watched through the window. Sheriff Roy strode over to where Doc Jordon was flopped, reached down, grabbed the man under the collar, and picked him up and dragged him outside. Once outside, he leaned down and lifted the doctor onto his shoulder much as a man might carry a big bag of flour. Seeing Tom again, Sheriff Roy said, "Come on over to the office with me, Tom. We'll see what we can do."

Inside the office, the sheriff poured a cup of coffee and forced a little down the mouth of the slumped doctor. Immediately the doctor growled, "Dan't dooo thaaaat!" Roy, however, just continued to dump coffee into the man's mouth. About half of it ran down the doctor's worn coat and onto the wooden floor.

After a short time the sheriff half dragged, half pushed the doctor outside and into the water trough. The doctor came alive enough to crawl out of the trough but then slumped into the dirt. "I shoulda done that first!" Roy exclaimed while he dragged the doctor back inside to pour more coffee down his throat.

After watching this rather spectacular scene, Tom again began to feel anger and resentment build up inside him. *Why did my pa have to have this happen to him? Why did the only doctor for over a hundred miles around have to be the town drunk? Didn't anybody know, didn't anybody care that my pa might be dyin' and even now might be dead?* Then, for an instant, Tom visualized his pa kneeling by the worn-out bedspread and crying to God for help. Something inside told Tom to pray, but something else told him not to. Whatever it was, won out, because Tom found he could not pray.

A groaning, moaning, half-talking, half-sputtering noise broke up Tom's thoughts and he heard Sheriff Cunningham say, "Now listen here, Doc! Jason Fleming is a sick fellow, and his son Tom has ridden all the way in to get your help. Now drink some more coffee!"

Tom stepped back inside. Doc Jordon now had his eyes open, and the dim light of the sheriff's office seemed to be hurting them, but at least he was showing signs of life.

Finally, Doc Jordan was able to hold on to his own coffee cup and started asking for the details about Jason Fleming. As Tom explained, the doctor started waking, and the look of an intelligent man started to appear.

"Tom," said the now almost-sober doctor, "go over ta my office an' get my black bag. You'll find it jus' behind my desk. Then go over ta the stable and tell Joe Booker ta saddle my horse fer ya and then bring 'im over here."

When Tom had done all this, he and Sheriff Roy helped Doc Jordon into the saddle and handed him his black bag, which he tied securely to the saddle horn. Just before they left, Sheriff Roy stopped Tom and said, "I'm really sorry I can't ride along with you, Tom; I'm expectin' trouble in town tonight, but I think things will be all right if I can stay here. I'll sure be a- prayin' for you, though." Then the sheriff stuck several pieces of jerky in Tom's shirt pocket.

Automatically, just as Tom's father had taught him, Tom said, "Thank you."

Tom and the doctor rode off slowly into the black night, heading toward the Fleming farm. Doc did not say much; and when Tom would say something, Doc just grunted or mumbled something under his breath that Tom could not hear, so Tom quit trying to talk to him. It was going to be a long ride to the farm. Several times Blackie tried to run, but Tom felt it would not do to ride off and leave the unreliable doctor.

Tom's young mind turned over repeatedly as he rode along. The events of the past few hours kept going through his head. He could not get out of his mind the last phrase the sheriff had said: *"I'll sure be a-prayin' for you, though."* *To think a full-size strong man and sheriff like that would pray! Or would he? Was it just an expression, or did he really mean it?* wondered Tom.

Tom ate the dry jerky and continued to roll his thoughts around in his head. He thought about his pa. Tom had really grown to love him. He was a large man, husky, not tall, but very strong, yet he had a gentle way about him, and up until today Tom had never seen his pa so fierce upset. Again, Tom thought about the prayer his pa had prayed. *Had it helped?*

Tom heard the doctor say, "Wake up, boy; you're gonna fall off that mare directly."

Tom straightened up and looked around about him. "How long have I been asleep?" he asked the now hung-over but wide-awake doctor.

"Oh, about an hour, Tom. I don't think I've seen anybody sleep in the saddle as well as you've been doin' without fallin' out! Yonder is the light of yer farm, isn't it?" said the doctor pointing toward a very yellow dim light.

As Tom strained to see, he felt his eyes blur over, probably from lack of sleep and rest. "I think so, Doctor," said Tom in a still-raspy voice caused from the shouting he had done earlier that day.

The doctor reached into his worn coat, drew out a large round watch and leaned out of the way of the moonlight to see the hands. "12:30. Now's about the time that a lot of sick folks make their decisions as to get better or not," he said, sounding more professional than ever. "Let's hurry up a little and git over there!"

The doctor lit out at a good gallop, and Tom took out after him, trying to catch up with him, but could not. The dust was so bad that Tom decided to slow and let it settle before continuing home.

Upon reaching the house, just as Tom was about to open the door, his mother stepped out and said that she thought it best that he not go in while the doctor was helping Pa. In almost a daze because his head was spinning from the exhaustion he was experiencing, he put Blackie up for the night and milked the cow. Lastly, he threw some hay to the plow horses, headed back toward the house and met his ma on the porch.

Ma sat down on the porch and leaned back against the house. She breathed out a breath of air that told Tom that she was also exhausted. The boy sat down by his mother, putting his head on her shoulder, and he started to tell her his adventures in bringing the doctor back. He shortly fell asleep.

The next morning the sun shone upon the Fleming shack and farmyard in the same way that it had for almost five years. This morning, however, a strong farmer named Jason Fleming did not greet it; it was greeted by only one young Tom, his son, who had just finished going through the most exhausting and trying day of his short life.

Tom woke to the crowing of the rooster and the mooing of the cow–and again the swirling of the birds above his pa's cornfields. As Tom lifted himself up from off the quilt that his mother must have put on the porch for him, he felt every muscle in his body ache. Slowly he rallied himself, although his mind felt fuzzy, and the full recollection of yesterday's events did not seem to want to enter his head. Tom sat just staring at the edge of where the bright light of the huge warm sun was shining.

Shortly the farmhouse door opened and his ma came out. "How do you feel, Tom?" she asked.

"I'm okay, Ma; how's Pa?" asked Tom.

Ma did not reply at first, and Tom did not try to force her.

"He woke up for a little while last night, Tom. He could not move a thing. He said to tell ya that he was sorry fer yellin' at ya the way he did," said Ma quietly.

Big tears came to Tom's eyes. This time Ma did not slap Tom; she had those same tears in her eyes, too.

"Yer pa's dying, Tom," she sobbed out.

Tom did not say anything. He only sat with those big tears dripping down his nose onto his dirty bare feet.

The doctor came out and said that if they wanted to see Pa again before he died, they had better come in now.

Tom looked at Ma and saw that she was drying her tears on her apron. Tom tried to wipe his tears off with his fingers, but he could not seem to get his eyes to quit watering.

Stepping into the room, Tom saw his pa for the first time since he had left home yesterday to get the doctor. Pa was lying in bed with his head propped up by two pillows. Tom noticed that Pa's face was very white. He walked slowly over to the bed and looked down at the man who just the day before had stood strong, proud and able. Now his pa was still–very still–so still that Tom was frightened. *How fast does a man go from the strong to the weak?* he thought.

"Pa?" Tom said quietly.

Pa opened his eyes. A very weak smile appeared on his face, and Tom heard in a muffled whisper the voice that only yesterday boomed at the birds. "Tom, I love you and I'm sorry I yelled at you so roughly yesterday. You're a very good boy, Tom, and I'm so proud of you! May God make you a great man to honor Him. Please forgive me for yellin' like that. No young boy your age should have to go through a thing like tha...." Pa's voice trailed off.

"Pa! Pa!" exclaimed Tom, and leaned over and hugged the neck of his pa. "It's okay, Pa, just get better! Please get better, Pa!"

The words were wasted because Pa never heard them. When Tom next looked into the eyes of his pa, he saw eyes that could no longer see. Tom turned and looked sadly at his mother and the doctor. The doctor leaned over and closed Pa's eyelids. Ma told Tom to stand back, and the doctor pulled the worn blanket over Pa's head.

Tom went to his cot and lie down, not ready yet to believe that his pa was dead. He heard the doctor consoling his mother. Then it occurred to Tom that maybe there was a reason why men drink and become drunkards. Again, Tom tried to pray. In fact he said, "Oh, God!" but what he wanted to say would not come out. Instead, he said, "Why did you let my pa die?" He felt that God had not been fair to him and that God had done him and Pa a great wrong.

The lowing of the cow from the barn interrupted Tom's thoughts. He got up, afraid to glance toward the bed that his dead pa lay on, and walked out toward the barn. The warm sun felt good on him, and the warm dust of the farmyard felt soothing to his bare feet. *Funny that I can even think of anything being good at a time like this,* thought Tom.

After taking care of the animals, Tom walked back to the farmhouse. Inside, the doctor sat at the table drinking something from a cup. Tom knew that it was not coffee. Ma had some scrambled eggs ready for everyone. Pa had always prayed at the dinner table before. Now who was to pray? Ma looked up to heaven and, with tears running down her cheeks, said, "God, I don't understand what you've done here, and, God, I don't know why you took Pa, but have mercy on us!"

Ma bowed her head and cried alone for a while. Doc began eating his eggs, and Tom tried to eat his too. He had eaten two bites and was chewing on the third when he felt something burning in the pit of his stomach, then in his chest, then in his throat. He got up and ran outside toward the barn. He stopped near the water trough and let loose of all the material in his stomach. Then he fell face first into his mess, cried, rolled in the dirt, and screamed, "Pa, Pa! Yur dead! Yur dead! Oh, why'd ya have to die Pa? Why? Oh, God, why'd ya take my pa from me? It's not fair!"

Tom lay in the dirt sobbing his heart out for as long as one body can cry, and then seemed to cry some more. After that, he lay there just breathing heavily until he fell asleep. Later he awoke with the burning sun blazing down upon him.

Tom got up and stumbled over to the water trough his pa had built. He climbed in and just lay in the cool water for about thirty minutes. Finally, Tom got out and walked toward the house. He noticed out back of the house, near the well, near the two trees his pa had planted not too many years ago, the doctor and his ma were digging a hole. Tom knew what it was. He walked over and offered to help.

"I think Pa would like it here, don't you?" Ma tried to ask in as cheerful a manner as she could muster.

"Yeah, I guess so, Ma," replied Tom sadly.

It was not long before the Doc and Tom had a box built. Ma dressed Pa in his best clothes–which had several patches on them–and combed his thin hair. The doctor and Ma together carefully laid Pa's body in the coffin. Then together they all half carried half dragged the coffin out to the grave. Ma leaned down and kissed Pa's lips one last time. Tom looked down upon his father just before they nailed the lid in place. He reached inside and gave his pa one last squeeze on the neatly folded hands. He cried. Tears fell from his eyes, and mucous ran from his nose.

Ma brought the family Bible out to the graveside. That big old book meant something to Tom. He had been told how it had belonged to his Grandfather Fleming and great-great-grandfather– and maybe another grandparent –until it had come to this country after passing over the ocean, which Tom had never seen.

Now, Ma stood reading it over Pa's coffin and saying something about Jesus coming and comforting one another with these words and some other things that did not make any real sense to Tom. Besides, Tom did not see how just words were going to help anybody. They would not bring Pa back.

Using ropes and Blackie, the experienced doctor helped them lower the coffin. Ma said something about "dust to dust and ashes," and then threw some dirt on top of Pa's coffin. Tom then helped shovel the prairie sod over his Pa. Pa was buried.

Slowly the three walked back to the farmhouse. As Doc prepared to leave, Ma brought him the only dollar she had and offered him the shotgun. Doc took them both.

"Thank you, Doc Jordon. You've been more than helpful, even though Jason died," she sobbed out and ran into her house.

The doctor looked sadly toward Tom. "I'm sorry, Tom. Goodbye."

Tom gave the doctor just a little wave and watched as the man slowly rode away.

Quietly Ma cleaned up the house for a while and then offered to make some supper. Tom said that he did not think that he could eat anything. They retired for the night shortly after the cattle were given their care.

CHAPTER TWO

Tom sat next to the window of the dusty stagecoach as it bounced along the sandy, granite road. He had been riding a long time without talking and was getting extremely restless and tired of the hard seat.

"Ma, can't I ask the man up top to let me ride up there with him? I'm so tired of this cage and bouncin' I could just scream! And these here clothes make me itch!" declared Tom.

"Just be patient, Tom. We should be at the way station before long and then I'll let you ask, although we may be stayin' for the night," replied Ma with a slight coarseness caused from the long ride and dust. "Just look at that beautiful desert out there, Tom! Isn't it somethin'!" she exclaimed.

"Yeah, somethin' all right. All you could ever grow in it would be them cactuses, and they're worthless. What good is it, Ma? I wanna go back to the farm!" stated Tom angrily.

There was a silence for a long minute, and then Ma said, "It ain't no use arguin' no more, Tom. I've already decided, and it's final. There's no way you and I could've ran that farm without your pa. Why, we almost starved and froze to death last winter **with** him! What do you think would've happened **without** him?"

"Ah–Ah, Ma," Tom replied with a quiver in his voice as the hard-riding stage hit a bump. "We coulda made it, if you just woulda let me try. There was still a lot of corn left, even after the birds. Why, we coulda made it; I know we coulda!"

"Enough is enough!" interrupted Ma. "What I've decided is decided. Here comes the way station now."

The old stagecoach pulled up to a small dust-covered ranch house and stopped with a final lurch. Tom jumped out and ran around to the well and water trough. The windmill overhead was turning slowly from the slight breeze so that the storage tank rising ten feet above the water trough was leaking a little water over the top. Tom picked up the tin can hanging next to the pipe that ran from the tank to the trough and filled it with water running out of the pipe.

"Ahhhhh, boy, is that good!" exclaimed Tom. "I can't hardly believe there's such delicious water in the desert. Want a drink, Ma?" asked Tom.

"You bet I do, after that dusty ride!" replied Ma as she took the tin can from Tom's gracious hand.

As Tom's ma drank of the cool desert water, Tom's gaze landed on a boy about his size and age. The boy was wearing light blue coveralls and had no shirt or shoes. His skin was very dark brown, tanned from all the summer sun.

The boy had noticed Tom, but he went on helping the stagecoach driver loosen the four horses and then led them over to the water trough near Tom and Ma Fleming, smiling as he looked at them.

"We'll be spending the night here," yelled the driver. "I'll get your bags in just a few minutes."

"Well, I'll go mosey into the house and see if anybody needs help with the supper," said Ma. "Tom, don't you wander off now."

"Okay, Ma," replied Tom as he noticed the boy smiling at him.

"Hi!" said the young boy. "My name is Pete Smith; what's yours?"

"T-Tom F-Fleming," stammered Tom. Tom was not used to having other boys his age around, and now his words came awkward to him. "N-Nice to meet ya. Nice place ya have here."

"We like it," replied Pete. "Wanta come with me over to the barn to put the horses up for the night?"

"Sure!" replied Tom.

Together the boys put the horses in the barn for the night, and Pete explained to Tom all about the way station. Pete was a superior talker, having gained much experience from working at the stage stop with his parents. Tom helped Pete curry the horses, and soon both boys hurried for the house.

Inside the stage stop, Tom saw a long wooden table with twenty chairs seated about it. A steaming bowl of beans was in the middle, and a huge platter of meat was sitting next to it.

"Just in time, boys!" said a strange voice from the kitchen. "Have a seat anywhere handy there. We're just about ready to eat."

Tom figured that the lady must be Pete's mother. Mrs. Smith was heavyset and about the sturdiest woman that he had ever seen.

The five people sat down at the table, and Mrs. Smith placed some delicious-smelling rolls on the table. The stage driver and Mrs. Smith started right in eating, so Tom figured that no one was going to pray.

"Yer pa ought to be home any time, Pete," said Mrs. Smith. "Henry went to town early this mornin' to bring back a load of hay. It's real hard to keep supplies out here in the desert."

The words were not out of her mouth good when the front door squeaked open and a fairly tall, dusty man walked in.

"Sorry I didn't get home before dark," said Henry Smith. "I just didn't feel like pushin' them horses any harder in this heat." He sat down and began eating.

"Boy am I tired! There's been some big happenin's in town. The bank was robbed last week, and the sheriff landed a bullet in the leg. I guess he's gonna be okay, but he prob'ly will develop a limp for the rest of his life. They haven't caught the men yet. There was two of them. Pass the bread please," said Mr. Smith.

"Which way were they headin'?" asked Mrs. Smith with a frightened look on her face.

"No one's sure, but they think they headed east out of town, out this way. You didn't see anyone, did you? They said one man had a pretty long beard," answered Mr. Smith.

"Did they get away with the money?" asked the stage driver.

"Yep, ole Jess at the bank says he figures they got away with over eight thousan' dollars!" answered Mr. Smith.

"Eight thousand dollars! Why, that's more money than any one man can shake a stick at!" replied Ma Fleming.

By the time supper was finished, the group had made plans to keep someone up as a sentry all night.

"Hey, Tom, do ya wanta go swimmin' with me?" asked Pete.

"Swimmin'?" asked Tom with a look of amazement.

"Sure!" exclaimed Pete with a big grin on his face. "Every once in a while I go swimmin' in the big water tank out at the front of the place. It's almost seven feet deep! You can swim, can't cha?"

Ma said that he could go swimming for a little while, and soon two young, naked, wiggly bodies were splashing, yelling, and having a great time in the tank.

"I have a big rock in the bottom of this tank," said Pete.

"Watch!" Pete dived to the bottom of the tank and reappeared with a rock about the size of a double fist. "Think you can do it?" asked Pete.

"I'll try," said Tom just before he went under. In a few seconds, he came back up with only some green slimy stuff and said, "I can't find it!"

"Of course ya can't!" laughed Pete, "I didn't drop it yet!"

Tom reached out and tried to dunk Pete but found Pete gone, and a sudden jerk on his leg told Tom that he was about to get dunked himself.

After the boys had tired out, they clung to the sides of the water tank and talked. Tom told Pete about the farm and the death of his father. Pete listened with interest.

"Where are ya goin' now?" asked Pete

"Ma wants to go to California. I have an aunt over there that runs a sewin' shop that my ma is gonna work for. Ma is real good at sewin," answered Tom.

"Have you gone to school yet?" asked Pete

"No, I've never been, but my ma has taught me how to read and write some. How 'bout you?" asked Tom.

"Well, I used to, but when we moved out here from Red Rock about three years ago, it became too far away to go to school. I can read and write a little, too," answered Pete.

The boys were silent for a while. The moon started to rise over the distant mountains and was nearly full so that the boys could see around quite well. They talked and swam around some more.

Suddenly Pete said, "Sh-h-h-h! I think I hear horse tracks being made."

Both boys got extremely quiet, and the water in the tank leveled off.

"Look over there!" exclaimed Tom quietly pointing towards the road leading to Red Rock.

Not too far down the road could be seen two horsemen riding quietly towards the ranch house.

"Do ya think that they're the bank robbers?" asked Tom.

"Could be," whispered Pete.

Tom started to go over the side of the tank to warn the people in the stage stop, but Pete pulled him back into the water.

"Sh-h-h-h! It's too late. They'll see ya!" Pete whispered forcefully.

Almost as he said it, the two men stepped off their horses at the bottom of the water tank. Tom and Pete peaked over the side of the big tank in time to see the two men head toward the door of the ranch house. One man had a beard.

"Oh, no!" whispered Pete. "This'll prob'bly mean that we are gonna be robbed again!"

"Again?" asked Tom.

"Yes, again! We've been robbed three times!" answered Pete.

As if Pete were some kind of a prophet, the two boys watched as the two men drew their guns and then knocked on the door. When the door opened, the men barged in and shut the door.

"What should we do?" asked Tom.

"My dad says that it's best to give them what they want and that way avoid gettin' hurt. I'm sure tired of this, though. My parents have lost a lotta money on accounta of these hold-ups," whispered Pete angrily.

"I wish I had a gun! I'd stop 'em!" exclaimed Tom.

"Yeah, or even a big club!" exclaimed Pete.

The two boys looked at each other and said together, "Or even a large rock!"

Pete dived down and came back up with the rock.

"Wait!" exclaimed Pete, "There's two of them, and we only have one rock."

"Yeah, that **is** a problem. Maybe we could also jump on 'em!" exclaimed Tom.

Both boys perched near the tank edge in a manner that they felt would keep them from being seen. The quiet desert breeze blew over them, and they both started to shiver. Tom started shaking so hard he felt that he was going to fall. Just when he knew that he was going to have to get back into the water, the front door opened and the two men walked out backward. Each had a big sack in one hand, and their gun in the other. They slowly edged towards their horses, and just before mounting, they stuck their guns into their holsters.

"Whoop!" went the sound of Pete's rock on the head of the man with the beard. At the same time Tom leaped out onto the back of the other man knocking him confused into the dirt. Henry Smith saw what was happening, ran to the outlaws' horses, and pulled a rifle from one of the sheaths. Tom had somersaulted some distance away from the man, and Mr. Smith aimed the rifle at the robber as he sat up in the dirt.

"If I didn't know better, I'd say that I was attacked by a naked little kid!" said the outlaw mingling his words with profanity.

The outlaw put his hands up, and the stagecoach driver went around behind him and drew the revolver from his side. Tom hurried back up the ladder and got back into the water tank.

The warm water felt good to Tom and started to relax his tense nerves almost at once. Tom thought that his hard-beating heart would surely splash water out of the tank.

The boys peered over the side of the tank and saw Mr. Smith and the stage driver take the two outlaws to the barn. The outlaw with the beard also had a large bump on the head and had to be aided to the barn.

Tom and Pete hurried down the ladder and dressed as soon as their mothers went inside the stage stop. The boys went to the big brown, dusty barn and watched as the two men tied the outlaws securely to separate posts.

"Go get these men's horses!" ordered Mr. Smith.

"Yes, sir!" replied Pete with the sound of anxiety in his voice as he turned and ran to get the outlaws' horses.

Tom and Pete led the horses into a stable towards the center of the big barn and started removing the saddles and saddlebags. Tom thought that in the saddlebags he might find all that money if these men were the outlaws that had robbed the bank.

When the stage stop owner and stage driver finished securing the outlaws, they went through the men's saddlebags and found what they expected. The bags contained more paper money than Tom thought existed in the world.

After giving the outlaws something to eat and drink, the group retired to the ranch house for the night. Tom's mother gave her son a lecture about doing dangerous and foolish things and scolded him quite soundly for jumping upon the outlaw. Tom felt that this was quite strange because after all, if he had not jumped on the outlaws, they would have gotten away.

The two boys spent the night on a couple of small mats up on the flat roof of the porch of the ranch house. It was cooler up there according to Pete. After two hours of restless wiggling and talking, the boys finally went to sleep.

Some time in the night, Tom heard a couple of adult voices talking but did not wake up enough to listen. Then in his dreams, as he was about to jump on the outlaw for the hundredth time, the morning sun hit him square in the face and he bolted upright. Pete was gone, and the smell of delicious, hot bacon filled the air. Tom jumped down from the porch with a sigh of delight and turned to face his mother who reached for him and gave him a big hug.

"Tom," she said while no one else was around to see or hear. "I didn't mean to be so hard on ya boy. It's just... well, I..." Ma Fleming developed big tears in her eyes. "I didn't mean to be so hard on ya, but you're all I have left except for yer aunt, and if anything happened to ya I just don't know what I'd do. I prayed a long time last night and really thanked God that when ya jumped on the outlaw he didn't turn and shoot ya through the head. I'm proud of ya, Tom, but I'm worried for ya too. Don't go and do foolish things like that any more!"

"Okay, Ma," Tom answered rather carelessly. "Where is Pete? What have they done with the outlaws? What are they gonna do with the money?"

"Pete and his pa have tied the outlaws tightly in the stagecoach and have just sat down for breakfast like we should be doin'. Go wash yer face and git in there," answered Ma Fleeming.

The stagecoach was soon on its dusty, bumpy ride again, only this time it carried the two prisoners and the money that they had stolen from the bank in Red Rock about thirty miles away. Behind the coach were tied the two horses of the robbers, and on the top of the blackest horse rode Tom with a grin from ear to ear.

"This is more like it," thought Tom as the horses trotted behind the dusty stagecoach. There was a sad feeling inside of him, though, as he thought of having to leave Pete Smith behind at the stage stop. Pete was the first boy that Tom had ever developed a friendship with during his now eleven years of life.

The horses trotted as the coach slowly rolled along the trail while Tom was enjoying the ride and doing some recalling of the last twelve hours of his life.

Tom had not thought much about the possibility of himself dying before; but when he thought of how his ma had developed those big tears in her eyes, he realized that he must have done something dangerous. Tom recalled the words of his mother: "I thanked God that when you jumped on the outlaw he didn't turn and shoot ya through the head." It bothered Tom that his mother had prayed for him like that. Tom had begun to think that God didn't care about him after what had happened to his pa. But now, maybe God **did** care. *After all,* thought Tom, *what if the outlaw had seen me coming and shot me?* Tom's mind was mixed and twisted over this matter. He could not quite figure whether God cared for him or not.

These thoughts had put Tom in a daze, and he tried to push them out of his mind as the miles dragged by. He was soon able to do so because the road became rougher and rockier as they passed through a mountainous section. Tom had never seen mountains like these until he had gone west. Now they were something to look at with awe. Tom wondered how they got there.

The next few hours of Tom's life became a foggy blur to him. For an instant he felt something slug him onto the ground. Then he felt rocks and dirt passing by all around, tearing at him, choking him, and bruising him, until he came to rest next to a huge prickly pear cactus. Blurred vision and hearing kept Tom from clearly perceiving that someone was holding up the stage.

The boy dropped into unconsciousness, but woke briefly to find himself inside of a very fast-moving, rough-riding stagecoach. The intense burning, gnawing pain in his shoulder caused him to cry out in distress.

Tom looked over the edge of the seat he was on and saw the stage driver lying in a pool of blood. With immense effort and with a fear that no one was driving the coach, Tom lifted himself up and looked out the window towards the driver's seat. To his amazement Tom saw his mother cracking a whip at the horses, and heard her yelling furiously for them to go faster. The coach hit a chuckhole, and Tom fell back inside.

CHAPTER THREE

The residents of the small town of Red Rock were used to the stage coming in pretty much on time and without much of a commotion. Today, though, they welcomed the stage early and in a manner that caused more excitement than even the recent bank robbery had.

Before the stage was recognizable, the people heard it coming and saw a cloud of dust behind it that told them something was wrong. Almost everyone dropped their lunchtime activities and gathered in the street.

"I need a doctor! Where is the doctor? Somebody help me!" yelled the red-faced Elizabeth Fleming before the stage had actually entered the east side of the town. Ma Fleming repeated herself several times using different intonations that only a woman in distress can make.

At first the people were speechless at such a sight, but they quickly directed Ma to the doctor's office. The doctor, his attention aroused by the commotion, was standing in front of his office.

The people had the doors open before the stage was stopped completely. They quickly carried Tom and the stagecoach driver inside Doc Raymond's office. Both victims were unconscious as the doctor and Frank Woods, the local general store owner, started working on them.

"Press right here on this wound, Frank, while I check the driver," ordered the doctor. He checked the driver's pulse, rechecked him, and then sadly and slowly pulled a cover over the man's head. "It's too late," he said quietly.

Doc then turned to Tom as Mrs. Fleming entered. She hysterically asked, "Is he gonna live? Will he be okay?"

"I don't know yet, ma'am. I'll do the best I can to help him," replied the doctor calmly.

"Oh, God, please, please don't let my boy die!" screamed Ma Fleming, and then she burst into uncontrollable sobs.

Doc motioned to a townswoman. "Clara, please take this lady to your place. I'll send word as soon as we know anything."

That afternoon and night found Tom's mother and Frank Woods in the room above the doctor's office sitting by Tom's bed as Tom unconsciously tossed, turned, and worked off a fever. Frank kindly brought Elizabeth Fleming her supper and tried to cheer her up as she wiped her son's forehead with a damp cloth.

"I've seen a lot of cases similar to this in my many years of helpin' the doctor, and I can honestly say that I'm sure he's gonna make it okay," said Frank reassuringly.

"Do you think he'll lose his arm?" asked Ma Fleming.

"Nah, Doc said that he was very lucky 'cuz the bullet entered and left his shoulder without hittin' any major parts," answered Frank.

Sometime late in the night Tom's fever broke, and Tom fell into a deep sleep. Late the next morning Mrs. Fleming awoke in the chair she had been in most of the night. A feeble voice said, "Ma! Ma!"

Ma jumped up and leaned over Tom, kissed him, hugged him gently, started crying and saying, "Praise God! Praise God!"

"Ma, my arm hurts! Where am I?" asked Tom all in the same whispered sentence. "I'm thirsty!"

Tom's mother poured the boy a glass of water, pulled herself together, and tried to answer Tom's questions.

"I'm sorry your arm hurts, Tom. I'll get the doctor right away. We're in the little town of Red Rock, and you've been unconscious since about 11:00 o'clock yesterday mornin'. We were in a stagecoach holdup!" answered Ma.

Ma left the room and soon returned with Frank Woods and Doc Raymond.

"Well, I see our young patient is waking this morning. How does the shoulder feel, Son?" asked the doctor.

"My shoulder hurts really badly, Doctor!" said Tom in a whispered moaning voice.

"Yes, I knew it would, Tom, and so you are going to have to take to drinking at an early age or endure the pain. A shot of whiskey every couple of hours or so for a day or two will get you through the worst of it," said Doc Raymond.

Tom's mother nodded that it would be all right and Frank Woods produced a shot glass and a bottle of strong whiskey.

"Here, Son," said Frank. "Drink 'er down!"

Frank held the glass to the boy's lips, and Tom gulped the whiskey down, choked, wheezed, gasped for air, and complained about his stomach hurting.

Doc started changing Tom's bandages; and before he was done, Tom was in a state of semi-consciousness.

"Mrs. Fleming, Tom is going to be all right. His temperature has come down, his color is coming back, and the wound looks like it will heal just fine. His arm and shoulder will be okay, but it will be some time before it's back to normal. You should wait at least two weeks before you try to travel with Tom. Even three weeks would not hurt. As soon as possible, we need to move Tom over to the boarding house or hotel or wherever you prefer. I use this room, as you can see, for emergencies, and so try to keep it ready."

"Of course, Doctor," said Ma Fleming.

Frank offered to help Ma get herself established at the boarding house. "Be real glad to help, Mrs. Fleming. I have a young man at my store who can cover 'til I get back."

After helping settle Mrs. Fleming, Frank invited her to breakfast at the Red Rock Cafe. Walking across the dusty street, Ma saw the little cafe and thought that it was charming.

Seated at a small table by the front window, Ma Fleming was delighted to see Clara Newman come to their table as the waitress. "Clara, how nice to see you again!" exclaimed Ma, using her best English. "I can't thank you enough for helpin' me when I was so upset yesterday. Doc Raymond said Tom is gonna be all right!"

"I'm so glad to hear that, Elizabeth! I was worried. Listen, I'm busy because I'm short of help, and business is good. I'm owner, cook and waiter! You wouldn't be lookin' for work, would ya?"

"Well...I, uh, uh, maybe, until Tom can travel!" exclaimed Ma.

"Let me know," said Clara after she had taken their orders.

"How can this town be so busy?" asked Ma as she watched the street.

"Well, the ranchin' business has become very profitable, and the Red Rock area has been growin' in ranches and cattle, creatin' a bigger need for the town," explained Frank Woods.

The two ate breakfast together and talked. Ma found that Frank had lost his wife two years ago when he was forty, and Frank learned that Elizabeth had lost her husband two months ago when she was thirty-eight. They soon discovered things of interest to talk about.

Just as Ma and Frank were finishing breakfast, the sheriff of Red Rock limped in with the aid of a crutch. He ordered coffee and sat down by Frank and Elizabeth.

"How's the leg, Sheriff? asked Frank.

"Sore, real sore, but healin'," said the sheriff.

"Well, the posse couldn't come up with a trace of a thing yesterday! Those outlaws just seemed to vanish. I need you to tell me about the holdup, Mrs. Fleming," said the sheriff.

"Yes, of course, Sheriff," replied Ma Fleming, and she told all about how the two outlaws had been caught at the stage stop and went on to say...

"We'd been climbin' into those mountains east of town when the stage was ambushed. Several shots were fired. The driver stopped, and two men approached the stage on foot. The driver went for his rifle, and they shot him right out of his seat! It was horrible! One man, with a deep voice, ordered me out of the stage. Their faces were covered. When I stepped down, I saw Tom lyin' back along side of the road; he'd been ridin' one of the outlaws' horses we had tied to the stage.

"The men untied the two outlaws in the stage and took the money and horses and started to leave. One of the outlaws–the one with the deep voice–stopped beside Tom and me and got down. He carried Tom onto the stage. He said he was sorry the boy was hurt, 'cuz they hadn't meant to hit him. He even helped me put the driver on the floor and told me to git up and drive the stage hard for Red Rock where I could find a doctor. Then he galloped away after his three buddies who'd already left into the mountains on the north."

"Well, you don't say!" exclaimed the sheriff. "A gentleman outlaw! Kin you tell me anything at all about how they looked?"

"Well, their faces were covered, so I, uh, well... the one had the deep voice. They wore reg'lar rancher-type clothes... guess I can't remember much. The two outlaws that we had caught, and then later got away... they were both tall. Oh, yeah! The outlaw with the deep voice was tall and muscular. The other was short and skinny... Now let me see... the other two... one had a beard and he was older than the other one.... In fact the other one was quite young."

"Is that all you can tell me, Mrs Fleming?" asked the sheriff.

"Yes. If I think of anything else I'll let you know," answered Elizabeth.

"Thank you, and sorry to interrupt your breakfast," said the sheriff as he left.

"He really is a good man," said Frank watching the sheriff limp away. He then paid for the breakfast and excused himself after explaining to Tom's mother her possibilities for lodging the next three weeks.

Elizabeth chose the boarding house across the street and down a little from Clara's cafe. She secured a room and went back to Doc Raymond's office to check on Tom.

The boy, in his alcohol-induced slumber, was muttering some strange sounds, but appeared to be okay. Ma went to see the doctor about taking Tom over to stay with her. Doc helped Ma carefully carry her injured son to the boarding house, and up the stairs to the room. After giving further instructions, the doctor left, and Ma settled down to looking after her wounded son.

Two long days later the doctor took Tom off the alcohol, and before the week was out, Tom was getting tired of staying in bed. Once when his mother was out, he tried to get up and walk across the room. He felt his heart beat hard, his arm started aching, and a great weak feeling come over him. He got right back into bed.

During this time of healing, the doctor came to see Tom often to check the wound. His mother accepted the offer of Clara Newman's and went to work as a waitress. Tom, therefore, was often alone much of the day–and a few times even late after dark.

One day during Tom's second week of recovery, the local town preacher, Reverend Maxland, stopped to visit Tom. The boy was glad for the visit and had some pressing questions to ask the preacher.

"Why did God cause my pa to die, me to get shot, and the outlaws to get away?" Tom blurted out almost before he had finished shaking the reverend's left hand.

"Hang on there, young fellow! You've asked me a mouthful, and those kinds of questions take some time and understanding– which I probably can't answer in one nice, simple explanation," answered the preacher.

"But why have Ma and me had all these problems? My pa and ma both loved God, and Pa read the Bible, and we went into town when we could ta go ta church. How come all these bad things are happenin' ta us?" asked Tom in somewhat of a demanding voice.

The eagerness in the boy's eyes and face disturbed the preacher because he did not really have a good answer for the boy.

"Well, Tom, it isn't for us to question God. But take everything that happens to us as His will for us. If we do, things will work out all right, and things **will** get better," said the pastor. He then, in a rather nervous fashion for him, asked Tom if he would like him to pray for him, and Tom nodded his head.

"Oh, God, hear our prayer for this young boy. Heal his body and give him rest. Quiet his heart concerning these trials he is going through, and give him peace concerning your great will." The preacher added the Lord's Prayer and then left.

Tom lay quietly thinking of what the preacher had said. He felt that the man had not answered nor tried to help him with his miserable, swirling thoughts.

Ma Fleming came in with Tom's dinner just after dark and explained that she had to go back down and work some more because the cafe was very busy. Tom ate his supper and lay back on his pillow and fell asleep.

Someone shook Tom on his good shoulder, and he awoke with a start to a dark room. "Ma, is that you?" asked Tom.

A deep voice from a few feet away spoke. "No, Tom, it ain't yer ma. I'm a friend of yers, though. Ya see, when ya were shot, I helped yer ma put ya in the stagecoach."

"You're an outlaw?" asked Tom, frightened.

"Yeah, I'm one of the outlaws. I mean ya no harm!" said the deep voice.

Tom could barely see the man's outline as he stepped in front of the window. "What do you want?" he asked.

"I don't want anything. I just have felt bad 'bout what happened to ya, ya bein' a young kid and all. I wanted to tell ya personally that I'm sorry. I don't know if it was one of my bullets that hit ya, but still I was with the others; could've been. How's the arm?" spoke the outlaw slowly.

The calm, slow, southern deep voice of the outlaw caused Tom to relax and trust the man. "My arm is better and is gonna be all right, the doctor said," answered Tom.

"You and yer ma have enough money and food?" asked the man.

"Yeah, I think so. Ma's workin' at Clara's cafe," explained Tom.

"Well, I want to give ya some money anyways," said the outlaw moving closer.

Tom felt a wad of money pushed into his good hand, and he could dimly see the shadow of the man as he leaned near. Tom was scared and shaken but said "thank you" without considering whether he should take the money or not. The gentle manner of the man caused Tom to be bold enough to ask the man a personal question.

"Mister, do you believe in God?" asked Tom.

"Kid, sometimes I do and sometimes I don't. If things goes good for me, I say I believe in God. When things goes bad, I say that I don't. Usually I say there's no God. Most everythin's just good or bad luck. Hey! Why don't ya call on the preacher? He kin help ya! See ya later, kid."

The outlaw went out the window and onto the roof and was gone before Tom had a chance to explain that he had already talked to the preacher. His words *"Usually I say there is no God"* went through Tom's mind several times. *Here's a man that don't believe in God, is an outlaw and a wanted man, yet he cares enough to ask how Ma and me are fixed for food and money and even gives us some money. On the other hand, the preacher believes in God, but had a hard time answerin' my questions. He didn't even bother to ask how Ma and me are fixed for food and money and didn't really seem to care much. I think that there is prob'ly no God,* 'cuz if there was, there wouldn't be so many bad things allowed to happen. If there's no God, everything's left to luck. It was bad luck that Pa died, good luck for the outlaws that they were able to get away, and bad luck for me that I got shot.

Tom hid the money under the mattress of his bed and fell into a restless sleep.

CHAPTER FOUR

Tom awoke to a bright ray of sunlight streaming in through the second floor window of the boarding house. His mother had already left for work. As his mind cleared, Tom suddenly remembered the outlaw's visit and the money underneath his mattress.

His good hand raced to the spot where he had hidden the money, and pulled out the roll of bills. Now, in the bright sunlight, Tom could count the money. Ten, twenty..., seventy, eighty..., one hundred dollars! "Wow! Wow! Wow!" he exclaimed aloud, as his heart beat hard and his mind raced through all the ways he could spend the money.

Then, sadly, Tom realized he could not spend the money. Everybody would want to know where he got it. He figured he would just turn it over to the sheriff to take back to the bank.

Tom carefully rolled the bills back up and put them back under the mattress. Shortly, his mother came in carrying his breakfast on a tray.

"Well, ya look thoughtful this mornin', Tom. What's on yer mind?" she asked.

"This outlaw came in the window and...ah, ah, ah, ...," Tom blurted out, but stopped short of completing the sentence. *"Do I want to tell?"* he thought.

"Poor child," Ma said. "You've had a bad dream–and no wonder, after gettin' shot."

Tom's thoughts were fading into the possibilities of hiding the money for future use. The boy gulped down his oatmeal and

43

milk. *This ain't necessarily stolen money,* thought Tom. *And it may be that in the future Ma and me will need it.*

"Doc Raymond said you were to try gettin' up today and walkin' about a bit," Ma said, interrupting Tom's thoughts.

When Tom had finished the oatmeal, he tried walking about. To his amazement, he did well; his wounded arm in the sling did not hurt. After walking about the room a bit, the boy asked if he could go downstairs and outside.

"Let's see if I kin help ya over to the doctor's office. That way he kin check yer arm and give us his advice," said Ma.

"Well, hello, young fella," said the doctor as he stopped his buggy in front of his office. "How's the arm doing? Must be doing pretty good for you to make the walk over here!"

"I feel good, Doctor!" exclaimed Tom with a big smile.

"Well, come in and let's take a quick look at the wound; kind of tired myself. I was called to go out to the Jacobson's ranch late last night... just got back. Grandma Jacobson was ailing, so I went out to see what I could do. Weren't anything I could, though. She was eighty-six, God rest her soul," said Doctor Raymond.

"Does God really rest people's souls?" asked Tom as the doctor removed the arm sling and bandage.

"Well, Son, I reckon He does when the soul is a person like Grandma Jacobson. Why, she's been working around these parts for years, a-helping people, showing kindness and receiving little for it. We all loved her dearly. Sure, Tom, God's bound to rest the soul of Grandma Jacobson right in Heaven. She went to church almost every Sunday, or whenever she could," explained the doctor.

"Well, what about outlaws? Does God rest their souls; do they possibly go to Heaven?" asked the thoughtful patient.

"Well, the Good Book says that those kinds of people will go to Hell! Mrs. Fleming, you ought to come and bring Tom to the church Sunday. It's just down from Clara's, you know," said Doc Raymond.

"I think I will," replied Ma as Doc finished wrapping Tom's arm up.

"Your son is okay. The wound has healed over so it's good for him to be up and about, but take it easy; a little at a time," explained the doctor smiling.

Back at the boarding house, Ma stated what a Godly man the doctor was and left instructions for Tom to take things easy. Then she headed back to Clara's cafe.

Tom went back to his bed, and removed the one hundred dollars and hid it safely in some things in his suitcase. He wondered if he was doing the right thing. Would God maybe someday rest his soul in Heaven or Hell? Was there even a God?

A knock at the door startled Tom from his thoughts. Upon answering the door, he was greeted with a big smile from the face of Pete Smith.

"Pete! Come in! Seems like ages since we stopped at the stage stop where I met ya. I'm glad yer here. Did ya hear what happened to me?" asked Tom.

"Yeah!" replied Pete, "I come to see how you were. Does the arm hurt?"

The boys were soon engrossed in talk. Tom told Pete all about his experience, and Pete told Tom all he knew about what had taken place since Tom had left the stage stop a month ago.

"Pete! Pete!" Pete's dad called.

"Up here, Pa!" answered Pete.

"Come in, Mr. Smith," invited Tom as Mr. Smith appeared at the open door.

"Well, Tom Fleming, you seem to be doin' fine now. Sure glad to see that! They haven't caught up with the outlaws yet, huh? Well, that's too bad. They'll get caught one of these days and'll get their just desserts! We gotta go or we won't be home 'til way after dark. You get well now! Hear Tom? Good bye," said Mr. Smith as he walked out the door with Pete.

The next morning the funeral for Grandma Jacobson took place. From his wooden bench in front of Frank Woods' store, Tom watched people come into town. Buggies, wagons, horses–all loaded with people and their families dressed in black–passed slowly by the general store on their way to the funeral at the little white church.

About eleven o'clock, Frank Woods, also dressed in black, came out of the store. "Well, I'm gonna go on down to the funeral, Tom. Looks like I'm too late to get a seat," he said.

Tom walked with Mr. Woods. The youth figured that he himself wouldn't go inside the building since he was not wearing black and was not dressed for church.

Arriving at the church, they found that the building was full and overflowing. People were gathered around the doors and windows outside. Tom and Frank stood as near as possible to one of the windows towards the front of the building. Tom could not see in the window. Presently a pump organ started playing quietly, and Tom could hear a few people crying. Then someone got up to sing a song but, after the first few words, the person broke down crying. Tom could hear more crying and wailing, and what sounded like some people groaning. Tom knew how they felt because his own dad had died only three months ago.

Tom looked up and was surprised to see huge tears running down the face of Frank Woods. As he looked about, he saw that other grown men, cowboys, ranchers, and ranch hands, were weeping or on the very verge of it. **ALL** the women he saw were crying. Tom felt like crying too.

A man's husky voice spoke up from inside the church. Tom thought he would be Reverend Maxland, but he was not. "Dearly beloved, we are gathered here today to pay our last respects to one of the greatest ladies that God ever put on the face of the earth; we all know her as Grandma Jacobson."

The preacher went on to tell when Grandma Jacobson was born, when she died, and who her many survivors were.

"We all know what a wonderful woman she was. There is probably not a soul here today that has not benefited from her life. Most of us owe our salvation to her, and some of us owe our very life. In all the kind deeds she did and works of love, she never forgot to tell people about Jesus; something most of us are reluctant to do," continued the preacher.

The preacher went on and on for about an hour mentioning specific things that Grandma Jacobson had done, and with each new thing there would be an outburst of crying and signs of grief. Finally, the preacher announced that another song would be sung before the funeral procession took place.

A man's tenor voice sang out loudly and clearly. The man sang a song about what a friend Jesus is. Since the song was a favorite of Grandma Jacobson, it made many people cry out loudly from time to time. The soloist's voice cracked a few times, and in so doing helped Tom recognize the singer to be Doctor Raymond.

The hearse led the large group of people up a little rounded hill northwest of the town about a mile. The desert cemetery was without trees or grass. Before lowering the casket into the ground, the people had a chance to go look at Grandma Jacobson once more. There was much crying, and apparently, the daughters of Grandma Jacobson were grieving the most. They both looked old to Tom. When the time came for the lid of the casket to be nailed down, they asked repeatedly for "just one more look." Finally, one daughter kissed her mother on the forehead and sobbed, "Bye, Mother, we'll see you in heaven!"

As the casket was laid into the desert cemetery, Tom thought, *What a horrible place to put a person you love.* And Grandma Jacobson must have been loved by more people than any one else Tom could think of. *"Is there really a Heaven?"* pondered Tom.

Tom spent several days just sitting around the front of Frank Woods' store. On Sunday he and Ma went to church.

Tom tried to listen to Reverend Maxland but found him very hard to understand; the boy soon lost his attention to a fly buzzing around the heads of the congregation. The building was hot and sticky, and the people kept going to sleep. One man slept from the beginning to the end of the sermon. Tom nearly laughed out- loud when the man shook the preacher's hand and told him what a fine sermon it was.

****

One afternoon Ma told Tom that they were going to live in Red Rock for a while and that Tom would be starting school the next day. On that Monday morning, Tom went to the little building down the road a way on the west side of town, about half way between the church and the cemetery. The school had a large cottonwood tree shading it on the west side.

To Tom's surprise, about forty kids of all ages showed up and brought about much confusion for the little one-room school building which was equipped for only twenty-five to thirty students. All the kids were kind to Tom, and many of them wanted to talk about his bullet wound.

As Tom started telling about the holdup, a group of kids gathered about him; soon the whole school was listening to the account of the stagecoach robbery. He removed his shirt and showed the scars where the bullet had entered and where it had exited. Tom became an immediate hero in the eyes of all the kids.

"Good morning, students," interrupted the school marm. "I am sorry that we have not enough room for everybody. Will those age ten and younger take a desk, and those older may stand along the back wall for now."

Tom walked to the back wall as the other kids shuffled to their places.

"My name is Miss Taylor. I am your new teacher. I am very glad to have every one of you here, even though we do not have enough seats. The first thing we do at nine o'clock sharp every morning is to say the pledge to the flag of our great country, and then have Scripture reading and prayer," explained Miss Taylor.

Tom immediately liked Miss Taylor. He figured that the teacher was not very old because she did not have any wrinkles on her face beneath her blonde hair that she wore in a bun on the back of her head. She had a particular manner about her that made him feel wanted, and yet he knew right away that the pretty New Englander would allow no funny stuff.

The Bible reading that morning was from Psalm 23. Tom enjoyed hearing Miss Taylor read and pray. She sounded as if she really knew to whom she was talking.

****

A bench and table were added to the back of the school building to accommodate the extra-large number of children. The days passed quickly for Tom and soon turned into weeks as he enjoyed school and was learning how to read and write better. The now twelve-year-old lean, redheaded boy with a small scattering of freckles was beginning to feel good about himself, especially since he was getting stronger and getting his health back. The pain of losing his dad had lessened some.

Two more boys came to school three weeks after the year started. Tom introduced himself to the boy his age and learned that he was Howard Jacobson, a great-grandson to the lady whose funeral Tom had attended just before school started.

Howie, as he was called, was not overly glad to meet Tom, although he did manage to introduce his brother Frank. Frank was four years older than Tom and Howie, and was therefore quite a bit taller and stronger than the other boys were. Frank was the largest boy in the school, and very friendly to Tom. He explained to Tom that he and Howie had not been able to attend school any earlier because they had had to help with the roundup on their ranch.

During morning recess, Tom tried to speak with Howie, but the boy would not speak to him. The negative response gave Tom a funny feeling. *What have I done? What is the matter? Why does Howie feel that way?* he thought.

****

Ma Fleming and Tom had attended the community church every Sunday since they had first visited there. Ma was showing signs of feeling at home, as she began to get to know the people; however, Tom did not enjoy the preaching.

One Sunday Mrs. Raymond invited Tom and his mother over to their house for lunch after church. The doctor had a nice house built of stone. It was set off from the downtown area of Red Rock and had a white picket fence around its yard.

Doc and Mrs. Raymond were both very friendly to the Flemings, and Tom genuinely liked the doctor. The boy had quickly come to respect the man for his ability as a doctor– and for his religious beliefs. Tom marveled at the doctor as he prayed over the food on the beautiful hardwood table. "Dear Lord, we are grateful for the food that Thou hast provided for the keeping of our fleshly bodies. Bless this food to our bodies and help us to use the strength we get from it for Your honor and glory. Thank You for these dear folks, and bless them and their visit with us today..."

Before the doctor finished praying, Tom's mind wandered off to his thoughts about God. Tom was beginning to believe that maybe he was wrong trying to feel that there was no God. *After all, don't people like the doctor and Frank Woods and Miss Taylor and my own mother believe in God? The doctor believes in God, and he is certainly doing well. He has a nice home, a good job, and a nice wife. Has he had good luck, or is life more than luck?* thought Tom.

"Amen." The doctor had finished praying.

The closing of the prayer brought Tom back to his manners and the concern of the food before him. That day as Tom left the doctor's home with his mother, he had newly inspired thoughts of love and hope towards God. He had not felt this way since back on the prairie farm before his God-loving pa had died.

****

The cooler air of the October morning felt refreshing to Tom as he walked the half mile to the little schoolhouse Monday morning. The sound of a horse coming from behind caused him to look back and see Howie coming down the road. Tom waved; but as Howie got close, Tom realized that Howie was coming right at him on a hefty black horse. Tom jumped back out of the way and felt the brush of the saddle stirrups as the horse raced by.

"Now, why did he go and do that?" Tom said aloud to himself. Tom felt the color drain from his face and his fists clench as he thought about Howie trying to run him down. *What is the matter with that guy? Why is he mad at me?* thought Tom.

Tom entered the schoolroom just as Miss Taylor finished ringing her large handheld bell. "Stand for the prayer, children!" she instructed.

Miss Taylor began her prayer "Dear God, bless these ..."

As the class stood with their heads bowed and most of their eyes closed, Tom looked over at Howie standing against the far back wall. He looked as if nothing was wrong, as if nothing had happened.

As Miss Taylor led the morning Bible reading, Tom realized that he could not think about what was being said. Having almost been run down by a horse had made him upset and angry. The morning wore on with the little kids reciting, and then the older kids reciting and writing on their slates.

Miss Taylor announced, "We are going to have a multiplication quiz down. All ages may play the game; everyone stand up against the walls. We shall go around the room starting with Sarah on my left and work back around toward me."

Since the school year had started, Tom had worked hard on learning the multiplication tables; however, he was still having some trouble. He wanted to play the game but was afraid the other kids would laugh at him.

"7X9?" quizzed Miss Taylor.

"63!" answered Sarah.

"8X8?" came the next drill.

"64!" answered the next student.

Howie answered correctly to" 4X4" and on went the contest; hardly anyone was missing anything.

Finally, it was Tom's turn; he felt red and nervous.

"9X8?" asked Miss Taylor.

Tom did not answer. Miss Taylor repeated, "9X8?"

"62," Tom heard himself say, but he knew as soon as he answered he was wrong.

"No, you have to sit down. 9X8?" Miss Taylor asked the next student.

"72!" he answered.

The boy had gotten the answer right. Tom sat at his seat dejected and embarrassed. Things were bad enough, but he looked over at Howie and received a big sneer from him.

Tom was glad when the contest was finally over. He was determined that he would learn the multiplication tables perfectly–especially since Howie had stayed standing until next to last, finishing in second place.

After school Tom walked over to where Howie was tightening the cinch on his saddle and getting ready to mount his horse. "What was the big idea of trying to run me down this morning?" asked Tom as he pulled Howie back from mounting his horse.

"Look, you red-headed dumbbell, if you can't stay out of the way, you'll get run over! Can't ya see that?" said Howie as he gave Tom a shove away and mounted his horse.

The shove brought a reaction within Tom's feelings such as he had never felt before. He instantly wanted to shove back, to fight, to show the enemy that he was no "dumbbell," and certainly no one to be pushed around.

Tom jumped up and grabbed Howie around the waist with both arms. He dragged him to the ground. Tom's reaction did startle Howie, but not for long. He had been a long-time fighter and actually somewhat of a bully to smaller kids; but Tom was his size, although he may have weighed less. Tom, however, had never before been in a fight. After dumping Howie, he jumped up and just stood there a little puzzled, not really knowing what to do next. Howie got to his feet and instantly drove his closed fist at Tom's face, hitting him square in the nose, causing it to bleed. Tom stepped back startled; and then madder than ever, he started hitting at Howie with both fists as hard as he could. Tom sank a blow into his stomach and one into his face; in turn, he received a blow in the forehead. The boys fell to the ground wrestling each other, trying to get on top of the other.

By now the crowd of kids that were leaving school had gathered around and started yelling, "Hit him, Tom! Hit him, Tom! That a-boy, Tom! Don't let him get ya, Tom!" Hearing these voices, Tom realized that the kids were for **him** and against Howie. The screams also made Miss Taylor realize that something was wrong, and she came running out. "Stop it! Stop It! Break it up **now!** Stop it!" she yelled before she had reached the crowd.

Tom had just gained the position of being on top when Miss Taylor arrived and wanted to know what was going on. By this time, Tom's nose had bled down over his face, chin, neck, and clothes; the blood had been smeared with dirt all over his face. Tom turned and looked up at Miss Taylor as she broke through the ring of kids.

Miss Taylor stepped back. "I...I think I'm going to faint!" gasped the school marm. She fell back as several of the kids helped her to lean down against the front steps of the schoolhouse.

"Do ya give, Howie? Do ya give?" asked Tom as he pinned Howie's shoulders to the ground with his knees.

"No!" mumbled Howie.

Tom slapped Howie's face hard and then hit him once more. "Do ya give, Howie? Do ya give?" he asked again.

"Yes! Don't hit me no more!" Howie begged.

The crowd of kids all cheered as Tom let Howie up.

Frank Jacobson, who had been aiding Miss Taylor by helping her to go inside the building, now came over as Tom released Howie. Frank looked at the two blood-and-dirt-smeared boys and said, "Wha'd'ya know! Howie got himself whipped!" He then examined the two boys' dirty, torn clothes and blood-smeared faces and laughed and laughed. "Ha, ha, that's funny! Two twelve-year-olds fightin' a life-and-death battle! Ha, ha," He laughed.

"Howie, I always tol' ya that ya'd better quit pickin' fights. I tol' ya I wouldn't help ya, and I knew that someday ya'd meet yer match!" exclaimed Frank.

"Aw, shudup!" sobbed Howie, with big tears rolling down his face. "I'm goin' home!" With that, Howie mounted his horse and rode towards the Jacobson ranch.

Tom went over to the water trough with all the kids following him and congratulating him. He washed his face with the water coming from the pipe from the windmill. He was able to wash his face clean, but that would never sew up the torn school clothes that his mother had sacrificed to buy for him. The school kids helped dust his clothes off and continued to congratulate him for winning the fight. It was small consolation, though; he knew that his mother would be very upset.

Tom walked the distance to the boarding house rather slowly, not really knowing what to do next. The boy went up to their room and changed his clothes; he then headed for Clara's restaurant as he usually did after school. Before he got there, though, a commotion coming down the main street attracted his attention.

A group of men had assembled around a horse being led by the town sheriff. On the horse was a body that had been laid stomach down across the saddle.

Tom went and looked at the body. It was a gruesome sight. The man had been shot in the head, the bullet entering an eye and coming out near his opposite ear. Tom found out that the man had been shot while trying to steal horses from a nearby ranch. The awfulness of the man's wound had startled Tom somewhat, but he still looked at the horse thief when they pulled him from the horse. A sudden realization hit Tom. The man was the one that Pete had dropped the rock on at Henry Smith's way station, only now he had no beard, making it hard to recognize him at first.

"Sheriff! Sheriff!" Tom cried out. "This is one of the outlaws that we caught at Smith's way station, but later got away!"

The sheriff was glad for the news. That meant that now there were only three outlaws that had been involved in the bank and stage hold up left to find.

The dead man was photographed standing up between two townsmen and then dragged into the undertaker's parlor while Tom was watching. Tom wondered if this was the outlaw that had given him the one hundred dollars. He had almost forgotten about the hidden stash.

The sheriff soon came out of the parlor carrying the dead man's personal belongings. He explained to Tom that the man's possessions would be saved for a month, in case any relatives showed up. At the end of the month, they would be auctioned off to pay the cattle rustler's undertaker's bill.

Tom followed the sheriff to his office. "Sheriff, kin I see that gun?" asked Tom.

The sheriff emptied the bullets from the gun and handed it to Tom. "It's a Remington Army .44," he explained.

Tom ran his fingers over the smooth barrel and well-worn brown wooden handle. "I'd like to have a gun like this! How much'd a gun like this cost?" asked Tom, returning the gun.

"About fifteen to twenty dollars, but why would a young boy like you be int'rested in a gun?" asked the sheriff.

"Well, I've seen a lotta men carryin' one around out here, and I've never even shot one. I shot a shotgun my pa used to have, though!" explained Tom.

"I guess it's just the way of boys; always curious about guns," replied the sheriff.

****

Tom's mother was extremely upset when he told her about the fight with Howie. She insisted on going out to the school the next morning to see that Tom apologized to Miss Taylor and Howie. Miss Taylor made Howie apologize also, and the boys shook hands. Tom stopped by the sheriff's office on his way home. "Hi, Sheriff!" greeted Tom.

"Hi, Tom," replied the sheriff, kindly.

"When's the funeral for the horse thief?"

"We already planted him first thing this morning; no funeral for the likes of him!" explained the sheriff.

Tom walked from the office a bit startled. "Already planted–no funeral," he mumbled orally. The obvious difference between this man's life and death and that of Grandma Jacobson was causing Tom to consider that people that loved God were better off.

Out of curiosity, Tom walked to the graveyard and found the site of the outlaw's grave. Only an effortless stake had marked it. He gathered a few rocks and put them around the grave. He felt unhappy for the man.

****

Tom got a job working for Frank Woods every day after school and all day Saturdays. Because he was busy working in

Frank's general store, going to school and attending church, the time passed quickly, and soon school was out for the summer.

Howie and Frank Jacobson had to leave school early to help with the spring roundup on their father's ranch. The boys, having become good friends after the schoolyard fight, had invited Tom to come out to the cattle ranch and visit when school was out. So one morning after getting his work caught up at the store, Tom asked Frank Woods if he could borrow his horse to visit the Jacobson ranch.

"Well, Tom, that ol' horse of mine is kinda unhurried, but if you don't get too impatient with her she'll make it okay. So I guess so; go ahead, and have a good time," said Frank.

Tom walked to the livery and told the owner that he wished to use Frank Woods' horse, and that Mr. Woods had given him permission. The old man seemed to be bothered, but he stopped his shoveling long enough to show Tom where the saddle and bridle were kept, and then went back to cleaning out a stall.

Tom put the bridle and saddle on the old mare without much trouble and felt they were on securely. He mounted and headed through the town toward the Jacobson ranch, which was about four miles south of town. The horse started well and seemed quite eager to go, so Tom gave the horse free reins. About two miles down the road, however, the horse wanted to quit. She started walking slower and slower until she finally came to a complete stop.

Tom was puzzled. All he used to have to do to get Blackie moving was just sort of indicate which way to go and give a slight kick in the flanks, and off she would go. Tom tried kicking this horse harder and finally got the old mare to walk, but, only slowly. "Oh, brother!" Tom thought vocally, "I could walk there faster than this!" He tried talking, kicking, yelling, and hitting the horse, but she would not move above a slow walk.

Finally, they arrived at their destination around lunchtime, only to find that there was very little activity around the ranch house. Tom knocked on the door and was greeted by a lady, Mrs. Jacobson. He explained who he was and why he had come. Mrs. Jacobson explained that Howie and Frank were helping finish up the roundup about three miles southwest of the ranch house.

Disappointedly, Tom turned away and started to leave. A ranch hand came riding in and stopped near a corral not too far from the house. Tom went over and watched as the cowboy caught and tied ten horses to a string of rope.

"Hi, young fella! Wha'cha up to taday?" the cowboy asked cheerfully. "Haven't I done seen ya befo'?"

"Yeah, you prob'ly seen me at the gen'ral store in Red Rock. I've been workin' for Frank Woods part time," answered Tom. "I've come out to visit Frank and Howie."

"Well, I'll jus' tell ya what we're a-gonna do, young fella. You come on out to the roundup with me, and even help me see that I keep these fresh horses together," said the cowboy.

"Boy, that would be swell! But this ol' mare I borrowed wouldn' go three more miles in less than three hours!" explained Tom.

"Weelll," drawled the cowboy as he lassoed the tenth horse and tied it to the others. "Kin ya ride a horse preeety good? Ya wouldn' fall off or anything like that ifen I gave ya a reeeel good one, would ya?"

The cowboy sized up Tom for ability as Tom explained that his pa used to have horses and that he was a good rider and that he would not have any trouble.

With a sparkle in his eyes, the cowboy went to another corral and lassoed a brown-and-white pinto. "This here hoss has only been broke 'bout a week. He's got lots of energy and may buck a time or two when ya gets on. Do ya wan' him?" asked the ranch hand.

"O sure!" said Tom, already starting to unsaddle the storekeeper's old mare. Then, with the aid of the cowboy, he slid the bit into the new horse's mouth. It was much harder than with the old mare. The pinto did not want the bit in its mouth and reared its head. Finally, the horse was saddled and ready to ride. Tom climbed up into the stirrups; but before he had actually seated himself in the saddle, he found himself sitting on the ground in front of where the horse had been!

Pain went all over Tom's seat and up his backbone.

"Oh, ah, eeeeeeee, oh, oh, oh, ah, eeeeeeeeee," complained Tom as the cowboy quieted the horse down with the rope he still had tied to the horse's neck.

"What happened?" asked Tom.

"What happened?" repeated the cowboy. "You's done been had, Son, and I'm 'fraid to say, it was by me. I knowed that would prob'ly happen!"

The cowboy chuckled to himself, laughed a little harder and then harder until he was roaring with laughter. He tried to talk. "You–ha, ha, ha–should–hee, hee, hee, ha, ha– have seen the–ha, ha– expression... on–ha, ha, ha, ho, ho, ho, on, eeeeee–ya, ya, ya–ha, ha, ha, ha–f-f-f-face! Hee, hee, hee, hee, hee!"

By this time, the cowboy had sat down on the ground holding the rope in one hand, and a full-size red bandana in the other hand; he was trying to wipe the tears from his eyes.

Tom was not sure how to react. All he knew for sure was that his posterior and pride both hurt. He stood up and walked over to the pinto, adjusted the stirrups one notch shorter, and then declared, "I'm gonna ride this horse!"

The cowboy sobered up from his laughter and said, "Well, now, this time here's is what ya do! Hold that saddle horn with all yer might. Ifun yer feet come out of the stirrups, ya still hol' to the horn, got it?"

This time the horse tamer did not stand back; in fact, this time he held the horse's head until Tom was seated in the saddle, and then stood back. The horse again bucked, but Tom held on as the horse bucked and reared. Tom saw the sky, then the ground, then the sky, then the ground, then the tamarack trees that the horse bucked into; but Tom held on. The brown-and-white pinto bucked all around the ranch yard for several minutes, and all the time the cowboy was hollering, "'At a-boy! Ride 'em! Hang on, kid! At a-boy!"

Finally the horse tired and settled down. Tom could feel the horse's sides heaving as the animal snorted and inhaled great gulps of air. White foam had begun to form in certain spots on the horse's hot body.

The cowboy swore and said, "Well, I'll be. Ya shore 'nough kin ride a horse, kin't ya! Well, I'll be!" and the cowboy swore some more.

CHAPTER FIVE

Tom felt exhausted as he put Frank Woods' old mare in the livery late that night. The day had been a long but exciting one for him. Now he dreaded having to face his ma after staying out so late.

"Tom, where've ya been all this time? Frank said ya went out to the Jacobson's ranch. What in the world kept ya so late?" Ma asked with her voice raised and an angry but relieved look in her eyes.

Tom sat down on the edge of his bed and said, "Ah, Ma, can't I tell ya tomorrow? I'm so tired!"

"No, young man, I want an explanation right now!" answered Ma harshly.

"Well, I went out there and they were still havin' their roundup and I had to ride another horse **five more miles** south of there. I had a grand time. Howie and Frank were glad ta see me and showed me how the roundup worked. They even fed me beans and hardtack from the chuck wagon. I saw how they rope and brand calves," explained the boy.

Tom went on and told his mother all about the cowboy who had pulled the joke on him and how he had been bucked off.

"And ya know what?" Tom continued as he lay back on his bed. "When I got out to the roundup with that cowboy, I found out what the other men call him. Ya know what it is?" asked Tom.

"No, what do they call him?" asked Ma.

"'Tricky'! Ha! No wonder! I guess I'm not the only guy who had a trick pulled on him by that cowboy! Ma, I'm **so** tired. Some of the cowboys showed me some rope tricks just before we ate supper...and time just flew by, so I came home after dark and I was...," Tom said as his eyes closed and he faded into sleep.

Ma watched his heavy eyelids close. The anger she had felt changed to love and compassion for her young cowboy as she took his shoes off and pulled a light sheet over him.

****

Tom woke with the sun streaming through the windows. His ma had long since left for work at Clara's. He dressed and went down to the restaurant and ate in the kitchen as he usually did. Since the breakfast business was in a lull, his mother sat down to a cup of coffee at the table with him. Once again, she scolded him for staying out after dark.

"Ya know," Tom said, not paying attention to his mother's scolding, "I got ta ride a brown-and-white pinto yesterday that could really run! He just seemed ta like ta run! Boy was it great! Ma, can I get a horse?"

"A horse?" Ma asked. "We don't have a pasture to keep it in, and we can't afford the livery."

"If I earn the money, can I, huh, can I?" asked Tom excitedly.

"Well, I..., I..., we'll see. How much would ya need fer a good horse? And how much would the livery cost?"

"I'd need about fifty dollars for a horse–or maybe one hundred–'cause I wannna git a really good one. I don't know about the livery–I'll ask," answered Tom.

The boy worked hard the rest of the summer for Frank Woods and did some dishwashing at Clara's. Whenever he could, he visited Howie at the Jacobson ranch and got to ride the pinto that had bucked him off. He talked to Howie's dad about the spotted horse. The cattleman explained that he did not really want to give up the horse because it had turned out to be a first-class cattle horse. Nevertheless, when he saw Tom's saddened face, he changed his mind and told Tom that he could have the horse when he had earned seventy-five dollars; he agreed to hold the horse until Tom could raise the money. Tom was elated; but as school time approached, the young boy was several dollars short of his goal.

Tom's birthday arrived on Sunday, August 27. Frank invited Tom and his mother out for a birthday picnic after church that afternoon. Tom answered Frank's knock on the boarding house door as the man came to pick them up for the outing.

"Come in, Mr. Woods; Ma's about ready," explained Tom.

Frank and Elizabeth were still in their Sunday best, but Tom had changed into "something comfortable," as he called it.

"I have a special birthday present for ya, Tom," said Frank. "It's down in the buggy."

Tom's eyes lit up. "Ya do? What is it?" he asked. Tom started to say, "*I hope it's not more school clothes like Ma got me*," but closed his mouth, realizing that his ma had worked hard for little pay to take care of them.

Down at the buggy Frank took Mrs. Fleming by the hand, helping her into the front seat. Tom thought his ma looked happy, and he felt glad for her.

"Now, Tom, this is your birthday present from me," said Frank as he pulled a wrapped package out from under the seat.

Tom took the package and sat in the back seat as Frank headed the buggy through the streets. At the east edge of town Frank turned north and headed up a canyon lined with cottonwood and sycamore trees.

"Well, what are ya waitin' for, son? Aren't cha gonna open it?" asked Frank.

Tom tore the package open and gasped as he saw the contents. He pulled out the Remington Army .44 that had belonged to the cattle rustler and bank robber. The holster was there, too. The boy ran his fingers over the smooth barrel and the worn brown wood handle as he had done the first time he had seen the gun when the sheriff showed it to him.

"The sheriff told me ya liked it; and when he auctioned it, I got it for a good price. Now, here's the deal, Tom. Your mother said it'd be all right for me to give it to ya on the condition that the gun stay in my possession and you only shoot when I'm with ya. When ya get a little older, oh, say sixteen, you can keep it with ya, if your mother permits," explained Frank.

"Wow, that's swell!" exclaimed Tom. "I'm really gonna take care of it! Can we shoot it today?"

"Yes! I brought two boxes of reloads with me, and we can shoot most of 'em. It's **never** good to shoot all your bullets 'cuz ya never know when ya might need 'em. A gun's worthless without bullets," explained Frank.

Frank drove the buggy on up the road until they came to a particularly pretty picnic spot, close to the creek bed. The leaves of the cottonwood trees were starting to turn their beautiful fall colors.

After they ate, Tom and Frank shot the pistol. Tom enjoyed the shooting practice, and by the time the bullets were almost used up, he was learning to keep the gun down and aim in such a way as to come close to most of the targets–and even hit some. Frank praised Tom for how well he did. Tom asked to save a few bullets to put in the gun belt.

When the shooting practice was over, Frank put the gun in the holster, rolled up the holster, and put it under the seat of the buggy. After another snack, Tom scouted around the area while his mother and Frank chatted. He wandered down by the creek and threw rocks across the small stream for a while. Then he hiked north along the creek, exploring bushes and trails along the mountainside.

Finally, Tom saw where the road ended; only a cattle trail wandered off across the creek and on up the canyon. With much curiosity Tom explored a couple more miles and decided he better be getting back. As he turned to leave, he promised himself he would return for more exploration. He had fallen in love with the sights and sounds of the creek and canyon that were not as bare of vegetation as the rest of the desert area near Red Rock.

Tom walked quietly back to the picnic spot. Occasionally quail would fly out in thick clusters as he drew near. They startled him at first, but he got used to them and he noticed several long-eared rabbits running in and out of the bushes.

When Tom reached the picnic spot, he saw Frank leaning over, kissing his mother. Startled, Tom stood staring. The not-so-young lovers must have felt his gaze because they looked up suddenly. Ma blushed; Frank cleared his throat.

"Well, Tom, did you have a nice hike?" asked Frank.

"Y-yes," stammered Tom. "I th-think this is a very b-beautiful canyon. I wanna explore it more sometime. I wonder why people and cattle haven't settled in here."

"Too rough," explained Frank. "I've hiked up there a ways myself. On up a few miles, there're some beautiful pools of water carved out of solid rock from waterfalls. There is also sheer mountain cliffs maybe one hundred feet or more high! Maybe we can hike up there sometime, although the only chances I have ta get away from the store is usually Sundays. You need to watch out for rattlesnakes 'round here!"

****

When school started that week, things seemed different to Tom. The interest he had in his work the year before had faded. Many times Miss Taylor would catch him staring out the windows, scold him, and slap his hands with her ruler.

When his mind wandered, Tom would think about Howie and Frank not yet at school. He knew that they were helping with the fall roundup and cattle drive that had started already. Tom longed to be helping with the roundup and long trail drive.

He longed to be on the back of the fast pinto. Often he imagined himself riding out to rope a calf, galloping fast across the plains and driving cattle toward Pueblo, Colorado, as he knew that was where Mr. Jacobson marketed his beef.

Other times Tom dreamed of shooting the .44 and hitting his target: quail, coyotes, deer, and other animals as suited his imagination. Tom also dreamed of exploring the canyon and seeing the beautiful pools of which Frank had talked.

Slowly school wore on for Tom, and finally Howie Jacobson returned without Frank. Howie explained that his older brother and his dad had decided Frank was big enough and old enough to work full time on the ranch. The boy had just turned sixteen.

Tom invited Howie to explore the canyon with him, and one Saturday the boys set out to do so. They found the canyon was as Frank Woods had said. After hiking up the canyon about six miles, the boys found the pools of water. The last two were right up the narrowing creek. The creek contained huge boulders and had steep mountain walls on either side. The water in the pools was crystal clear, and the boys could see to the sandy bottom. The water that spilled over from one pool made a beautiful twenty-five foot waterfall. The boys both wanted to go swimming but decided that the water was too cold in January for such fun.

Howie and Tom became closer friends, and often Tom would spend the night on the Jacobson ranch. He practiced the art of roping and often got to ride the speckled pinto that he loved so much. He still had been able to save only fifty-five of the seventy-five dollars needed to buy the horse. He hoped to have enough by the time school was done.

****

The relationship between Frank Woods and Elizabeth Fleming grew that winter until they announced their engagement. The wedding date was set for June 27. Ma was worried about how Tom would feel and talked to him about it.

"Tom, how do ya feel about me marryin' Frank? He'll become yer stepfather, ya know."

"Ma, I feel kinda funny about it. Like you're betrayin' Pa or somethin'. Ma, why did my real pa have to die? Frank can never take the place of Pa!"

"I know, Tom. I don't think he'll try to. I think he loves you and me and wants ta care for us the best he can. I don't think he wants ta take Pa's place. I'll always love the memory of your pa, Tom. There never was a greater man, and I'm proud of the boy he gave me," comforted Ma.

****

January and February crept by for Tom. One night in March, Tom was awaked by the noise of gunshots and loud shouting and laughing.

"Lie down, Tom; it's just some of those noisy cowboys with nothin' else better to do this time of year–although I do wish they'd do their drinkin' and carryin' on where I don't have ta hear it," whispered Ma.

Tom lay back but could not sleep. Eventually he got up and looked out the window. He could barely see down to the saloon and the tail end of some horses hitched to the post out front. Tom checked to see if his ma was sleeping and then dressed quietly and slipped out the window onto the roof. He realized that he could walk across the roof of the boarding house quietly. He slipped down the ladder nailed to the back of the boarding house and sneaked quietly down the alley toward the saloon, trying to be careful not to be seen or heard. As he neared the saloon's back door, he could smell the strong odor of liquor and tobacco. Tom shivered in the early morning air. Laughter and music came from within.

The back door of the building opened with a squeak. Tom tiptoed into the dark storage room. He realized that probably no one heard the squeak because of the noise inside. He was able to look between the rough boards and peer into the main room of the smoke-filled saloon. Several men were sitting at a large table playing cards. The barkeeper was standing behind the counter looking tired, as if he wished the game would end so he could close. Beneath the counter was a sawed-off shotgun.

Tom watched the men playing poker. Shortly he sneaked out, walked down the alley, climbed onto the boarding house roof, and quietly re-entered the window to his room. His mother was still sleeping.

The excitement of what he had done gave Tom a thrill, and on many following nights, he sneaked out to watch what went on in the saloon. He saw many things that a boy his age should not have even known about.

One night a man became so drunk and sick that he wobbled around the saloon until he stumbled out the back door, nearly scaring Tom from his hiding place. Tom peeked around the back door at the drunk, went out, and hid behind a garbage barrel. The drunk threw up several times, gagged, and started dry heaving. Much of the vomit ran down his chin and onto his clothes. The man lay down in the dirty alley and pulled his legs up to his chest. Apparently, the man was asleep.

Tom started to move from his hiding place but stopped when a shadowy figure rounded the outside corner of the saloon. The figure proved to be the man that Tom often saw sleeping in church. Instead of helping the drunk, the church member reached down, took the sleeping man's wallet, and frisked his body, removing a watch with a gold chain; then he hurried off. Tom rushed back to the boarding house and lay in bed thinking about what he had seen. *That man shouldn't have done that. He goes to the church where they talk about helpin' others*, thought Tom.

The next Sunday Tom was wondering if the man would be in his usual place in church. He was. Tom did not hear any of the sermon. All he could think about was how the sleepy church member had stolen the drunk's valuables and now sat in church acting as though nothing had ever happened.

****

June 27th came, and the wedding of Elizabeth Fleming and Frank Woods with it. The church ceremony was splendid. Tom thought his mother looked prettier and happier than ever in her new calico dress. After the wedding, the new Mr. and Mrs. Woods took the stage out of town for their honeymoon.

Arrangements had been made for Tom to stay with Howie Jacobson for one week. Tom was thrilled. This gave him a chance to go out to the spring roundup and live with Howie and the cowboys during the busy time of roundup. He also got to ride "his" horse–toward which he was still saving money.

That week Tom realized that he had grown considerably in a year. He discovered that with the young pinto under him he was able to lasso and hog-tie the young calves that had been driven in from the surrounding hills. Once, Mr. Jacobson saw Tom lasso and hog-tie a spirited young calf and help hold the calf down as another cowboy pressed the red-hot branding iron into the calf's flank. The ranch owner praised the boy for doing such a good job and told him he could have a job any time he wanted one.

The week was over all too soon, and Tom returned to Red Rock and to a new home, for now he and his ma were to move into the little apartment above the general store. Since the apartment was so small, a special little room was made for Tom to sleep in downstairs, in the back of the store.

As Tom unpacked his suitcase, he found the one-hundred dollars the stagecoach robber with the low voice had given him. He had almost forgotten about it. *If I could just use this money, I could buy the pinto, a saddle, and maybe a new pair of boots*, thought Tom. However, he knew that he could not spend the money and the pinto was still not his. He would have had enough money this spring, but Frank had talked him into buying a Winchester rifle the sheriff had up for auction. Tom had not enjoyed the rifle as much as he had enjoyed the pistol because he could not hold the rifle long without his arms getting tired, and the rifle's kick made his arm sore. He wished he had spent the money on the horse as he had originally planned.

The rest of the extremely hot, dusty month of July went slowly for Tom. His work at his stepfather's store bored him, and he did not like to wash dishes at Clara's; but he did so, trying to earn enough money for the horse.

Tom's life would have been too boring for him except for his almost nightly "sneaky snoops." Sleeping down in the back of the store made it especially easy for him to go out without being caught. Soon Tom discovered that there were other interesting places to observe at night besides the saloon. One was the sheriff's office and jail; another was the funeral parlor.

One night as Tom was sneaking a look through the back window of the jail, he knocked over the wobbly wooden barrel he was standing on. Instantly Tom ran and hid in the old outhouse belonging to the building next door. Through the weathered cracks he could dimly see the deputy checking the area in the alley. Tom knew the man would probably check the outhouse; he would be trapped!

When the deputy turned away from the direction of the outhouse, Tom opened the door slowly and, quietly reaching down to the ground, he groped for a rock. When he found one, he carefully tossed it towards some bushes away from the building. Hearing the noise, the deputy walked toward the bushes, and Tom stepped out of the outhouse and hid behind it. He felt his heart beat hard with excitement. Although he was scared, he somehow enjoyed the thrill of the event.

The deputy walked toward the outhouse, and Tom listened as his steps came closer. As the lawman opened the door, Tom felt himself tremble. Then the door shut, and the deputy moved to look behind the stinky building. Tom moved in the other direction to the front of it and then took off running down the alley as quietly as possible at an angle the deputy could not see. He crossed the street to Frank Wood's place, ran into the alley behind the general store, and sneaked quietly back to his cot. A moment later, he heard footsteps run down the alley. He realized that the deputy must have almost caught up with him. As he lay in his cot laughing to himself, the excitement of the adventure gave Tom a taste for more.

One night in early August, Tom heard gunshots coming from the saloon. He sneaked out to see what was going on. He poked his head around the corner of the store in time to see two men carrying a wounded man toward Doc Raymond's office. Someone sent for the doctor who soon appeared to help the wounded man.

Tom quietly approached a window of the doctor's office. Underneath the crack in the curtain, he could see the doctor getting the unconscious man ready for surgery. The patient was Tricky, the cowboy.

Doc Raymond bared the man's chest and frowned. He said something to the man helping him and then started to probe for the bullet embedded in the man's chest. Blood gurgled from Tricky's chest, and Tom felt sick. The boy sat back on the boardwalk feeling dizzy. Someone was coming his way! Tom held still, and the person did not seem to notice him as he passed.

Tom heard a commotion coming from the saloon as the cowboys, townsfolk, and the deputy talked about the shooting. He took one last peek under the curtain and saw Doc Raymond pulling a dull gray object from Tricky's chest.

The next day as Tom packed supplies into a rancher's wagon, he felt a longing to go where the wagon must be going, to a roundup.

"Thanks, Joe," hollered Tom to the driver as the wagon pulled away. Then he walked into the dimly lit store and found Doc Raymond talking to Frank.

"I think he's going to live," the doctor was saying; "but it'll be some time before he's up and around. That's one lucky cowboy!"

Tom knew he must be talking about Tricky and was glad to hear he would live.

****

As the hot, uncomfortable month of August drew to a close, Tom lay in his cot, not able to sleep. He opened the window near his cot, but no wind stirred to help cool the stuffy room. He fanned himself awhile, then got up and dressed.

Tom stepped quietly into the dark alley and noticed that the full moon was shining brightly. When he reached the end of the alley, he saw that the silvery moon was bright enough to cast an eerie light on the buildings. The town was quiet–unusually quiet–and the lack of air movement made the night seem extremely hot.

Walking west, the restless boy decided to go out to the schoolhouse just for the sake of something to do. Arriving at the old windmill in front of the building, Tom found no water running out of the pipe, so he took a drink of the cool water in the trough. The moon was so big and full that Tom could see around the school well. He saw a lamp still burning in Miss Taylor's cottage next to the school building. He would have liked to have talked to Miss Taylor but knew that he would be scolded for being out so late.

Tom sat down on the ground, leaning against the watering trough, his back away from Miss Taylor's cottage. *What a nice person Miss Taylor is*, thought Tom. *I'm glad she's my teacher, and I'm glad she goes to church too.* As Tom thought to himself, he reached his finger out and traced circles around the big bright moon. It seemed as though he could touch it. Coyotes howled in the not so distant mountains.

It's strange that such a person as Miss Taylor and the sleepy church member both go to the same church. It seems that man doesn't belong in a group with her, or my mother, or Frank Woods, or Doc Raymond and Mrs. Raymond.

Well, thought Tom as he heard someone approaching and slid low behind the watering trough; *if it's not the doctor himself. I wonder if maybe Miss Taylor is sick.*

The bright moonlit night clearly showed Miss Taylor dressed nicely as she came out to greet the doctor. She put her arms around the doctor's neck as Doc Raymond put his arms around her slender waist. Tom gasped as he plainly saw the two kiss for a lengthy time. Miss Taylor invited the doctor in. Tom sneaked back to town, back to his cot, with an awful feeling of depression and hurt upon him.

Somehow the night passed, but not without Tom's tossing and turning on his cot as visions of Doc and Miss Taylor spun through his head. In one dreamy blur, Tom visualized the two helping the sleepy church member rob the drunk in the alley; but before they finished, Frank called out...

"Tom, come on, boy, it's late! Up! We've work to do today!"

Tom moaned as his sleepy eyes fought to stay closed; but Frank persisted, and soon the young boy was seated at the small table in Clara's cafe, where his mother still worked.

Throughout the day, Tom's thoughts went back to the scene of the night before. He determined that he did not want to go back to church–and that he would not.

When Doc Raymond waved to Tom, while Tom was unloading a supply wagon in the street, Tom's hand rose and waved in reflex. Tom felt awful. He wanted to confide in someone. He wanted to tell what he had seen, what he knew. He wanted to know why people he thought were "good Christian people," as the townsfolk referred to the churchgoers, had done the exact things they weren't supposed to do, and that by their own standards.

"I wonder how Mrs. Raymond would feel?" muttered Tom as he rolled a keg of nails past Frank.

"What'd ya say, Tom? asked Frank.

Tom started to speak but found he couldn't. *What can I say? Should I say anything?* he wonder. "Oh, I was just thinkin' 'bout how I'd like to get that horse," he lied. "I'll have enough money before long, ya know, although I'll still need a saddle and bridle."

Frank eyed Tom in an unusual manner. "How much money do ya have, Tom?"

"Sixty-five dollars," answered Tom quietly.

"You sure you don't have any more?" asked Frank.

"Yes, why? What makes you ask that?" asked Tom.

"Oh, nothin'," replied the storeowner. "We'd better finish unloadin' that wagon. I'm expectin' another one tomorrow— maybe even today!"

When Sunday came, Tom decided to go to church after all; but to his surprise, Frank stayed behind, and Tom and his mother walked alone to the church. Overhead the sky was turning gray as dark clouds began to form.

During the sparsely attended church service, Tom was quick to notice that Doc and Mrs. Raymond were in their usual places and Miss Taylor in hers. The singing was as good as ever on the part of all except Tom. He just could not get himself to sing the familiar words "Trust and obey, for there's no other way to be happy in Jesus, but to trust and obey."

Tom's mother noticed and nudged Tom. But he still did not sing.

After the service, Tom watched as Doc greeted people, including his mother and him. "Morning, Mrs. Woods, Tom; fine sermon, didn't you think so?"

"Why, yes, just fine," replied Ma.

"And good morning to you, Miss Taylor," greeted the doctor.

Tom did not hear the rest. His thoughts were withdrawn. He did not realize, until now, that people could put on such good acts.

As Ma and Tom walked towards the store, Ma asked, "Tom what's the matter? There's surely somethin' the matter! You've been mopin' 'round fer three or four days now. You wouldn't sing in church, and you didn't so much as say 'hi' to Doc Raymond who helped ya so much when your arm was bad hurt!"

"Ah, Ma, it's nothin; you wouldn't understand," answered Tom.

"Tom, did you steal some money from Frank?" asked Ma.

Tom stopped and looked at his mother and said, "Ma, what in the world would make you say a thing like that? You know I've always been honest, just like you and Pa taught me! No, I didn't steal any money whatsoever! **Now** I know why Frank's been actin' so funny! He thinks I've stolen some of his money!"

The two walked on in silence and ascended the stairs to the little apartment above the store. Tom was about to open the door for Ma when the door burst open and the usually calm face of Frank appeared. This time, however, his face was changed–horribly changed. Anger clearly showed.

"Come here, boy!" yelled Frank. "You stole my hundred dollars, didn't ya? Huh? Didn't ya?"

Frank grabbed Tom by the arm; the normally gentle man had become like a mad bull.

"Tell us the truth fer a change!" Frank yelled louder.

"No, I didn't steal yer money!" replied Tom tensely.

Frank went to the table and picked up a roll of bills. Tom understood. Frank had stayed home from church to search his belongings and had found the one-hundred dollars the bank robber had given him.

Frank tossed the one-hundred dollars to Ma and said, "Elizabeth, I found this, along with the sixty-five dollars Tom had earned, in his suitcase! The boy's a thief and a liar! That's what's been botherin' him ever since he stole the money Wednesday night! I don't know how he found where I hid it, but he did! Now what have ya to say fer yourself, boy?" Frank shouted.

Before Tom could reply, Frank produced his razor strap.

"I'll teach ya to not steal and lie, boy!" Frank yelled.

The strap came down across Tom's bottom as Frank held tight to Tom's arm. The stinging pain brought an immediate outcry to Tom's lips. "I didn't do it! I didn't do it!" yelled Tom. "A bank robber gave me the money!"

"You'll have to do better than that, Tom!" Frank yelled as he brought the strap down repeatedly. "Lie some more, will ya, boy?"

The strap came down repeatedly across Tom's back. The more Frank beat, the angrier he seemed to get. Tom cried loudly, "Stop! Stop! You're killin' me! It hurts! It hurts! Please stop!" sobbed Tom.

"Frank, not so hard, not so rough; he's just a boy!" pleaded Ma. "Stop, Frank!"

"No!" shouted Frank, "not 'til he tells the truth! Tell the truth, Tom!"

"I didn't do it! I didn't do it...," sobbed Tom, but he was unable to finish his words because the strap came down across his face, across his head, across the back of the neck. The pain was awful for the nearly fourteen-year-old boy. Although he was tall and strong for his age, he could tolerate no more. He was nearly hanging from Frank's hand.

"I did it," whispered Tom in a muffled sob.

The beating ceased, and Tom fell to the floor. He pulled his legs up to his chest as Frank looked at him. The stepfather threw the razor strap down and stomped toward the door.

"And after all I've done fer him," he muttered as he left the room.

Tom lay sobbing uncontrollably. The stinging pain that racked his body made him feel as if he were on fire. His head throbbed and felt too big for him. Large welts appeared on his face. Ma tried to get him to get up and lie on the bed after the worst of the sobbing and crying was over. He managed to crawl onto the bed.

Tom lay there sobbing as Ma washed his wounds silently. Large welts and black-and-blue areas appeared. In one place on his back the skin was broken and bleeding. His neck was almost as red as his red hair.

"My goodness! My goodness!" muttered Tom's mother. "Why'd ya do it, Tom? My goodness! It doesn't matter, though; Frank shouldn't have whipped ya so much!"

Tom started to say something, but his badly bruised mouth would not allow him to talk. Besides, he did not know what to say. He lay breathing hard. He felt he was in a position where he could not speak the truth without causing more harm.

Tom turned onto his side and moaned. Thoughts ran through his head. A list of people he had thought much of had suddenly changed to a list of people he thought little of: Miss Taylor, Doc Raymond, and now his stepfather. Tom knew that his mother was only confused. He still felt love for her. Tom knew that Frank was misled too, but that did not excuse the awful beating he had received from him when the man lost his temper. He hated his stepfather.

Tom thought about running away. He knew he absolutely would **never** go back to church again. He decided he would **never** pray again either. He decided that there definitely was no God. He thought of the bad words he had heard the cowboys use so freely, and he cursed God in his heart, using those words. He cursed silently to himself and blamed his beating on bad luck.

Finally, Tom lapsed into sleep. When he awoke, his mother was sitting on the bed with a bowl of hot soup for him. The sun was going down. He could hear thunder in the distance.

"Here, Tom, try to eat this," Ma said sympathetically.

Tom sat up and tried to clear the gooey matter from his eyes. His legs and back were stiff from the beating. His mouth was swollen from the belting across the face. Slowly Tom sipped the soup and felt better for it. He tried to talk to his mother, but his words were slurred because of his swollen face.

"Don't talk now, Tom," said Ma soothingly.

After sipping the soup, Tom got up slowly with much effort and much pain, and headed for his cot downstairs. He had trouble going down the stairs, but with his mother's help finally slumped down on the cot in his small room. Sleep did not come. Soon Tom heard his mother and Frank fighting. It was the first time, which he knew of, that they had fought. He knew that they were fighting over the awful whipping Frank had given him. As his body sweated from the humid summer heat and the welts covering his body, Tom made plans to run away. Lightning crashed nearby.

CHAPTER SIX

The hot rain poured from the black clouds as the young solitary figure inched his way up the muddy trail.

"If only I could see," mumbled Tom as a branch brushed his hat off. He was puzzled. In the darkness, he now felt lost. Several hours earlier, under cover of darkness and a thunderstorm, he had packed his belongings, taken a bag of food from Frank's store, and headed up the canyon he and Howie had explored in part. Now in the pitch-blackness he was soaking wet and lost. The bag felt very heavy on his shoulders.

Tom sat down, resting and shivering under some scrub brush as rain poured off his hat. A bright bolt of lightning flashed across the sky followed by a crack of thunder, scaring the runaway. But the flash revealed to him something on the hillside. Lightning flashed again, and this time he knew where he was and what he had seen.

"Oh, yeah! I've gone further than I thought," Tom said out loud as he got on his feet, picking up his Winchester. Slowly he headed towards the object he had seen. The continued lightning helped him make his way to the old prospector's shack. Suddenly, brilliant lightning bolted through the black sky sending branches of light in every direction. Tom stood startled–not only because of the lightning and thunder, but because he had seen smoke coming from the shack. *Who could be there?* thought Tom. *I heard that the old prospector that used to work the minin' claim was dead!*

The water-soaked runaway slowly eased himself up against the tin cabin. Rain was hammering on the rusty roof. There were no windows to look into. *Who could be in there? Way up here? S'pose the person inside tries to make me go back to Red Rock. I've just gotta get out of this rain,* thought Tom.

"Hey! Anybody here?" yelled Tom as he rapped on the tin-covered door. He thought he heard boots hit the wooden floor inside.

"Who's there?" a startled voice tried to yell above the noise of the rain pelting the tin roof.

"Tom Fleming, and I hav'ta get outa this here rain!" he yelled.

The man opened the door a slight bit, looked through the slit, and then opened it wider. Tom stumbled into the dimly lit shack as thunder boomed through the canyon and hills. In the light from the pot-bellied stove, the tall muscular man motioned to Tom to stand by the old stove as he slid more firewood into the blackened cooker. The rain was so loud on the roof that talking was almost impossible. The stove grew hotter, and the man signaled to Tom to take his shirt off and dry it near the stove. Tom did. He also sat down and, leaning back on his bag, dried his shoes and socks.

The rest, the warm stove, and the stuffy shack soon put the young boy to sleep. He slept until the rain came to an abrupt stop. The almost-sudden stillness brought an uneasy feeling to him and he jumped up, not sure where he was. His mind cleared and remembered the past eventful night with clarity. It had been a hard, long night.

Tom opened the creaky door of the shack and noted that the sun was up. Far down below, in the bottom of the canyon, the usually calm creek roared like a mighty river. The sound of large boulders could be heard falling and banging as the force of the flooded creek moved them along.

"Well," a voice from behind Tom spoke. "I see that my young friend has survived the night all right. That was some storm!"

Tom whirled around, feeling some fright. His fear was eased somewhat, however, as he noted the man when the light shone in upon him. The stranger's face was smiling–peaceful and kind looking–although it had the appearance of being weather worn. But what had startled Tom at first restartled him when the man spoke again.

"Well, I think we'd better see if we can fix up some grub. I'll kindle the fire first," the man said calmly.

*What was it? Why does his voice scare me? This man, this voice, somewhere...*thought Tom.

"How'd cha like some flapjacks this mornin', kid?" asked the man.

"Yeah, I'd really like that," said Tom as he felt his stomach growl.

Tom's thoughts flew around in circles in his head. *Yes! Yes! This is the man! The large build, the deep voice... Yes! This is the man...this is the outlaw! The man that gave me the hundred dollars. There's no doubt about it! Does he know who I am? How could he not?* thought Tom.

"Do ya know who I am?" Tom asked the man who was pouring water into a tin dish and stirring in flapjack mix.

"Yeah, I know who you are. You're Tom Flemin'. Tom Flemin', I'm guessin' that ya may be thinkin' that ya know who **I** am," answered the man.

"Did ya give me a hundred dollars?" asked Tom.

"Yeah, I did," answered the man.

"Oh," replied Tom, not knowing what to say.

The man kept preparing the flapjacks and finally poured some batter right on the now-hot pot-bellied stove. Neither person spoke. The man turned the flapjacks. Silence filled the room until the flapjacks were done and the man handed the hungry boy some on a tin plate.

"Thank you." Tom spoke as if his tongue were made of the very flour in the flapjacks. He gulped down the breakfast like a ravenous wolf. The exertion of the night before had left him extremely hungry.

Finally the man spoke. "Well, I guess ya realize that ya spent the night with an outlaw. I'm sorry fer yer sake."

"Don't feel bad 'bout it," Tom replied. Somehow, the man did not fit the description of most outlaws Tom had seen or heard about.

"What happened to yer face, kid? How'd ya get them black-and-blue marks on ya?" asked the outlaw.

It was easy to explain to the outlaw the complete details of the whipping Tom had received and the unfairness of it all. After all, the lawbreaker was the one and only man that knew for sure that Tom had not stolen the money. In fact, Tom was so much in need of lifting the burden from his shoulders that he went on to tell the outlaw about the other hypocrisies that were eating at his mind. First, he told all about Doc Raymond and Miss Taylor. Then he related about the sleepy church member. When he was through, he realized that the outlaw had sat still listening carefully, taking in every word.

The outlaw reached into his gray shirt pocket and pulled out the fixings for a smoke. Tom watched with interest as the man poured tobacco onto a little white paper, rolled the paper and licked the roll. The outlaw lit the cigarette and sat smoking slowly, seeming to enjoy every bit of the moment, and yet his eyes were focused out in the distance revealing that he was in deep thought.

Finally he spoke. "I know all about it, Tom. Church people (the man swore); righteous people, (the man swore again); holier-than-thou people (the man swore at them with some particular names); I knows just how ya feel, Tom."

Tom delightfully quoted back the outlaw's swear words and included some of his own. "Frank Woods I hate you! Frank Woods you're a...," and Tom swore with deep meaning.

Tom was a little startled at himself for saying those kinds of things, but somehow he felt good by doing so, kind of as if the saying of the words brought some revenge.

"Tom, I must admit that I've seen a few of those kinds of people who were okay and really seemed to be all they said they were. I've seen a few, a very few and far between," said the man.

"One time, 'fore I got into this rotten life; I met a woman that I fell in love with. She fell in love with me, too, I think. She ran a little tradin' post and did a mission work with the Indians. Her name was Mary." The man paused for a moment; it was obvious that the thought of Mary was pleasant to him. "It's a wonder that those Indians didn' scalp 'er. For some reason the Indians were attracted to 'er. The same Indians that'd scalp you or me on a moment's notice would've given their lives for the woman. She was a very pretty woman. I got to know 'er when I drove a mule train goin' to 'er tradin' post. The Indians never bothered me; they knew I was goin' to the woman's tradin' post. I tell ya, Tom, she was really somethin'!"

It struck Tom as being funny that the man should be talking so to him. Yet wasn't it interesting that Tom himself had been able to unload his own burden on the man–a complete stranger? A friendship was developing, and Tom didn't even know the man's name.

The man continued: "I fell so in love with the fine-looking woman that I made deliveries to 'er post in record time. I could be tired and worn, yet I'd push my poor ole mules jus' to hurry up and see 'er lovely face. It was somethin' like seein' an angel, I guess. When I'd finally get there and see 'er sweet face and hear 'er lovely voice, I'd jus' forget I was tired. I'd jus' forget it! She might ask me to move this heavy keg here or there, or unload those heavy sacks and stack 'em here or there, and I'd do it, and all the time I'd just keep stealin' peeks at 'er and not even be feelin' the heavy materials that it took several men to help me load onto my wagons. It was really somethin'! I'd usually spend a night or two just 'restin' up' before I'd make my return trip. She'd bring me a hot meal out to my tent and we'd talk for hours. She really liked to talk to me. Somehow, we'd always end up talkin' 'bout Jesus or somethin' like that. She always wanted me to receive Jesus. 'You got to receive Jesus,' she'd say. I never did understand what she meant though.

"Finally, one time when we were 'bout done talkin' for the night, I leaned over and kissed 'er, and she kissed back. Boy! I tell ya, I thought the world had become paradise. I felt good all over!

"The very next trip I brought 'er some special little presents like women always like, and when just the right moment came, I asked 'er to marry me, even though she was a little older than me. She didn't smile. She cried. Finally, I says, 'Mary, what's wrong?' She just cried some more. Finally she tol' me that she loved me but she couldn' marry me 'cause I hadn' received 'er Jesus. I tol' her that I **would** receive Jesus, but she said, 'No it don't work that way.'

"Well, I kep' goin' back there and deliverin' my supplies, but Mary was never the same. Oh, yeah, she was a perfect wonderful lady, happy lookin' and smiley as ever, but she never would talk to me personally again, 'less it was about Jesus. I think she was 'fraid she'd break down and marry me.

"Not long after that, I got in with the wrong kinda people and got involved in a bank robbery and shootout. I was so ashamed of myself that I couldn't go back and see Mary. That was forty years ago. I guess I'm tellin' you all this 'cuz I just wanted you to know that there **are** people in this ole world that are good people. They **say** it, they **look** it, and they **are** it. But as I said before, they're few and far between."

"Well, I'll keep my eyes open for those kinds of people," said Tom. "Although I think I know of one—my mother—although she ain't perfect either, but she's a whole lot better than those hypocrites like Frank Woods. Someday I'm gonna get back at Frank Woods. I hate him!" exclaimed Tom.

"Ya gotta be careful, Tom. Sounds like ya think a lot of your ma. If you were to do somethin' to Frank, it'd prob'ly hurt yer ma too, seeing how she's married to 'im,'" replied the outlaw.

"I guess you're right. Say! Here we've been a-talkin' like this and I feel like we're friends, but I don't even know what to call ya," said Tom.

"Just call me Jed; Jed the outlaw," said the man sadly.

"Now lookie here, Tom. There's prob'ly gonna be people out lookin' for ya today. The sun's out...quit raining. What ya gonna do?" asked Jed.

"I don't figure anybody 'll be comin' up the canyon lookin' for me. At least not for a day or so. Ya see, I figure that Frank and Ma 'll prob'ly go out to the Jacobson ranch lookin' for me, 'cuz I spent a lotta of time there, and they know that I liked it out there. I was thinkin' of goin' out there and seein' if I could help with the fall roundup and cattle drive to Pueblo, but I know that Frank would be out there and drag me back to that crummy store of his and prob'ly beat me again for runnin' away. I don't think the cattle drive started yet. In a few days I'll try to sneak near the ranch and keep an eye on the roundup, and when they're gone far 'nough toward Colorado that Frank 'll not be lookin' for me, I'll join up with 'em. Mr. Jacobson told me he'd give me a job anytime," explained Tom.

"Well!" Jed exclaimed as he blew smoke from another cigarette. "I reckon that you'll be needin' help, and I reckon I'll be glad to see if I kin help ya. Besides, if someone's gonna comb this canyon lookin' fer ya, I reckon I'd best be movin' on too. Tell ya what; how about you 'n me both joinin' up with that cattle drive?"

"Can ya?" asked Tom, with a doubtful look on his face.

"Kin I? Why I was a-punchin' cattle 'fore you were even a twinkle in your pa's eye!" exclaimed Jed.

"Naw..." laughed Tom. "I didn't mean that. Can you join up with the cattle drive and not get in trouble with the law?"

"Well, that all depends 'pon who sees my face. It's true that I'm wanted in several states fer deeds which I'd jus' as soon not mention," answered Jed.

"You mean like the bank robbery and the shootin' of the stagecoach driver?" Tom inquired anxiously.

"Yeah, stuff like that. Tom... ya know, Tom, if I had this ole life to do all over again...," said Jed, and he hesitated for several moments before continuing. "Ah...," and Jed swore, "I'd prob'ly do it all over the same way as before. There must be somethin' better in life than this, though. 'Member I tol' ya how I got into a bank robbery with some men and was ashamed to go see Mary after that?"

"Yeah, I remember," answered the interested boy.

"Well, there were four guys involved in that. Started one day when I was in a dirty little saloon in New Mexico. I'd jus' come back from Arizona with my mule train. I was hot, tired, disgusted. Lotta work, those mule trains. I had a mule die on the way back and an axle break on a wagon and another wagon turn on its side 'fore I made it back. Well, I'd made a little money. Not a whole lot, but it kept me alive long enough to make another trip, just to turn around again and do it over again. Anyways...I was sittin' thinkin' 'bout what else I could do to make a little money besides drive mules, when four cowboys rumbles into the saloon and ordered drinks. One of 'em was my brother, Ned. We'd been on a trail drive together several times.

"I asked Ned how things was goin', and he tol' me 'not so good.' He and his buddies had just finished a trail drive that spring and were come on back down the Goodnight-Loving Trail to help with another roundup and trail drive. Ned had made 'bout seventy-five dollars on the last drive, and he and his buddies had gone into Pueblo to celebrate the end of the drive. And Ned got drunk and fell asleep in a saloon and never woke up 'til the next mornin'. His money was gone. Someone had stole it. So ya see, he was still a-feeling pretty low. His buddies had helped him out and spent most of their money, like them cowboys always does, and now they was all a-feelin' low.

"Somehow we all got ta talkin' 'bout this problem of always bein' low on money. Ya see, Tom, ya could help with a whole big roundup and cattle drive, spend two or three months of yer life a-sweating and eating nothin' but bacon and beans, and only come out with 'nough money to buy yaself a shave and a haircut and a good saddle. But if ya wants to do a little drinkin' and have a little fun, too, there's jus' not 'nough money for that.

"Anyways... we somehow done went and planned the bank robbery. An' it went off slick as snot, 'til one of the fellows didn't tie his moneybag onto his saddle good and it fell off 'fore we got out of the town good. Well, he stopped and went back for it, and the rest of us stopped to cover 'im. Just as his hand grasped the bag, he was shot right through the head and fell down like a bag of flour! The other two guys started shootin' at the townspeople while I went and grabbed the money bag and had my horse shot out from under me! I ran down the street and jumped up behind Ned, and off we went!

"Some mess we made there. Heard later that our guns killed three towns-people! Anyways... we made it to an ole abandoned cave to hide out just like we'd planned. We talked 'bout how it was too bad that ole–I forgot his name–got shot dead. But we all realized that it meant more fer each of us. We counted the money, divided evenly, and spent the night in the cave. On 'bout mornin', I woke up and saw one fella 'bout to make off with the money of all of us! Just as he mounted his horse, I hollered at 'im and he turned and shot at me, barely missin' my ear! Ned and me grabbed our guns and chased out after the fella in our stockin' feet! We took a clear aim at the man, shot at him once, and the man dropped out of his saddle!

"That was the first time I ever shot a man directly. We buried the body; I felt real bad 'bout it. I searched the man's personal belongin's. We found a old letter in his pocket from his wife. Since I never learned ta read, we saved it and later had someone read it to us. His wife tol' 'bout how bad conditions were fer her and their son back home, and she was begging him to come home.

"Just after we decided to leave the old cave and had been on the trail fer a hour, one heavy dirt storm blew up. Boy! It was a dirt storm like I'd never seen 'fore and ain't never seen since! We had ta get off our horses and try ta find shelter and cover our faces 'cuz we was chokin'! Well, we put our bandannas over our faces, with our faces to the ground against our arms. The storm lasted nearly a hour! When the air cleared, we got up an' realized that our horses had run off. An' so had my money. Ned had grabbed his saddlebag which contained his money and the money of the fella which we had shot.

"We finally sent the other money to the fella's wife. We never knew if she got it. Ned bein' the kinda fella he was shared his money with me, which didn' last long, and we showed up fer the fall cattle drive, broke as ever, only now the law was lookin' fer us. Boy! When it comes to money, my middle name has been 'Bad Luck'!" explained Jed.

"Yeah boy! I guess so," said the long-quiet Tom.

Jed continued. "Tom, ya see, I robbed a bank; it didn' do me no good. I drove mules. It didn' do me no good. Only thing is, 'fore I robbed the bank I didn' have the law on the lookout for me. I'd have been better off if I hadn' robbed the first bank. I've been involved in two others since then. One you know 'bout. But where's the money? I'm broke agin."

"Well, it was awful nice of you to give me that hundred dollars when I was hurt," Tom cut in. "Only I didn' use it right. I couldn'. My ma would've just insisted we give it back to the bank, and I didn' know for sure that it was bank money."

"Ah, it **was** bank money, kid; where else'd Jed the outlaw get one hundred dollars right after the Red Rock bank had been robbed? Well, kid, I've prob'ly talked to you 'bout these things more'n anybody. Funny thing. You've gotta keep quiet or you'll get Jed in a heap of trouble," explained Jed.

"Don't worry, Jed. I'm not gonna tell anybody anything," promised Tom.

"Tom, the way I see it, money 'n things ain't worth all the trouble and time we spend on 'em. Just think of the people killed 'cuz of it. If people had a little food, they oughta be happy. Only thing is, though, they ain't. 'Cept Mary. Now **she** seemed to be quite happy. She only lived in a shacky mission cabin, sold stuff to the Indians, and told 'em about Jesus. Took any profit from the things she traded the Indians and bought stuff for the Indians— like medicine, food, and clothes. She often **gave** medicine and blankets away! Mos' people ain't happy tryin' to git all they can, but Mary was happy **givin'** all she had away! More I think about it, the stranger it was. Maybe there's somethin' to this Jesus thing. If I could talk to Mary again, I'd listen closer to what she had to say," explained Jed.

There was a pause in the shack. It was quiet for a while. The fire had burned out; the sun was up bright and warm. The shack grew stuffy; a rat rattled paper and trash in a dirty corner. Jed seemed to be recollecting memories about Mary, so Tom sat still and didn't disturb him.

Presently Jed said, "We'll go over the mountain in the mornin'. I know a place we can hide and wait for the cattle drive to come by. Say! Where'd ya git that pistol? That's Ned's pistol! Where'd ya git it?"

Reluctantly, Tom told Jed about the dead cattle rustler that the sheriff had brought into town for burial. Jed sat, staring out the shack's open door. Tom felt badly and now wished he had never seen the gun. Jed took the gun and looked it over closely. He ran his weathered fingers over the well-worn brown handle and examined the marks. "Ned was the only real friend I had in this life. He was the best friend I ever had. That's why I had ta stop the stagecoach you and your ma was with. I **had** to set 'im free! You see, he was my younger brother! Jed and Ned, the only sons of my father. Tom?"

"I'm sorry, Jed," answered Tom.

"Tom, will **you** be my friend?" asked Jed.

"Sure, Jed, always," answered Tom.

"I want you to have his gun. I hope you learn to shoot as straight as Ned. He could kill a fly at two hundred paces! Ned used that old army gun ta kill many blue coats! I want you to take care of it," said Jed quietly.

"I'll take care of the gun, Jed," replied Tom solemnly.

****

The beautiful fall morning wore on as Tom and Jed sat in the shade of the tin shack and became better and better friends. Tom took a liking to the outlaw as the man recounted his experiences as a boy growing up with his now-dead brother, Ned. In fact, Tom felt sorry for the man when once the big fellow broke and cried at the remembrance of his brother.

"Sorry, Tom, I guess ole Ned meant more to me than I realized," he said as he brushed aside his tears with a big, rough hand.

"I understand...I felt the same when my pa died," said Tom.

Silence gripped the two as man and boy sat and thought about their departed loved ones. The noon sun drove the shade away, and the humidity rose, making things uncomfortable.

"Let's go into the ole mine, Tom. It'll be cooler in there," suggested Jed.

The two spent the afternoon talking and resting in the cool damp mine. "I wish I could go back to Red Rock and visit Ned's grave. I bet the poor fella didn't get a decent burial. They prob'ly stripped him of everything. He prob'ly didn't even get buried with his boots on," said Jed mournfully.

"Yeah, you're right," remarked Tom, as he recounted to Jed how quickly his brother had been buried.

****

The sun was starting to strike down from the west as the two new buddies made their way back down the soggy canyon toward Red Rock. Jed had decided that he wanted to visit Ned's grave before they turned east to join up with the cattle drive. Not only did he want to visit the grave, he also wanted to leave a few things inside the coffin for Ned. That thought made Tom's blood run cold.

"But Jed, won't your brother stink?" complained Tom.

"Naw, it's been over a year. 'Sides, you don't have ta look; just point out which grave it is," answered Jed.

The last rays of sun were disappearing as Jed and Tom arrived at the cemetery. They had hiked in from the north over a large hill, avoiding the town. Jed's horse had been left back on the other side of the hill. Only a shovel and saddlebag were taken along.

"Okay, Tom! Which grave is it?" asked Jed.

"I'm scared, Jed!" answered Tom.

"Tom, you've gotta help me. You said you'd be my friend. Show me quick, 'fore the sunlight is completely gone!" pled Jed.

"It's over this way. Here it is, right here. No marker, but here're the rocks I put around it," explained Tom.

"That was real kind of ya, Tom," said Jed.

Jed set to digging heartily as Tom sat and watched. The wet, packed desert quickly gave way to the muscular hands and back of Jed. The blackness surrounded both Jed and Tom as the silvery stars came out to stare at the lonely pair. The blackness surrounding the two was broken only by the starlit night. Jed never broke his digging stride as Tom listened to the "chink, clank, clonk, chink, clank, clonk" of the shovel. Tom could see only a faint shadow of Jed as he dug. A less-than-full moon appeared, revealing the wet desert and the lonely couple. The familiar sounds of barking coyotes echoed in the nearby mountains.

"Chink, clank, clonk, chink, clank, clonk, chink, clank, clonk, thud." The sound of the shovel hitting the wood paralyzed Tom. Jed cleaned the dirt off the wooden coffin lid and threw the dirt out of the hole. The moon seemed to shine brighter as Tom heard the creaky sound of rusty hinges. The coyotes laughed loudly nearby as Jed lit a match and looked in upon the deteriorated remains of his brother. Tom sat glued to his spot, barely daring to breathe.

"Hello, Ned," Tom heard Jed say, but the young boy did not dare to look into the hole. "Sorry to bother ya like this, Ned. I've missed ya; wondered what'd happened to ya. I see they did leave yer boots with ya. I'm sorry 'bout the fight we got in last time we were together, Ned. I'm real sorry. Do ya forgive me, Ned?" Jed paused as if to give Ned time to reply. "Thanks, Ned. I'm gonna leave a few helpful things with ya, Ned; maybe you can use 'em wherever yer at now. Hope it kinda makes things right between you and me." He turned to the quiet boy and said, "Tom, hand me that saddlebag and blanket!" The command startled Tom. He clumsily handed down the blanket and saddlebag. Tom wondered if maybe he was having nightmares and wished he would wake up. He shivered in the damp night's air. Jed placed the saddlebag in the already-rotting coffin and covered his pitiable brother's remains with the blanket as lovingly as a dedicated mother tucks in her children at night.

"Bye, Ned; bye, my unfortunate brother," said Jed quietly with a hushed sob in his gruff voice.

CHAPTER SEVEN

"You've gotta tell me all about it, Tom," said Howie Jacobson as he reached into the cook's pot for more beans. "Sounds like you'll be in a heap of trouble if your step-dad catches up with us!"

"Don't call him my step-dad! I tell you, Howie, if he comes out here and tries to get me, and if I get the chance, I'll put a bullet right between his eyes! I hate him! You don't understand yet! He beat me to within an inch of my life for something I didn't do! I had to say that I did it before he would stop beatin' me! Look for yourself! I still have the bruises! Some fine Christian man he turned out to be!" exclaimed Tom as he swore to show his madness.

"Well, don't cha holler at me; I didn't beat ya!" replied Howie.

"Yeah, I know; sorry, Howie. I just get so stirred up thinkin' about it, that's all. I really hate the man! I hate him!"

"Ok, Ok!" Howie interrupted. "Tell me what happened since you ran away from Red Rock. Oh, and don't worry about yer–a-a-a–I mean, don't worry about Frank Woods looking for ya here. He was out looking for ya two days ago and done decided you weren't with us."

"That's good. When I left Red Rock, I hiked up into the canyon we explored and met Jed in the old prospector's shack. We decided to ride out to here where the cattle trail crosses the Pecos River and wait for you. Jed seemed to be able to figure out about when you'd be here. We only waited a half day before you came. What do you know about Jed?" asked Tom.

"Not much," explained Howie as he lay back on his sleeping roll. "He's worked for us several times. He comes and goes kinda quietly. I think he's wanted for something, but that's none of my business though. My dad likes him 'cuz he's a good worker, knows how to move steers.

"We're glad ya came along when ya did, 'cuz we're short on help. Ole Tricky got himself shot and won't be along to help for a while. Tricky got a little too tricky at a poker game in Red Rock. My dad let me come this time instead of going to school 'cuz we're so short on help. You'll prob'ly be helpin' with the horses tomorrow. Boy, am I tired, Tom! See you in the mornin'," Howie slurred his words as he drifted off to sleep.

****

"Come and get it! Get up! Get outa the sack!" yelled the cook as he beat a large spoon on a pan. "If ya don't come on, I'll throw it in the river! Come on, boys!"

Tom ate beans and bacon with the men before the sun was up, and was cheered when Howie told him that the speckled pinto was available for him if he wanted it.

The cook hollered, "Hurry up and eat yer Pecos strawberries (as he called the beans) an' come on!"

"Our job today'll be for us to get the remuda safely across the river and to collect firewood for the cook," explained Howie to Tom. "See that large skin tied under the cook's wagon? We have to fill it with driftwood after crossin' the Pecos 'cuz as we go up away from the river, firewood'll get scarce. We also have to do anything else the cook tells us. We might be needed to help fill the water barrels on the wagon."

The crossing of the river went without problems. The cowboys let the cattle drink their fill and then started pushing them north. Tom and Howie helped fill the large water barrels and then filled the skins under the wagon with firewood.

"Talk is," explained the worried-looking cook, "it may be a time 'fore we get to the next water; bad business for a cattle drive."

As if to confirm the statement, Mr. Jacobson, the owner and trail boss, rode up to the chuck wagon and explained that his scouting had revealed that the next water would be the Canadian Royal River about four days away. "So in case we need them, fill every canteen and pot you fellows can find," he ordered.

"Well, Tom, you look a little distance from home. It's okay with me, though. I met Jed up front of the cattle and he explained things. We need extra help, so you learn Howie's job; you're pretty good with the horses. I'll use Howie in other areas. I might need you to help ride night watch because we've been a little short of help, and some of the boys are extra tired. I'll pay you same as Howie, if you work hard. Good luck, Tom. See you at noon," explained Mr. Jacobson.

As the morning progressed, Howie explained to Tom how his job as the horse wrangler worked. Tom enjoyed riding the speckled pinto and soon understood how the cowboys would come and go picking a fresh horse from the remuda, that Tom was driving.

By lunchtime, the cook had already driven ahead of the cattle and had set up his cooking equipment for the cowboys. Lunch was more bacon, beans and hardtack. Mr. Jacobson explained that the wranglers would keep pushing the cattle constantly until they got to the Canadian Royal. "I know it's tough fellas, but we can't let the cattle get too thirsty or we'll have nothing to pay your wages with when we get to Pueblo. We'll take a brief rest at midnight and another one in the morning."

The day wore on, and Tom enjoyed his work extremely much. He was able to drive the horses very leisurely and was occasionally interrupted by a cowboy that would come and want a fresh horse. Tom would then help the man catch and saddle his rested horse so the wrangler could quickly return to his position with the herd.

Why in the world didn't I leave the school and Frank Woods behind long ago? thought Tom as he trotted up to the horses to steer them in line with the herd. *This is great! Much better than school, and much better than working in the store, and much better than being around a town full of hypocrites!*

However, as darkness settled in the West and the cowboys ate their fill of food from the cook's big pot, Tom had a strong yearning to lie down and sleep. There wasn't much talk around the chuck wagon as the boys ate; only a few mutterings to the cook about how he had better keep the coffee hot and ready. Tom's head had nodded, and one of the cowboys called Rusty said, "You'd better git some of that coffee down yer insides while ya can. It's gonna be a lengthy night."

The night **was** long, and Tom became very saddle sore and had to walk leading his horse whenever he could. The moon finally came up and showed one fourth of its brightness as Tom walked along, often stumbling on the rocks in the way. Howie was riding drag, trying to keep the straggling cows moving.

Except for the shuffling sound of the cows' hoofs and the mooing of the cattle and an occasional sound from a cowboy, the night was quiet. The tiredness and loneliness crept over Tom with sickening emotional feelings. The cattle drive that had been such a wonderful thing at the beginning of the day had now degenerated to a level of distaste in Tom's mind. He wondered about his mother and thought about how worried she might be about him.

****

The rising sun found a medium-size herd of cattle moving slowly north in the eastern New Mexico Territory. Ten cowboys and two young men were driving the three hundred cattle as the cook set up his equipment in time to welcome the punchers to a substantial breakfast of bacon, beans, and hardtack.

The breakfast and rest were a welcome relief to Tom as well as all the men. Rusty told Tom that a piece of lambskin laid in the saddle would help his saddle sores. Tom fell back asleep against the sandy wheel of the cook's wagon, and Howie fell asleep in the seat of the wagon. When Mr. Jacobson saw the excessively tired boys, he told the cook to let them sleep until he was ready to move and then send them back to work.

The cook was extremely tired also, but did not have the heart to wake the exhausted boys to help him. He let them sleep until he was ready to roll and catch up with the herd.

"We should be near the water by nightfall," explained Howie after the cook woke them up. "We'll have made a four days' trip in less than two!"

The extreme heat and dust made Tom and other dehydrated cowboys go to the chuck wagon many times for a drink from the barrels. He became so tired in the late afternoon that he actually fell asleep in the saddle as the horses plodded along through the dust.

In Tom's mind he was dreaming about Frank Woods beating him. As he dreamed that the leather strap was coming down upon him, he fell out of his saddle. One shoe caught in the stirrup! The tired pinto hardly noticed and started to drag Tom.

"Whoa boy! Whoa!" commanded Tom.

The pinto stopped and Tom pulled his twisted leg free. Looking around, Tom was relieved to see that no one had noticed.

"They're moving!" a cowboy hollered.

Tom saw the cattle starting to move faster and then begin to dash. He did not understand what was happening. Quickly Tom swung back into the saddle as the pinto also started scampering with the remuda.

Rusty appeared suddenly and pulled up along side of Tom. "The cattle smell water and are gonna run for it. The horses'll do the same. When they get to the river, don't let 'em over drink; chase 'em past if necessary!" yelled Rusty.

Just as Rusty had said, the cattle soon came to the Canadian Royal River. Some of the cattle plunged in and started to drink heavily, but most stood and cooled and drank slowly. The river was not wide, but it was deep at this spot. The remuda of horses that Tom was trying to care for seemed to pay him no attention as he tried to keep them from drinking too quickly after not drinking for two full days. Tom did manage to allow the pinto to drink only a little at a time.

For a moment it looked as if there would be disaster as the cattle all tried to crowd into the water in the same spot; however, the cowboys managed to drive some of the cattle further up stream so that the three hundred could all find a place to drink.

That evening after super was done; Howie and Tom helped the cook clean up. Jed explained that the cattle would be okay-although a few of them were very uncomfortable–but he thought they would probably live. "But if we hadn't a made that four-day trek in two days, the cattle would've over drank and died right on the spot," he said.

The next two days were spent very leisurely since Mr. Jacobson wished to give the cattle a rest and fatten them on the plentiful grass along the river.

The cook was up early on the third morning. "Come on, come on! Get out of the sack before I throw it to the birds! Come and get it!" he hollered.

Tom was rested, up, and ready to go as soon as the cook called. Before breakfast was finished, though, a tired-looking cowboy rode into camp. He turned out to be the scout for another herd of cattle coming up the trail. As he ate breakfast with the crew from the Jacobson ranch, he explained that his herd would be getting to the river in the afternoon and that they too had been traveling night and day.

Crossing the river turned out to be rather simple since it was not swollen. Tom had heard the cowboys mention that it was hard to tell what a river might do. Storms occurring miles up stream could cause a river to flood suddenly, though at this spot there might not be any sign of a storm. Tom was amazed at the way the cattle took to the water, almost as if they had been raised in a river. He watched the cowboys ride across on their horses. Then he tried too. He found that his small pinto was an adequate swimmer.

The uneventful river crossing was just the beginning of many monotonous days as the cattle moved slowly along toward their destination. Occasionally a cow would be startled and run off or get upset because she thought her calf was missing, but things would always settle down as a cowboy chased the straggler back in place with the ease and skill of many years of practice.

Tom plodded along too, hour after hour, watching his horses and helping cowboys saddle and re-saddle when a fresh horse was necessary. Some of the time was spent in deep thought for Tom. For the first time a funny, fearful feeling came over Tom as he realized that he did not know what he was going to do when they reached Pueblo. In his heart he knew, though, that he was not going back to Red Rock where he would have to be near Frank Woods. His hatred for the man grew as he thought about the undeserved beating. He often dreamed that he would someday grow up, ride back and rescue his mother from Frank Woods after he beat the man as he himself had been beaten. His hatred for Frank Woods was so intense that he often thought he would beat him to death or shoot him in the head several times.

Thoughts like this were traveling through Tom's head one day when he noted that there was a change in the scenery. Shortly, Howie rode up and said, "We'll be getting to Pueblo tonight! Tomorrow we'll help load the cattle on the train. Then we'll be all done!"

Loading the cattle on the train proved to be an interesting job. The cowboys herded them into the high wooden corrals where a buyer examined the luckless animals. After a price was determined, Mr. Jacobson told the boys to load the herd into the cattle cars.

It was the first time Tom had seen a locomotive and cars and the sight of the iron monster belching smoke and puffing off steam sent exciting tingles through his spine. He watched carefully as the brakeman waved a signal to the engineer as the first cattle car came to a stop exactly even with a long chute.

Jed gave Tom a long stick and told him to stand by the chute and poke the cows if they would not move up. Most of the animals were reluctant to enter the dreadful chute, so other cowboys also took sticks, poked, and prodded them until they moved.

It was not until late afternoon that the entire herd was loaded. Tom stood amazed as the black, smoking steam engine puffed slowly out of Pueblo with the entire herd of cattle. The train soon gathered up speed as all the weary cowboys stared at the black smoke disappearing into the east. The men all threw their sweaty hats into the air. They were ready to celebrate the ending of the cattle drive. Their tiredness gave way to celebration!

Back at the almost bare chuck wagon just outside of town, the cowboys got their things together as the trail boss handed out their pay. Tom began to feel lost as the cowboys took their wages and headed back to town. Some would be going back to Red Rock as regular ranch hands on the Jacobson ranch. Most of them would be going first to Pueblo to purchase a bath, a shave, a haircut and to spend their money on booze, "wild" women and poker. Many would be broke or almost broke when they left Pueblo.

"Well, Tom, how much do I be indebted to you? Let's see–about two-and-one-half months make it about seventy five dollars. That okay?' asked Mr. Jacobson.

"Do you remember that you were gonna sell me the pinto for seventy five dollars?" asked Tom. "How 'bout keepin' the money for the horse? I'll trade you my Winchester for the saddle and bridle."

Mr. Jacobson thought for a moment and said, "It's a deal! And, Tom, you're welcome to ride along with Howie and the rest of us as we depart back to the ranch."

"Well, thanks for the offer, Mr. Jacobson, but I'm not ready to go back. I'd appreciate it, though, if you or Howie would let my ma know that I'm okay," said Tom.

All the cowboys had left for town except for the Jacobsons and Jed. "Ain't ya goin' to town, Jed?" asked Tom.

"Naw, best not, Tom," replied Jed. "Too many people know my ole face in this place. I reckon I'd better be thinkin' 'bout what I'm gonna do this winter. Already the nights've been gettin' cool. Thought about goin' up into a mountain I know 'bout here in Colorado and doin' some trappin' this winter. There's money in it if things goes well. There's a cabin up there I helped a fella assemble a long time ago. It's prob'ly still up 'cuz we built it really good. Would ya be interested in goin' along? I'll teach ya what I know about trappin.'"

Tom thought for a moment. "Yeah, I think I'll try it, Jed. I don't know what else to do. I just spent all my wages to buy the pinto. What about the horses?"

"We'll make a corral and shelter for 'em before the first storm. They'll be all right. Need 'em to carry our supplies anyway. Speakin' of supplies, hows about I give ya my money and a list of things we need and have ya go into Pueblo and buy our supplies for us?" answered Jed.

Tom agreed to do so; and as the sun set, two weary, shadowy figures walked west from Pueblo leading two horses over burdened with a multitude of food supplies, pots, pans, traps, coats and ammunition.

Tom and Jed rested for the night as soon as Jed knew that they were far enough from Pueblo not to be bothered. The next morning Jed led Tom up a wide gorge that slowly narrowed and became steep. The two traveled quite some time before they climbed out of it. The countryside began to get more and more forested with oak and pine as they traveled upwards for several days.

By the end of the week Jed stopped. "I believe that cabin should be over that ridge just yonder. It's partly protected by the ridge itself," he explained.

True to his direction, Jed found the cabin where he had said it would be. Tom asked Jed how he could have found it just getting glimpses of it from between the towering pines at that distance.

"Just gut feeling, boy, just instinct," explained Jed and smiled.

To Jed's delight the old cabin showed slight need of repair. When he arrived at the only door and pulled the leather string, which moved the wooden latch inside, it still worked.

"A good sign, Tom, a good sign," Jed said smiling.

Inside the log shack, the two runaways found the old cabin dusty but undamaged. Soon a fire was going in the old cast iron stove, and the two were rewarded with a hot meal.

Within the week, the two trappers had fixed the cabin, constructed corrals and shelter for the horses, gathered feed, and cleared and cleaned the nearby spring. The two worked for several days. Jed felled a few trees so the wood could start drying for firewood. Even before a large supply of firewood was gathered, the winter's first snow began to fall.

Finally, the time came to start trapping and Jed cleverly showed Tom how to make a pair of snowshoes. The trapping of animals for their skins was novel to Tom, and learning to check a trap line was pleasurable to him. Tom was enjoying his new adventure.

In January, a dreadful storm brought a good deal of snow and cold. The two did not try to venture from the cabin except to check the horses. The animals were not faring well in such freezing weather.

"I fear the horses'll freeze if this storm doesn't let up, Tom," said Jed.

"What can we do, Jed? I'd hate to lose my pinto. He's just right for me."

"Well, if the storm doesn't break tomorrow, we kin try to squeeze the horses in here. It's much warmer, 'though it's still a little chilly in here even with the fire burnin' constantly," said Jed.

That night the storm worsened. The cabin proved sturdy but chilly as the two huddled near the stove. Staying awake feeding the stove, they heard the horses neighing.

A lull in the storm allowed Tom and Jed to leave the warmth and security of the cabin and wade through the waist-deep snow to get to the endangered horses. They were standing together in a corner, cold but not wet. The trappers had trouble getting the horses through the undersized door, especially Jed's large sorrel, but they finally succeeded.

Two days of existing with the horses in the cabin were necessary before the blizzard let up and the trappers were able to take the horses back to the outside shelter. While returning the horses, Tom discovered foot tracks in the snow around the cabin and horse shelter.

"Looks like maybe we've had some company, Jed! Other trappers, ya think?" asked Tom.

Jed examined the good prints closely and said, "Naw, Tom, this here's a Indian moccasin print; he has somethin' wrong with him. He's young."

"How do you know, Jed?" asked Tom.

"Cuz they're close together and look too deep. He was movin' very slowly. The print is too small for a grown man," explained Jed.

The tracks led into the horse shelter, and in one freezing corner of the shelter, they found a youthful Indian rolled in a blanket.

"Is he dead, Jed?" asked Tom.

"I don't see how he could be alive, Tom. Nevertheless, let's take 'im into the cabin and put 'im near the warm fire. Sometimes people who look dead when frozed ain't really. Let's just carry 'im into the cabin and put 'im near the fire. We'll carry 'im rolled up like he is," said Jed.

Tom sat by the boy near the warm fire while Jed went out and chopped more wood. The storm had passed, and the air outside was clear but extremely cold.

Jed built the fire up high and covered the Indian boy with a blanket he first warmed by the fire. Taking the boy's moccasins off, Jed saw his feet white and stiff.

"I'm 'fraid he's nearly froze. If he **is** alive and **does** live, he may be crippled. Let's warm some water slightly and try ta thaw his feet slowly," said Jed.

After soaking the boy's feet with the warm water, Jed also warmed some whiskey and tried forcing it between the boy's cold lips. After a few tries, a faint gasping noise was heard, and they knew the boy was still alive. Within a couple hours the young Indian opened his eyelids and revealed dark black, confused, frightened eyes. Jed gave the boy a teaspoon of warm water that he held in his throat for a long minute and then finally swallowed.

"That's good, Tom, good sign, good sign. We may have an Indian buddy here yet," explained Jed.

All through the night the two trappers watched their Indian visitor as he thawed out and slowly regained the movement in his arms and legs. Jed massaged the young Indian's feet with his strong hands for several hours. Although the young boy made several noises that sounded like grunting to Tom, he never seemed to show pain.

Tom made the boy some oatmeal and encouraged him to eat it with a spoon. Both the oatmeal and the spoon seemed to be new to the lad. Jed offered him some jerky, and the Indian readily ate.

Within two days the young Indian was well and able to walk around the cabin that Jed had kept particularly warm. To Jed's great surprise, the boy's feet seemed to be fine.

"Must've been all that tender love and care you gave him, Jed," said Tom with a little laugh.

The Indian boy tried to communicate with sign language, which at first did not make any sense to Tom.

"The boy said he got lost in big storm and couldn't find his way. He was 'bout to lie down and die when he spotted our cabin but was 'fraid to come to the door, so he went to the stable. He says he killed a deer not far from here and wants us to go get it for food if we can find it," interpreted Jed.

The three hunters had little trouble finding the deer that had been partly eaten by wolves. Jed hacked off a good portion of the frozen meat, and all three lugged it back to the cozy cabin. They worked together and soon had large strips covered with pepper and salt hanging by the fire to make jerky.

The now healthy-looking Indian boy called himself Hoga. By using sign language, he told Jed that he wanted to go to his people. Wrapping himself in his blanket and carrying a large pouch full of jerky which Jed gave him, the young Indian started out but stopped and turned back to sign to Jed and Tom an expression of gratefulness.

"He said he'll never forget us and always'll be our friend."

The cold, white winter in the mountains slowly turned to spring as the days grew longer and the snow began to melt.

"It was a good winter, Tom. We trapped a lotta furs and kept ourselves warm and comfortable most of the time. But our food supplies is gone 'cept fer the meat we trap. I reckon in 'bout a week we oughta head down the mountain and sell our furs. Maybe we kin go back to the Jacobson's ranch and herd cattle in the spring roundup," said Jed.

****

Selling the furs proved easy since in Pueblo there were several buyers that wanted to purchase the furs to resell in the East. The two also rented a room and purchased warm baths and meals, both of which Tom greatly needed. Then they left for the Jacobson ranch.

The long horseback ride to the ranch was agreeable. The weather was still cool and the nights pleasant. The pinto had become a part of Tom's life, and he loved the horse like a brother. The speckled mount had grown to consider Tom his master.

Tom enjoyed the roundup and branding and often thought of going to Red Rock to see his mother. Howie reported that Mrs. Woods had grown sick because of her worry about Tom's disappearance. She had come out to the ranch to ask Howie about him. He had told her that Tom had gone on the last trail drive to Pueblo and had then taken off with some cowboys.

Tom considered going to Red Rock but still felt such hatred for Frank Woods that he didn't go to town. Tom had already been practicing using the Remington .44, and with some advice from Jed had become a fair shot. The boy became more attached to the gun and wore it often. His fourteen-year-old frame had filled out enough that the belt no longer hung on him so awkwardly. The gun gave him a sense of control and pleasure.

Frank Woods is never gonna touch me again! thought Tom. If he does, I will shoot him. Well,—might anyway!

****

One hot summer evening when Tom could not sleep and the cattle were calm, Tom decided to strap on the .44 and finally rode to town. Other cowpokes were there, and the town was alive with the smell of booze and the noise of partying people at every saloon. Tom knew what went on there. He stopped by the sheriff's office to greet his friend. The sheriff seemed unusually interested in knowing all about Tom and wondered where he had spent the winter and with whom. Tom was awfully nervous. He told several lies to cover for Jed.

Going to the back of Clara's cafe, Tom found his mother working late. She was overwhelmed with joy to see Tom. She hugged and kissed him in the way only a joyful mother can. Tom was embarrassed.

"Oh, Ma, good night! That's enough!" insisted Tom.

"Well, Tom, it's just been so long!" said Ma. "Where've ya been and why'd ya stay so long? I'm so glad you're back!"

"I've been herding cattle mostly, and I'm just here for a visit, Ma," stated Tom rather bluntly.

"Well, sit down here and I'll get ya somethin' to eat, and we'll talk," said Ma.

Tom ate the delicious food while his mother talked on and on about how much she missed him and how sorry she and Frank were that he left and how delighted she was that he was okay.

"Ma, I'm not staying; I just come to see you and let you know I was all right," Tom stated somewhat apologetically.

"But, Tom, you're my boy; I love ya. You **have** to stay with me!" Ma said with a note of pleading in her voice.

"I love you too, Ma, and you're a wonderful mother, and I'll come back and visit, but I have to go," said Tom.

"Oh, Tom, why do ya have to go? Can't ya forgive and forget?" asked Ma.

"No, Ma! When ya get beat within an inch of yer life for somethin' ya didn't do, by a man who calls himself a Christian, ya can't forget **or** forgive! I hate him! When I think 'bout what he did, my blood boils inside me! I feel like killin' him! Moreover, I can! So I had better not stay!" exclaimed Tom as he talked loudly.

During Tom's explanation, his face got red and his eyes widened as rage showed on his young face.

"Why, Tom, you're showin' some of the angry character your pa used to. I didn't think you'd harbor such hatred in your heart for Frank after all this time," stated Ma.

"I'm sorry, Ma; it is there. If I'd been guilty of stealin' the one hundred dollars, I would've gotten over it. But **I** did **not** steal any money. I can't prove it, but I know it; so if I meet with Frank, I'm liable to put a bullet in him!" exclaimed Tom.

"My, Tom, I'm sorry to hear ya talk like this. Frank has said he was sorry he beat ya so badly, and that he just lost control. Tom, if ya didn't steal Frank's money but ya had one hundred dollars in your bag and Frank was missing one hundred dollars, what happened to Frank's money and where did ya get your one hundred dollars?" asked Ma.

"I don't know what happened to Frank's money. I did **not** steal it! If I tell ya where I got **my** one hundred dollars, you wouldn't believe me, 'cuz it's a very amazing thing!" exclaimed Tom.

"Tell me anyway, please!" pled Ma.

"'Member when we first came to Red Rock and I got shot and was stayin' in the boardin' house alone some evenings while you worked late here?" asked Tom.

"Yes," answered Ma.

"Well, one night while you were out, a man slipped through the window and talked briefly to me. He said he was one of the outlaws who robbed the stage and was sorry I was shot and then gave me the money," explained Tom.

"Tom, that **is** a extraordinary story, but not necessarily unbelievable. Why didn't ya tell Frank and me?" asked Ma.

"I tried to Ma, but Frank just kept beatin' me and said, 'You gotta do better than that!' Remember?" asked Tom.

"I think so, Tom. We heard rumors that you'd been seen with an outlaw. Was he the one?" asked Ma.

Tom froze. He didn't know what to say, not even to his mother. He did not want to betray Jed but did not want to lie to his mother.

"Tom, your reaction tells me it's true; and Tom, oh, my boy, you'll become just like the people you're with. If ya don't leave this man alone, you'll become an outlaw too!" Ma exclaimed fearfully.

"Ma!" gasped Tom.

The two sat looking at each other in silence until Ma started to cry.

"I don't want my only child becomin' an outlaw! Oh, Tom, you're only a boy fourteen years old, and ya come in here wearin' a gun, talkin' 'bout killin' my husband!" sobbed Ma Fleming Woods.

Tom sat still and said nothing until Ma quit crying so much. His mother's weeping and sadness made him feel bad.

"Ma, I promise ya that I'll **never** kill Frank–for your sake, even though I may feel like it!" exclaimed Tom.

A noise of horses in the street in front caused the two to hurry to the front of the restaurant to look out. The dim light from the stores was not bright enough to reveal who was on the horses, especially with the dust in the air.

"Sheriff has finally caught the outlaw," alleged an onlooker.

Alarm clamped Tom's chest. *Could it be Jed?* thought Tom.

Tom turned and gave his mother a kiss. "I'll be back. I'm gonna see what's up!"

Tom followed the posse down the street to the sheriff's office. From the shadows, Tom could see the sheriff remove a handcuff from the saddle horn so the prisoner could step down. Then Tom recognized the man as his best friend, Jed. Startled but wanting to be loyal to Jed, Tom followed the men to the front of the sheriff's small office until he saw the sheriff lock Jed securely inside a cell. When the sheriff saw Tom, he motioned to him. Tom stepped forward with his heart pounding hard.

"Well, Tom, we got your buddy, thanks to you," smiled the sheriff. "Yes, when you showed up in Red Rock I knowed Jed must be near because it had been reported to us that you were riding with him,"

"Who tol' you?" asked Tom rather angrily.

"Can't tell you, Tom, but it would surely do you a world of good to pick better friends. When you showed up earlier this evening, I knew I could believe the reports, because you had and have a new spirit of rebellion and haughtiness written on your face. I can usually tell where a man–or boy–is coming from just by the look on his face, the glint in his eyes, and the way he wears his gun. Most young boys your age don't yet wear a gun belt," explained the sheriff as he spit tobacco onto the ground.

"I see," said Tom. He dejectedly turned and left. Instead of stopping to see his mother, Tom mounted his pinto and rode back to the roundup. As Tom galloped into camp, he could hear the cowboys talking about the arrest.

Tom just lay down on his blanket thinking about the turn of events and his part in Jed's being arrested. Finally, Tom fell into a restless sleep.

CHAPTER EIGHT

T he snow was falling very lightly from the light, low clouds as Tom dismounted his beloved pinto and tried the leather latch in the old cabin's door. The latch still worked. *"Good sign, good sign."* The haunting words of Jed's remark came to Tom as he remembered how Jed had brought him here and cared for them last winter.

Inside, Tom found the cabin undisturbed. Apparently, no one had found or bothered the place since Jed and Tom had left it last spring. He sat at the table, his mind in a fog, as he looked about remembering the year he and Jed had spent together. The events of the past three months began to come to mind. Overcome by loneliness, Tom grieved for Jed as great tears of grief fell from his eyes. Jed had, in a way, actually become as a father to him.

The emotions and feelings Tom had hid to everyone came loose as he sat there and cried and sobbed, "Jed, oh, Jed, why, why?" Finally, he stopped crying and sat remembering…

Jed had had to sit in the Red Rock jail for over a month waiting for the circuit judge to appear for his fateful trial. Tom had visited him often until the cattle drive began. Tom recalled the conversation: "Tom, it ain't yer fault. I was gonna get caught some time. Besides I was tired of runnin' and always hidin'. I feel almos' glad to have been caught; 'cept, I prob'ly am gonna get the rope. Too many people saw me shoot some people in that bank robbery I tol' ya 'bout. Tom, I advise ya ta stay clean; earn your money; stay out of trouble. Sittin' here thinkin' 'bout things has caused me to think 'bout all my bad luck, but you know, Tom–it wasn't so much bad luck, as I was jus' foolish–wrong! Maybe there **is** somethin' to this sin thing, and the need for Jesus; like Mary tol' me!" Jed said.

"Ah, Jed, it don't sound like ya to go and get religious," smirked Tom.

"Tom, listen, think 'bout it! Look at me! Look at the fix I'm in! What would my life be like if I'd followed the Good Book? I wouldn't be here!" exclaimed the serious prisoner.

"But Jed, I know people who say they know Jesus, and go to church, and yet they do rotten bad things when they think no one is lookin'!" said Tom raising his voice.

"Yeah, I know, but there are some who do better, like Mary did, and your ma. Those kind of people are happy; maybe poor, but they're happy, because they have no guilt inside. Peace with God and man!" explained Jed loudly.

"Well, maybe, Jed, maybe," suggested Tom.

"Well ya jus' think real hard about it, Tom, so you don't end up like me,"

Jed stood up and walked about the small jail cell. "I'm so tired of this here cell, Tom. I've been here over a month. I hope I get the death sentence and not the life sentence."

"Maybe I could break ya out of this place, and we could go really far away–maybe to another country even!" exclaimed Tom.

"Naw, I'm not even gonna let ya try, Tom. Then you'd be a fugitive just like me. Always runnin', runnin', runnin', and hidin'. No good, Tom, ya got your whole life ahead of ya. Do better than I did!" Jed's voice became louder and almost angry, as he looked Tom in the eyes.

"Stay clean! Work hard! Earn your money! Get a nice wife, like Mary would've been. **EARN** a little farm or ranch! Go to church! **STAY** OUT OF TROUBLE! Don't break the law–don't **SIN!**"

Jed stopped, still staring into Tom's eyes. It was the moment of enlightenment and understanding for Jed. "Tom, that's it!

That's the whole problem! Why didn' I understan' before? I was tol'! Mary tole' me!"

"What's it, Jed? What do ya mean?" asked Tom.

Jed did not reply, so Tom just sat still thinking.

"I didn' believe, Tom, because I didn' see; but now I see!

Now I see–" Jed spoke sort of to Tom and sort of to himself.

Large tears started falling from Jed's eyes as he muttered, "Now I see! Now I see–why didn' I see sooner? Now I believe! Now I believe, Dear God, now I believe!"

Tom sat still, hardly able to believe his eyes and ears. Jed the outlaw–the strong, manly outlaw with the deep voice–now sat before him crying and praying. It seemed that Jed would never stop. He had gone on muttering in prayer–partly crying and partly praying–with Tom catching a few words here and there.

"Sin–lust–greed–that's me–God, that's me! Thank ya Jesus, thank ya, Jesus–"

Finally, Jed stopped crying, praying and walking in circles. In the middle of the cell Jed stopped and looked up toward the low roof and hollered, "Praise God! Praise God! I'm saved like Mary tole' me I could be!"

"Tom, I'm free! It's okay for me to die now! Things is right between me and Jesus! I'm free! I'm right with God! I feel good inside where it counts most! Tom, don't ya see? Jesus has forgiven me–and–and you, too!" exclaimed Jed.

"But I ain't killed no one yet, Jed," replied Tom quietly.

"Not just killin', Tom. I'm free of **all** my wrongs. Ya see, Tommy boy, I didn' understand the need fer Jesus, but now I do! We all need 'im, because we's all as guilty and crooked as a dog's hind leg. That's why Jesus came–that's why He died–ta pay the price that only He could pay. Jesus, 'God in the flesh,' as Mary used ta say, paid the price fer all of us. Paise God!" explained Jed earnestly.

Jed went on and on trying to explain things to Tom, but Tom did not or would not understand.

"Don't ya see, Tom? It takes a dark hour like this'un ta make a man understand his need fer God and ta think deep thoughts 'bout God, sin and his lostness. Otherwise many people don't think 'bout their sins, or God, much," explained Jed a little more quietly.

****

A blast of cold air came through the open cabin door causing Tom to snap out of his thoughts. "Gotta get the fire goin'," muttered Tom aloud; "A storm is comin'."

Tom found the wood box had only a few pieces of wood. He hurried around unpacking his horse and mule, but the darkening sky and storm had crept up on him until he had to go inside. He decided to bring the mule and horse into the cabin as he felt the temperature falling fast. The late August storm was unusually bad. Soon the sky was black except for lightning bolts, which seemed to be hitting all about the cabin.

"Some birthday present, God," said the now fifteen-year-old boy. As if God responded, the lightning bolts stopped. Tom built a fire. The light and heat seemed to help settle the animals somewhat; but his wood supply was low.

The untimely storm wore on into the night with a very heavy snow falling all around the cabin. The fuel for the fire was soon gone, and there was no way to get more until the storm broke. Tom made the pinto and mule lie down, covered them and him the best he could with his tarp, and then rolled himself into his fur coat left in the cabin from last season. Then he lay against his horse's belly. Tom's last bitter thoughts before going into an exhausted sleep were, *God? I don't need God! God helps those who helps themselves!*

During the night, the early storm quieted, and a beautiful morning sun shone upon the mountain ridge. The early storm had brought one foot of snow and an early cold. The sky was amazingly clear as the sunny morning began to warm up quickly.

The snow would not last long. Tom roused himself. The cabin was very cold and the animals quite impatient to go out.

After moving the animals to the snow-covered shelter, Tom went out into the snow with the homemade snowshoes Jed had shown him how to make last year. Finding firewood was a little difficult because of the snow. Tom stooped under some trees where the snow had not fallen so deeply to pick up a small branch. As he did so, he heard a slight noise near him. Suddenly he felt the presence of someone near.

Straightening up quickly, Tom reached for the old .44. He realized he had left it in the cabin. A thought in Tom's mind said; *Never leave your gun behind again!*

"Who's there?" Tom spoke quietly. "Anybody there?" He spoke louder. An Indian brave larger than Tom stepped out of his forest-hiding place: then another and another.

Oh, why don't I have my gun? thought Tom. *I can never protect myself from them!* Tom was about to run when a fourth Indian, one about his size, also stepped out into the open. The smaller Indian grinned at Tom.

"Hoga!" exclaimed Tom.

In very crude sign language, the two communicated. Hoga wanted to know if he was okay. Did he need help? Where was Jed? As best as he could, Tom said he was all right but needed firewood. He could not seem to explain that Jed was in prison.

The Indians helped Tom gather firewood and cleared snow so the animals could get to the autumn grass underneath. Soon the little cabin was warm and cozy, and Tom invited his Indian friends in for breakfast. They left, however, but soon returned with a young deer which they helped Tom dress.

Before leaving, Hoga made several gestures wondering where Jed was. Tom tried to explain, but the Indians seemed to think that Jed was dead. It struck Tom that maybe if he drew a picture of Jed in jail, they would understand. The Indians were amazed at the pencil Tom used. They each had to hold it and make some marks. The stick figure drawing of a man behind bars was all Tom could draw, but, whether they understood or not, the Indians at least quit asking about Jed.

****

Autumn faded into winter, but left Tom a chance to get things ready for it. He started his trap line again, just as Jed had shown him. The Indians came again. It was as if they were looking out for him. He realized that they really were because he and Jed had saved Hoga's life.

The trapping went well. The animals were plentiful, and before winter was half over the boy had furs stretched out all over the cabin. Things were going well and Tom sensed a goodly profit would come from the furs. However, he felt very lonely, and sometimes in the night when the winter wind howled, he felt fear. He resisted a strong urge to pray. Occasionally when he was snowed in and had nothing better to do, he would think of Jed. He had heard by means of the telegraph in Pueblo that Jed had been given a life sentence, which was to be served in the Arizona Territorial Prison at Fort Yuma.

Tom thought of the change in thinking that Jed had after he had accepted Jesus in his jail cell at Red Rock. Jed had wanted to tell his old missionary friend Mary about it, but did not know how to reach her.

The love Tom felt toward Jed was much like a son should feel for a loving father, and he felt puzzled by Jed's becoming religious when he himself felt so little need for God. *Still, I'll go to see him,* thought Tom. *I'll sell my furs this spring and travel to Fort Yuma by train, or I'll go by horse if I don't have enough money.*

When the spring came the fifteen-year-old lad, now nearing sixteen, put the cabin in order so that he might later return. This time he chopped a huge supply of firewood and enjoyed the work as he felt his heart beat hard in his chest and the blood surge through his strong biceps that had developed chopping wood.

His strength and stature had greatly increased through the long winter. Trying to bundle and tie all his winter furs to his mule and pinto was difficult, but he finally managed to do it just the way Jed had taught him.

As he was leaving, Tom saw his Indian friends on the ridge. He waved; they held their arms out straight. Tom thought about giving them something; however, they did not need furs. They too had had a good winter. Since they had moved closer to the cabin before he had arrived last fall, they had invited Tom to their village for meals, and their friendship had grown. He had learned a lot about their way of living. They had taught him much.

Now Tom wished to show his friendship more, so he invited them down from the ridge. He went into the cabin and brought out all his pots and pans and other hardware. He was also sure to give them all the pencils and paper he had. This they joyfully accepted like kids with new toys.

"Pencil," Tom said to them as they tried to repeat back. A final wave and Tom left for Pueblo, walking and leading the fur-laden pinto and mule down the mountain.

Although anxious to get back to civilization, Tom took a week to come to the bottom of the mountain range, which opened onto the road leading east, and west; Pueblo was to the east. The boy had traveled down the dusty narrow road only a short distance when he heard a horse coming behind him. In fact, when he looked back, he saw two mounted riders who quickly overtook him and his weighed down animals.

"Well, well, well, what have we here?" asked the man in front, as he drew out a fat cigar and lit it. He wore a somewhat worn and torn black tophat.

Tom smelled the cigar smoke and the sweaty, foul smell of dirty bodies mixed with alcohol. He realized that a couple of outlaws had stopped him. Tom looked at the beady-eyed man and asked him what he wanted.

"What I wants is them furs, young fella! Where'd ya get 'um?" asked the foul-mouthed leader of the two.

"I trapped them, and you're not gonna get 'em without buyin' 'em!" exclaimed Tom as he felt his anger rising and his heart thumping in his chest.

"Is that so, lad?" The cigar smoker spoke slowly and said calmly to his sidekick, "Shoot the kid, Frederick."

Tom made the mistake of looking suddenly at the outlaw to his left; when his face was turned, the outlaw in front lunged forward and slugged him square in the side of his head. Tom reeled backwards, falling against his horse. The pinto reared up, causing the man's horse in front to rear. Tom fell to the dusty ground as his pinto and mule ran off down the road.

The outlaw, not prepared for his horse to rear, lost his balance and fell off hard. He came up cursing and hollering, "Shoot him, Frederick, shoot him!"

Frederick raised his gun to shoot the stunned boy, but a sudden swish left an Indian's arrow deep in the outlaw's black heart. Tom watched as the startled man's gun fired into the air. The man's eyes opened wide with pain and fear as his body fell to the ground upon the arrow, forcing it to go completely through him. Blood squirted from the man's back.

In that short time, Tom regained alertness. Seeing the remaining outlaw draw his gun, Tom pulled his own .44 and shot him in the chest. The bullet the man had shot at Tom missed. The wounded man lay on the ground, bleeding profusely. He raised his gun only slightly and shot a bullet into the ground near Tom, then dropped his weak arm.

Tom looked around for the Indians, but he saw nothing. Shortly, however, Hoga appeared out of the nearby bushes. In the broken English that Hoga had learned from Tom, Hoga said, "Tom help Hoga; Hoga help Tom."

Tom kneeled down by the outlaw after kicking the gun out of his reach. The man's eyes still showed alertness, but he was bleeding badly. "I'm sorry, Mister," spoke Tom softly; "I didn' want to hurt ya; ya left me no choice!"

The wounded man's breath was coming hard and shallow; bright red blood covered the man's shirt and ran onto the ground. His breathing came short and fast. He tried to speak. "Water! Water!" Tom held the man's head up and gave him a drink from his own canteen.

"I'm dying! Not like this! Oh, God–not like this! Not shot down by a mere youngster! Snake Eyes killed by a boy! God, I'm sorry, I should've lived a better life. It's over now!" squeaked the voice of the bloody, dirty, wounded outlaw. "I'm dyin' and goin' to Hell! Torture! God, I should've done better! What is your name, schoolboy?" he asked grabbing Tom's arm with a desperate bloody hand.

"Tom," replied Tom softly.

"Tom, it weren't your fault. I had it comin'! I'm as good as dead; I can feel it comin'! Listen carefully! I have a valuable map in my hat; it'll lead you to gold. One piece of the map is missin'. The old Scottish man has it, Scotty. Now I did somethin' good; I told this boy about the treasure. God! Jesus, have mercy on me!"

Snake Eyes gasped for air but could not get any because his own blood had filled his lungs and was choking him. Panic filled the man's face as blood oozed out of his mouth. Tom thought the man's bloody face would cling to the terrified look forever; but as death came, the face relaxed and the man lay staring into the heavens.

Tom's stomach turned; he started to cry. He laid the man's head down carefully, walked into the brush, and threw up. He then sat down and cried. It all happened so quickly, and Tom was such a part of it. He looked down and saw the blood on his clothes. *What did all this mean? Now I'm a killer!* thought Tom.

Tom thought about how the man died calling upon Jesus to have mercy on him. The boy realized that he might have died the same awful way if he had been the one shot.

Hoga reappeared with Tom's horse and mule. The furs were still in place. After washing his mouth out and taking a deep drink of water, Tom felt better. He was amazed and thankful that his Indian friend had followed him secretly for a week. Together they loaded the dead men onto their own horses, belly down, as Tom had seen it done. He felt he should take the men's bodies to the sheriff in Pueblo and explain things rather than try to bury them.

Tom inspected the outlaw's hat. Inside the sweatband was a long, carefully folded paper with sweat stains on it. Opening it up he saw that it was a map to a mountain somewhere in Arizona, but the map did not show the precise location of the treasure. Tom inspected the hat of the outlaw Snake Eyes had called Frederick, but he found no papers.

After a somewhat sentimental farewell, Tom thanked Hoga and started out again for Pueblo. He hurried because he did not want to be with the two corpses after dark.

CHAPTER NINE

A large crowd followed Tom down the busy street in Pueblo as he headed for the sheriff's office late that afternoon. The sheriff had arrived before Tom reached the jail. He took one look at each dead outlaw, swore loudly, and exclaimed, "I don't believe it! I don't believe it, but it's good! It's great! We have finally caught up with two of the dirtiest, sneakiest criminals I've ever known of!"

The local newspaperman came running up and insisted on taking a picture. The sheriff directed Tom to the morgue where the sheriff removed the criminals' personal belongings. Then he headed back to his headquarters with Tom. "What's your name, young man?" he asked.

"Tom Fleming," answered Tom.

"Well, Tom Fleming, I'm sheriff Rod Bungard, and I'm awfully glad to shake your hand. You have brought in Snake Eyes and Frederick. These two rascals are wanted for just about **everything** you can imagine. By the way, there is a bounty on their heads! Looky here at this poster, and this poster!" exclaimed the sheriff.

Tom took the posters. He could clearly tell that the two men, he had carried in deceased, were the men on the posters. They each had a reward of five hundred dollars on their heads, dead or alive.

"As soon as I make my report to the federal government, I will get the reward money for you. Oh! We'd better get a good photograph of them!" stated the lawman.

The sheriff walked to his office entrance and started to leave, but another man stopped him. "Clem, I was just gonna ask you to go take a picture or two of those outlaws before we bury 'em. We might need 'em to assist this boy–er–young man–get his reward," the sheriff said.

"Already a step ahead of you, Sheriff!" stated the newsman; "and I'll be glad to furnish the pictures if he will give me the story of how he brought them in."

All this seemed like a dream to Tom, but he was glad for the news and glad he was not suspected of anything in the demise of the two men. He gave the sheriff a complete report of what had happened while the newspaperman listened, took notes, and asked questions. Tom even told them about Snake Eyes' dying words, asking Jesus to have mercy on him. He did not tell them about the treasure map, though.

When the sheriff and reporter were done with Tom, he went and sold his furs. The skins brought a good price and enabled Tom to rent a room in the hotel.

Tom paid extra for a bath of clean water, and after soaking for a long while, and scrubbing cleaner than he had been in almost nine months; he tried sleeping in the hotel bed that felt so soft. Sleep would not come at first because the scene of the death of the two criminals kept going through his head. Finally, however, he fell into a deep sleep because his overly tired body could take no more.

Late the next morning the sheriff received, from the telegraph office, a reply from the Federal government that his report had been received and that Tom would be getting a telegraphed check for one thousand dollars. The sheriff walked to the hotel to tell him the good news. The young man had just come down the stairs from his room, and the two met in the lobby. When the officer told him the news, Tom threw his crusty old hat into the air and shouted for joy. "Whoopee!"

Later, while talking with the sheriff, he learned he could take a train ride to Fort Yuma, Arizona.

Tom walked by the general store and barbershop to go to the livery to check about his pinto and mule. Finding his animals in fine shape, he went back to the barbershop. The sound of his boots on the wooden planks reminded him that he needed new boots and clothing.

The redheaded boy looked even younger than his almost sixteen years as he paid the barber the twenty-five cents. "Good luck," said the barber, "and congratulations on getting those two most wanted."

Luck? That's what it is all right. I hope my luck holds, Tom said to himself as he headed for the general store.

The store was not as busy as Tom expected. He pushed the wooden and glass door open and a little bell on the door jingled. No one appeared at first. Then an exceptionally attractive girl about Tom's age appeared from around the curtain in the rear of the store. The girl had a little white handkerchief in her hand and had obviously been crying.

"May I assist you?" she asked with difficulty.

As Tom walked toward the counter, he realized the girl was very distressed–and extremely pretty. Her long, brown, neatly combed hair hung over her shoulders. A red ribbon tied on top made her especially cute. Tom got close enough to see the girl's pretty face and the wet streaks running down her rosy cheeks. When the girl looked clearly into Tom's eyes, he felt compassion for her. He also experienced something more that made his heart leap inside his chest.

"May I assist you?" the girl asked again.

"Ma–maybe I sh–should ask that of ya–you," Tom stuttered. "Is s–something wrong; are you okay?" asked Tom.

"There is nothing you can do. My father is dreadfully sick; the doctor and my mother are with him now. He has been in bed for a week, and my mother is worn out–and if my father dies, I don't know what we'll do." The girl started crying again. Tom, always uncomfortable around girls, felt completely helpless.

"I'm sorry," he muttered.

"What is your name?" the girl asked.

"T-Tom; what is yours?" stammered a surprised Tom.

"Mandy. Mandy Whitman," she answered back sweetly.

"Pretty name, Mandy. Don't worry; your dad will get better!" said Tom, not knowing what else to say. "It's springtime; I just know he will!"

"Thanks, Tom. I think I can wait on you now. What did you want?" asked Mandy as she wiped her eyes and nose

"Clothes, just some good, new clothes–nothing fancy–just some new ones, perhaps an extra set because I'm gonna travel ta Fort Yuma, Arizona, soon," explained Tom.

Mandy started to explain where the men's section of clothes was. "Oh, down that row–"

"Mandy!" Mandy's mother called as she came around the heavy curtain. "Your father is getting better; he's regained consciousness and is talking a little! The doctor says he'll probably be up and around in a few days! Praise God!" Mandy hurriedly left the store to see her father.

Shortly Mandy reappeared with a much-changed countenance and told Tom the good news. She directed him towards the men's clothing. To his delight, he realized she was showing him clothes for a gentleman, not for a boy. She pointed to a curtained area in the corner where he could try the clothes.

Tom chose the clothes he wanted. They included, among other things, a new hat and a pair of boots. He paid for them with the cash from his furs.

"Thank you, Tom. I hope I see you again," Mandy said in a marvelous way that made Tom blush. Her pretty brown eyes fluttered ever so slightly.

"Ya–you too," Tom choked out; "I mean, me too! Thank you! I mean, you're so welcome!" Tom turned abruptly; embarrassed and confused he ran into the cold potbelly stove and somersaulted over it. "What the–," he started to swear but withheld the words because of Mandy's presence.

Mandy ran around to Tom. "Are you hurt?" she asked in an incredibly comforting female tone.

"Yeah, I'm all right," Tom said, confused and now more angry at himself than embarrassed.

"I hope you didn't hurt your nice new clothes! Let me brush you off!" Mandy offered.

Tom had a wonderful feeling as Mandy's tender, pretty, slender fingers slid over his clothes. "Well, good-bye again Mandy," Tom stated foggily, and he tripped on the threshold as he stumbled through the door. Once outside, he took a deep breath of air and said to himself, *Boy is she something, really something!* In a bit of a daze he continued down the wooden sidewalk back toward the hotel but walked right past it. Suddenly, realizing what he had done, Tom turned around to retrace his steps. The sheriff was crossing the street toward him.

"Got something for ya, Tom. Can't believe it came already, but put this here check for one thousand dollars in that new vest pocket and head towards the bank; it's your safest bet. First, I need you to sign this certificate of receipt. Here, sign this," instructed the sheriff as he handed the paper to Tom.

Tom took the paper and looked at the pencil as if he had never seen one before. He looked at the pencil and back to the sheriff.

"What's the matta with ya, boy? Are you sick? I said sign the receipt!" exclaimed the sheriff.

"What?" asked Tom rather quietly.

"What is the matta with you, kid? You **are** sick! I said, 'sign the receipt!'" exclaimed the sheriff again.

Tom took the receipt and wrote his first name.

The sheriff looked at it and said, "No, no, no! You also have to sign your last name!"

"Oh," replied Tom quietly and added the name Fleming. "Thanks, Sheriff."

"I think ya got a problem, son. You have a haze across your face! Been eatin' good? Ya betta go see the doctor! Put the money in the bank! See ya later, Tom," said the sheriff who then walked away briskly.

The money felt good to Tom as he headed toward the bank. In fact, Tom felt good all over. He did not feel his feet on the boardwalk. *Wait a minute,* thought Tom as he snapped to his senses. *What if the bank gets robbed? Then I lose all my money!*

He thought about ways to spend his money. He even considered sending a large amount to his ma, but figured he would not for fear it might benefit Frank Woods in some way.

"May I help you, young man?" the voice of the teller interrupted Tom's thoughts.

"Ah, ah, well... yes! I, ah, want ta put some money in your bank, but I don't wanna lose it," stammered Tom.

"Well, that is why you put it in! Say! Aren't you the young fella that brought Snake Eyes in? I'll bet you want to deposit the reward money, don't ya?" asked the teller.

"Yes, but what if your safe gets robbed? Has it ever been robbed?" asked Tom.

The teller looked a little sheepish, "Maybe you better talk to the president, Mr. Blackstone. Mr. Blackstone!" the teller called.

An older man with slightly graying hair looked up from behind a large oak desk.

"You need to talk to this customer, sir," explained the teller.

"Yes, of course. What can I do for you? Come around the counter, son, and have a seat here by my desk," said the president with a friendly gesture. "Are you Tom, the young man that brought in Snake Eyes and Frederick?"

Tom nodded his head and explained his fears to the owner.

"Well, Tom, I wouldn't lie to you. Yes, my bank was robbed about two years ago. A couple of drunken cowboys came in here, shot up the place real dreadful, and demanded I fill up a carpet bag with money. Therefore, I did. They headed west on Main Street out front. When the sheriff heard the shots, he came running. When the robbers saw him coming, they turned south by the general store and went behind some buildings until they got themselves cornered by the sheriff and some towns folks; so they gave up. Drunk cowboys; dead end street," Mr. Blackstone explained.

"So you got the money returned?" asked Tom.

"That's the sad and strange part, Tom. Those two men somehow hid the money! Three thousand five hundred dollars! It was never found! Nothing could get the cowboys to talk. There is still a five hundred dollar reward for the return of it, though," said the bank keeper solemnly.

"Probably somebody found it and they ain't talking 'cuz they'd rather have the three thousand five hundred than the five hundred," suggested Tom.

"Perhaps," said Mr. Blackstone. "Anyhow, we still have money, and business goes on. The safe is good–but what can you do when someone is pointing a gun at you? Same for you, Tom! If you keep your reward money in your pocket, you can even more easily lose it or have it stolen."

Tom carefully filled out the form for a deposit, but chose to keep out two hundred dollars. That was a lot of money to him, but nonetheless, he wanted to spend some.

While walking back down the main street, Tom felt the lump of money in his pocket. Deciding he needed a wallet, he went back to the general store. He knew that was an excellent excuse to see the beautiful girl again.

Tom pushed the door open, and the bell clattered. He could see that Mandy was busy waiting on an elderly lady buying some material. The store smelled similar to Frank Wood's store: a mixture of feed, leather, hard goods, cedar and mothballs. Unlike other stores, this store had a pleasant fragrance added by the feminine touch that made a person want to linger there.

Mandy's eyes met Tom's again. It seemed to Tom that her eyes twinkled at him. The lady buying the material asked, "How much is this?" but Mandy did not answer. "How much is this?" she asked louder.

"Th–three cents!" stammered Mandy. Tom walked around the store looking at the items but not **really** seeing anything. He kept glancing at Mandy and the lady, wishing that the customer would make up her mind and be done.

"May I help you?" Mandy's mother had just appeared from behind the curtain at the rear of the store.

"Ah, ah, ya...yes, I was–I wanna buy a wallet," said Tom nervously.

"Well, I hardly think you'll find one in this section!" said the lady with a look of amusement on her tired face.

Tom looked down and focused his eyes on the material in front. He felt his face blush red as he saw ladies' undergarments on the shelf.

"I, ah, well–it's because–I, well–I couldn't find your wallets!" Tom blurted out finally.

"They're over this way," she said kindly.

Tom looked over the wallets carefully until he found the one he liked. He was relieved to hear Mandy's mother say, "You may pay the girl at the cash register."

Tom waited while Mandy finished with her customer.

"Hi again," Tom said nervously, but a little more relaxed by Mandy's charming smile. "I...ah... just wanna buy this here wallet, Mandy," he said looking into her brown eyes.

The couple stood staring at each other. Apparently, Mandy found Tom's presence a thing of interest to her, too.

"Well, of course," she said, clearing her throat slightly and giving out a slight giggle.

Tom paid for the wallet, and Mandy said, "After you left earlier, my mom said you were the young man that brought in Snake Eyes and Frederick!"

"Yes, I did," Tom said, not sure if he should be proud of himself or not.

"Are you a bounty hunter, Tom?" asked Mandy.

"No! I just had to fight them or they would have shot me," explained Tom.

"Oh, I see," said Mandy very sweetly. "You must be awfully brave!"

Tom felt embarrassed and uncomfortable, but loved the attention the girl gave him. "Well, I did what I had to–I, ah...did not like shooting the man; I never killed before."

Mandy walked around the counter and stood close to Tom.

"Tell me about it, Tom," Mandy said, with sympathy in her voice.

The closeness to Mandy, the fragrance of her perfume, and the beauty of her face and long brown hair almost overcame Tom.

"I, ah... you see, I was trapping furs in the mountains this past winter and I ah..." Tom stopped.

"Yes, Tom?" Mandy encouraged as she stepped slightly closer to Tom so that he could feel the slightest frill on her dress. All the love-smitten boy could do was stand there with a brainless look on his face. The feelings of love toward this beautiful girl had overcome him so fast that he did not know how to react.

"Mandy!" Mandy's mother called. "Will you come here?" she said as she appeared from around the curtain. "Oh! I... didn't know you still had a customer!" she said and noticed the red-faced Tom and the closeness of the two. Mandy stepped back.

"Tom was just telling me about how he brought in Snake Eyes and Frederick," explained Mandy.

"Well, I trust you're not a bounty hunter, young man!" stated Mrs. Whitman, rather harshly.

"Oh, no, Mother! He's not a bounty hunter; he shot them in self defense!" exclaimed Mandy.

"What are you then?" asked the girl's mother.

"I, I, I... am a trapper and a cattleman, ma'am," explained Tom.

"Oh, well, that's better."

"Mother, can Tom go to church with us tomorrow?" asked Mandy suddenly without asking Tom first.

"I guess so, dear, but someone has to stay with your father."

"Tom, you will go with me, won't you?" asked Mandy, looking at him with expectant eyes.

Tom's feelings of love for Mandy overpowered his abhorrence of churches. "Ya-yes," he stammered.

Mandy's mother disappeared around the curtain again as if to leave the two alone. Tom's tongue regained its ability to function again as he told Mandy all about his past winter: how he had made friends with the Indians, how they saved his life, and how he brought the two dead outlaws in. He also told her about his reward money.

"I didn't really need it, though. I earned plenty of money trapping for furs. Mr. Blackstone said his bank was robbed once, so I didn't really want to put my money in the bank, but I did."

"Oh, yes. I remember that, Tom! The robbers rode along the street here and got themselves cornered out back. They never came out with the stolen money and never told anyone where they hid it! Strange, isn't it?" exclaimed Mandy.

"Yeah," replied Tom with interest. "Do you think the money is still around here somewhere? Maybe they threw it on the roof or something!"

"It may be around here, Tom, but I don't see how. The townspeople combed the area here and all around. So they would have found it if it was possible. Maybe somebody else stole it!" exclaimed Mandy.

"Do you think that would be stealing?" asked Tom. "I mean the person that found it didn't rob the bank."

"Well, of course, if you have something that belongs to somebody else and you know it, it's stealing," said Mandy sweetly. "Besides, the bank offered a five hundred dollar reward."

"Well, I think I'll take a look around, too," Tom said with a faraway look in his eyes.

"Oh, don't be silly, Tom. The place has been searched and searched," smiled Mandy.

"Well, actually, I have to use the outhouse," said Tom somewhat awkwardly. "By the way, did they search it?"

"Of course! Well, good-by, you can pick me up for church at 10:30 tomorrow morning. You **will** come with me, won't you?" Mandy asked very sweetly.

"Yes!"-exclaimed Tom, without thinking about his promise to not go to church. "Is it far?"

"No, we can walk there in about fifteen minutes," she said.

Taking the side door from the general store, Tom found himself on the dusty side street by the store. Walking slowly toward the outhouse, Tom looked around to see that the street dead-ended with wood-framed buildings all around the dead end. There was no space to get through, not even for a person walking.

He walked to the outhouse. "Boy! This one is a terrible stinker," he said aloud.

Tom latched the door and used the outhouse. While putting his clothes in order, he leaned over and his new wallet fell out of his vest into the human waste below.

"Oh, no!" Tom said rather loudly. Looking down into the waste, he could barely see the wallet in the dim light. Opening the door and getting down on his knees, he could clearly see the ruined wallet below. He knew he could not reach it with his arms. "Maybe I'll just forget it," he mumbled, as he let out a breath of air. *Naw...can't do that...over two hundred dollars in there!"*

Mrs. Whitman arrived at the open door of the outhouse and Tom stood up.

"Young man, what are you looking at now?" asked Mandy's mother with a clear look of amusement on her face as she gave out a little giggle.

"I, ah, well...you see, I was... using..." Tom stopped, his face turned as red as his hair.

"Well, go on," said Mrs. Whitman with a laugh.

The woman's good-natured laugh enabled Tom to feel more at ease, and he found his tongue again.

"I dropped my new wallet down there!" Tom exclaimed while pointing down the hole.

"Go ask Mandy for a clothes hanger and pliers and see if you can't fish it out. I'll go use a different facility," said Mrs. Whitman rather matter-of-factly.

Tom swore to himself as he walked back to the store.

"Mandy, I...ah, dropped... I mean... your mother asked me to borrow a clothes hanger and a pair of pliers," stuttered Tom.

"What does she want them for?" asked Mandy.

"Oh, well...she'll tell you later," explained Tom and hurried off to the outhouse, where he jerked on the door only to find it latched.

Startled at the realization of the mess his wallet was in, Tom halted for a moment, and then walked backward cursing to himself. Feeling angry, he kicked his new boots into the dusty street, sending dust and dirt flying around everywhere.

"I'm jus' gonna forget it!" murmured Tom. "Only money–two hundred dollars–I got more." Then he thought back to how hard he had worked in the past to earn that amount of money, and he knew he had to get it out.

An elderly man hobbled out of the building shortly. "Okay, sonny, all yours!" chuckled the man.

Tom opened the weathered door wide and looked down the stinky hole. "Yuck!" he said aloud. He swore as he bent a hook in the clothes hanger he had straightened out. "Why me?"

Tom took a cavernous breath of air and leaned down to the hole.

He could just barely reach the wallet with the hanger. The hook caught the edge of the wallet, and Tom was able to lift it carefully upward. Tom's breath was running out, and he exhaled deeply. As he did so, he lost his position and the wallet fell even deeper. "Plop."

"Oh..." Tom swore loudly, left the building, and threw the pliers and wire down. Then he kicked more dirt into the air several times.

A person walking past noticed Tom and stopped to ask what was wrong. Tom explained the problem. The man went and looked down the hole. "If it were me, I would forget it, unless you have an awful lot of money there!" he exclaimed.

Mrs. Whitman came by, "Did you get the wallet?"

"No!" Tom answered rather abruptly.

"Well, I'll sell you another one for half price since you had such an awful thing happen," she offered sympathetically.

"Thanks," Tom whispered, realizing that did not help get the wallet out.

A local barkeeper came by. "What's the matta?" he asked.

Soon a dozen people were discussing the problem. The small group started to draw others who wanted to find out what the problem was. Tom heard bits of their talk like, "A thousand dollars reward money down the hole!" Then the sheriff showed up.

"What's wrong here?" he asked. The sheriff thought that a longer wire might work, so he hurried off to the blacksmith's shop to get something. Within a few minutes, the sheriff produced a longer wire with a sharp bent hook and a small lantern with a wire hanging from it.

"What's that fer?" asked Tom.

"The lantern can be put down the hole to give ya plenty of light," explained the sheriff.

With the lantern being held by the sheriff, Tom reached way down with his arm and wire and once again snagged the wallet and began bringing it up very slowly. When he had it almost to the top, he noticed that there was a ledge built under the bench and the top boards at the far end of the outhouse. Between them, a carpetbag had been stuffed.

Tom carefully continued to pull the wallet up until he got it out. He turned around with the gooey wallet hanging from the wire. A large crowd had gathered around. Clem, the newspaperman, had set up his camera and tripod. At that moment he hollered, "Hold still; don't move!" The picture was taken, a cheer went up from the crowd, and everybody laughed. Then Tom realized he must have looked exceedingly foolish standing there with his drippy wallet on the end of a wire, with the outhouse behind him. "Why'd I let my picture get taken?" he mumbled.

Someone hollered, "Next time, use the bank!" and everyone except Tom roared laughing. His red face turned redder as he felt his pride hurt. He had started to tell the sheriff about the carpetbag, but his injured pride caused him to clam up.

The crowd began to disperse, and Mrs. Whitman brought Tom a pail to put the wallet in. He then carefully removed the money, threw the empty wallet back down the outhouse, and walked to the pump to wash his hands. Looking about, he wondered if Mandy had seen what had happened.

Tom decided to go for a ride on his pinto while he thought about recent happenings. He turned and headed west and rode through Main Street, observing parts of the town he had not noticed before.

The west edge of town opened into a rocky area with scattered trees and flat terrain. Tom spurred his pinto slightly and took off into a smooth gallop. A mile later, he slowed when he noticed a pleasant forested area with a small trail leading down towards a creek. *A nice place to go to think,* he thought.

Tom dismounted and walked his pinto until the trail ended. There he found someone had tied a horse. Seeing a footpath among the trees, he quietly followed the trail. The area was green, cool, and quiet. He thought it was a very pretty place and stopped to look and listen to the water in the creek as it splashed down its course.

Funny how a creek makes such interesting noise, thought Tom. *Sounds almost like a voice.* Quietly he walked towards the babble. His experience trapping with the Indians had taught him how to walk very quietly. He also remembered how he used to sneak up on people in Red Rock and saw people doing things they should not have been. The "voice" grew louder as Tom approached a small clearing by the creek. He realized that he was hearing more than the creek.

In the clearing was a large log about thirty feet long. A man was kneeling at the larger end of the log, praying. Tom felt startled at first; then realizing the man did not know he was there; he just stood still and listened.

The man's prayer was long and about many things. He often paused from asking God for something to praise God for something. His prayer included many people by name, including prayer for Mandy's father. Tom noticed that the man's black suit was new looking. He had taken off the jacket and laid it neatly on the log.

"...and thank you for allowing Snake Eyes and Frederick to be caught up with so no more innocent people will be hurt by them," the man prayed.

The sunlight coming through the trees in the clearing showed brightly around the kneeling man. The scene was so beautiful to Tom that it reminded him of a picture he had seen of Jesus kneeling in prayer. Tom began to think that this man was the local pastor, but he noticed that he packed a pistol on his hip. *Would a preacher carry a gun?* thought Tom.

Slowly, quietly, Tom backed away being careful not to disturb the man. Tom rode his pinto back into Pueblo leisurely. He believed that he had been allowed to see something extraordinary. *Or was it just luck?* His thoughts troubled him, and he began to think deeper.

A man that prays alone, secretly, must sure believe in what he is doing, because nobody but God is there. The scene came to Tom's mind again. *I guess it did seem like God was there.*

The night seemed long to Tom as he wrestled with his thoughts in his bed. Believing he would find the stolen money under the outhouse, he knew he should return the money to the bank. The thought of three thousand five hundred dollars as compared to five hundred dollars was a great temptation to him.

Tom remembered what Jed had told him about money—how that stolen money lasted only for a short while and "then you were worse off because you are in trouble after that." *Still,* he reasoned, *I didn' steal the money. I only found it.* His mind wanted to convince him that it would be okay to keep all of the money.

The next morning Tom realized that he had forgotten it was Sunday and that the restaurants were closed. Digging hungrily in his saddlebags, he found a piece of jerky. With it was the map Snake Eyes had given him. He had almost forgotten about the treasure map. He studied it again. *A mountain in Arizona?* he thought.

Mandy was ready for church when Tom arrived. Her long brown hair streamed beautifully over her left shoulder. The white dress she wore had pretty frills of red ribbon on the shoulders. Tom noticed everything about her, although he tried not to be obvious. He thought Mandy was beautiful, but he hardly knew what to say. He felt he should say something as they stood just outside of Mandy's door. Mandy's face seemed so clean, bright, and happy.

"Mandy, I, ah, I...," stammered Tom.

"Yes, Tom?" she said sweetly.

"Well, I jus' wanna say, I... that... ah, well...," Tom just could not get the words out. He felt his face turn red. He could only stand there turning the brim of his hat around and around in his hands.

Mandy stepped closer to Tom. The smell of Mandy's fresh perfume and the look of her pretty eyes staring at him overpowered him. He just could not speak. He tried, but only got a squawk out of his throat.

Mandy seemed to understand. "Here, Tom, take my arm and walk me to church like the proper gentleman that you are."

The walk to the freshly white painted church building seemed too short to Tom. He never felt his boots touch the ground. He knew he was walking the most wonderful and beautiful lady in the world down the street. He also reasoned that he was that perfect gentleman. Something inside his heart said, *I'll always be a perfect gentleman with Mandy; she **is** special.*

Tom was not surprised to see that the pastor of the church was the man he had seen praying.

"Howdy!" said the man to Tom as Mandy introduced him. "I'm Joe Jacobson, and I'm real glad you came with Mandy, Tom." Tom noticed that the man was not carrying his pistol. The service began with singing and Tom was aware that everyone sang especially loud and with enthusiasm. There were people of all ages in attendance–even some boys and girls Tom and Mandy's age. Tom was struck with the happiness these people had and could see that Mandy really liked her church and pastor.

During announcements, Mandy introduced Tom to everyone. They all recognized that it was Tom that had finished Snake Eyes and Frederick. The people were obviously pleased.

Pastor Jacobson's sermon was a story from the Bible about a boy that had talked his pa out of his inheritance and had run off and spent it all until he was broke and hurting. Pastor Joe first read the story from the Bible, and then he talked about it. He acted out some of the scenes and even got down on his knees once and acted like a pig that the boy fed. The pastor held everyone's attention and made people both laugh and cry. No one noticed when the pastor preached overtime.

The preacher finished by encouraging everyone to "Come home" like the boy in the story finally did.

"Come home to Jesus," the pastor pleaded. "If you're not living right, come home to Jesus; He'll forgive you and give you a new chance. If you don't know Jesus, he wants you to be his child."

Tom was very confused inside. The message had been interesting and made so much sense to Tom, but he remembered how he had seen people in Red Rock say one thing and do another. *Was this Jesus genuine? Had He really made these people happy? Is that why there was something extraordinary about Mandy? Is that why her face showed such radiance?*

CHAPTER TEN

Tom and Mandy walked home from church rather slowly. It was obvious that they were in no hurry to get back. The sun was setting in the west and the sky was beginning to darken.

"Tom, how did you like the service? Isn't Pastor Joe a wonderful preacher? I could just listen to him all day! He makes a person want to know Jesus better, like a close friend," said Mandy.

Tom was quiet. He was not sure what to say. He had to admit that Pastor Joe had made him listen and that he had made a lot of sense. Tom had even felt the urge to go forward, but he did not because he remembered all the appalling things he had seen the church people doing in Red Rock and felt that maybe there was something going on here in Pueblo like that.

"Tom, you didn't answer me! Didn't you like the preaching?" Mandy asked rather concerned.

"I, ah, well–yes, I liked it fine, Mandy. Pastor Joe's a good preacher. What'd ya say his last name was?" asked Tom.

"Jacobson, Pastor Joe Jacobson, and I think that he's magnificent!" exclaimed Mandy.

Tom was glad that Mandy was so cheerful; that was partly what had attracted him to her.

"Yer church and yer pastor sure make ya happy, Mandy," said Tom meaningfully.

"Yes, they do, Tom. They make a lot of people happy, because they have Jesus in their hearts," replied Mandy.

I don't know if I could ever be like that. I have really awful feelings about church people, Mandy. Not you of course," stated Tom.

"Why, Tom?" asked Mandy, as she pulled on his arm to stop their walking. Looking into his eyes, Mandy understood. Tom had been hurt really badly by people that had called themselves Christians.

"Tom, you've been hurt badly by someone that was a Christian, haven't you?" asked Mandy, sort of exclaiming it as a fact. "I want you to tell me about it."

"Are you sure, Mandy? It might make you feel bad."

"Yes, tell me anyway; I want to understand what happened to you," answered the Christian girl tenderly.

"Well, my ma and I went ta a church in Red Rock, and my ma really liked it. There were some people there that said the kinds of things 'bout Jesus like ya do, but they did some really bad things when they thought that no one was a lookin'. I mean **really bad** things, Mandy," explained Tom.

"I guess I don't understand. They shouldn't be that way, but that doesn't change Jesus. No matter what others or we do, Jesus stays the same. It was not Jesus that sinned, and He is our Savior," explained Mandy.

"For yer sake, I hope yer pastor and church are all that they seem ta be, but ya may be really disappointed in the future when ya find out some things about them people that ya don't know 'bout yet," replied Tom.

"Well, I'm sure that I would be disappointed," said Mandy as she gave a gentle nudge on Tom's arm to continue walking. "But I will never be disappointed in Jesus. You're right, Tom. I would be very disappointed to find something out bad about Pastor Joe, or any other of my Christian friends. But I will never be dissatisfied in Jesus!"

"You really have a lot of faith in Jesus. I hope fer yer sake that yer Jesus really is real," said Tom thoughtfully.

"He is, Tom; **He is**," spoke Mandy slowly, but forcefully.

"My father wants to talk to you when we get back tonight. He is feeling much better and he wants to meet you and has something to talk to you about," said Mandy. "I told him all about you."

"Like what?" asked Tom somewhat nervously.

"Oh, you'll see!" exclaimed Mandy with a mischievous smile on her face.

Tom and Mandy entered the back door of the general store, into the part of the building that was the living quarters of the Whitmans. Once inside, Tom could see that the area was divided into three or four small rooms. The area actually seemed like a house, and was very tidy and cozy. Mandy turned up the wick in the lamps and the room lightened. The room was a kitchen with an expensive looking oak table in the middle. The table had very neat-looking place cloths and another ornamented glass lamp in the middle of it.

"Yer house looks real nice, Mandy," complimented Tom.

"Thank you. Mother and I work–" another voice interrupted Mandy.

"That you, Mandy?" Mrs. Whitman called from the next room.

"Yes," replied Mandy.

"Is Tom with you?" asked Mandy's mother.

"Yes, he is," she answered.

"Well, if he doesn't mind, bring him into our bedroom to meet and talk with your father," instructed Mrs. Whitman.

Mr. Whitman was sitting up in bed, propped up with two large clean, white pillows. The room smelled strong of aromatic medicine. Mr. Whitman held out his hand and Tom stepped closer and shook it.

"Nice ta meet ya, Sir," stated Tom politely. "I'm glad ta hear yer gettin' well."

"Well, Tom, it's nice to meet you, too. Mandy has spoken very highly of you. I can see that you are polite and have good manners as she said. Where did you get them?" asked Mr. Whitman in a voice only slightly above a whisper.

"My ma and pa, Sir. My pa was always a perfect gentleman, and I suppose I copy him," replied Tom, while mentally picturing the way his pa had always lovingly cared for his mother.

"Mandy said your father died. Sorry, it must be hard for a young fellow like you. I almost died too, but as you can see, God is healing me. I feel my strength and health coming back. Mandy, hold that lamp a little closer to Tom. My goodness, you sure do have the reddest hair I've ever seen!" exclaimed Mr. Whitman, but actually, he wanted to get a better look at Tom's face and countenance. Mandy's Father cleared his throat. "How old are you?" he asked.

"Fifteen and will be sixteen in August, Sir," answered Tom.

"Well, Tom, we have a problem, and Mandy and Mrs. Whitman think that you might be willing to help. What do you plan on doing for the rest of the month or so?" Mr. Whitman asked.

"Well, I got a couple of ideas. I could go on back ta Red Rock and help drive cattle up this way again. I don't really have to though, 'cuz of my earnin's from trappin' and the reward money fer the outlaws. I've actually been thinkin' of travelin' ta Arizona territory ta see an old friend in prison at Fort Yuma," explained Tom.

"A friend in prison? How is it you have a friend in prison?" asked Mr. Whitman.

"Well, I don't know where ta start ta explain that, sir–it's kind of a long story," said Tom nervously.

Tom groped for words. He realized that having a friend in prison did not impress these people. "I can tell ya though, that my friend in prison now says that he loves Jesus–kind of like Mandy does." Tom could not believe he had said that.

"Well, perhaps you can tell me all about it when I'm stronger," said Mr. Whitman with a slight smile. "To get to the point, we need some help here in the store until I get well. Business has been good, and Mrs. Whitman and Mandy have been doing well but they are getting behind. We have many supplies coming in on the train this week, and some of them are exceptionally heavy. Too heavy for the ladies, but I know that wouldn't be a problem for those sturdy muscles of yours!"

Tom hesitated; he really wanted to get going to see Jed, but then he also realized that Mandy was looking at him with those pretty brown eyes.

"Ah, ah, ah, well, I..." stammered Tom.

"Why don't you think about it tonight and let us know in the morning?" suggested Mrs. Whitman. "If you decide to stay, we could use you tomorrow. If you don't, then we'll have to try to get someone else."

"Ok, I'll sleep on it! Well, I'll be on my way. Good night," said Tom.

"I'll show you out," offered Mandy happily.

Mandy opened the door, and both she and Tom stepped out into the night.

"Please stay and help us, Tom. I just **know** that God wants you to stay and help us. My folks will pay you well! Thank you for walking me to church," Mandy said sweetly.

"Yer welcome, Mandy; my pleasure! Good night," replied Tom.

"Good night, Tom. You're special," replied Mandy as her soft hand gave Tom a squeeze on his hand, and then she slipped back inside her home.

Tom turned to go, but in the darkness, he set off in the wrong direction, while mentally recounting those last words that Mandy had said and reliving the tingle that the squeeze on the hand had sent through his body. Wham! He had run into the outhouse especially hard! Confused and dazed, he stood still trying to figure out what had happened. The aroma of the building told Tom where he was, so he turned around and headed the right direction, rubbing the knot on his head.

Just before entering the hotel where he was staying, he realized that his hat must have been knocked of when he ran into the outhouse. Somewhat disturbed at himself for not picking it up, Tom went back to get it. The smell of the building reminded him of all the trouble he had when he dropped his wallet down the outhouse. It occurred to Tom that he ought to inspect the bag he had spotted to see if it really did contain the three thousand dollars the bank robbers stole.

He entered the outhouse and carefully reached into the black hole, back into the area in which he had seen the carpetbag. Tom found the dusty bag and carefully pulled it out. Sweat ran down his forehead as he released his breath. The bag was closed with leather straps that were hard to unbuckle in the dark, so he decided to take it back to his hotel room.

Tom walked back quietly and dusted the bag as he went.

"Pew—stinks badly!" muttered Tom to himself. Trying not to be noticed, he quickly passed by the hotel's front desk and slipped up the stairs to his undersized room. As Tom unlocked his door and was just about to step inside, somebody in the lobby cursed and said, "What stinks?"

Quickly, Tom locked the wooden door behind him, sat on the edge of his bed, and unbuckled the straps on the stinky gray bag as his heartbeat hard. His hands shook as the last strap came loose and he pulled open the foul bag. Inside, as he anticipated, was the money. It was lying in a jumbled mess as would be expected. Some of the money was still in bundles; there were no coins. He leafed through the money and restacked the green bundles.

Tom became acutely aware of the awful smell. The room and bag reeked of human waste. As his stomach began to turn, he dropped the bag of money to the floor, went to the windows, and slid them both open as far as he could. He stuck his head out the window and breathed deeply, still aware of the very strong odor around him. A minute of the fresher air helped him, so he went back to the bag and closed it up and rebuckled the straps.

"What am I gonna do?" muttered Tom out loud.

Tom stuck the bag in the closet and closed the brown wooden door tight. Since the room seemed to smell better, he went to bed where he tossed and turned most of the night until he woke up feeling cold because the night air coming through the windows had chilled him. The restless sleeper got up, closed the windows, and sat back on the edge of his bed. He sat thinking about Mr. Whitman's offer, then about the money.

I guess I can go see Jed later, he thought. *But what am I gonna do with the money?*

Tom lit the kerosene lamp and walked to the closet. Before opening the door, he could smell the pungent odor coming from the polluted bag inside.

"Good grief!" exclaimed Tom aloud. "This I can't believe!" and he cursed out loud. Opening the door proved the worst. The smell rolled out into the room. He closed the door quickly and opened the windows again. He swore.

Tom sat on his bed thinking. He lay back down and drifted off to sleep considering whether he should take the money to the bank or not. He decided that he would leave the money where it was for now. "I didn't steal the stinky stuff," he muttered as he fell off to sleep.

The crowing of a rooster on the roof outside the open windows woke Tom as the sun came up. He washed his face in the basin, looked in the mirror, and realized he was going to have to start shaving more often or grow a beard. He combed his hair, lathered his face, and shaved, thinking about how he would look to the world's most wonderful lady.

Tom went to the restaurant where the waitress, an older heavyset woman, eyed him with one eye as she took his order of eggs, bacon, and hash browns.

"Something wrong?" asked Tom.

"Well, Sonny, I don't normally tell customers this sort of thing, but you have a very awful smell about you," she said under her breath quietly.

"I do?" asked Tom knowingly.

"Yes," she whispered.

He understood and excused himself and went to purchase a bath. He did not want to stink when he went to see Mr. Whitman and especially Mandy.

Tom took the bath, washed his clothes, and wrung them out tightly hoping that they would quickly dry on his body by the time he went back and finished breakfast.

While Tom walked to the Whitmans' store, he considered what he was going to do with the stinky bag of money.

"Good morning, Tom," greeted Mandy in a very pleasant voice as she let him in. "Did you decide to work for us?"

"Yes," stated Tom rather matter-of-fact like.

"Oh good!" squealed Mandy with obvious delight as she turned to go tell her dad.

****

Working for Mr. Whitman turned out to be a bigger job than Tom had realized. His first job was to take a wagon to the train depot to pick up a large order of goods. Tom arrived at the busy depot just as the westbound train approached the town. The massive steam engine was smoking and shooting out steam and the bell was ringing as the whistle was blowing to announce its arrival. Tom got up as close to the engine as he dared. Fascinated by it, Tom wished he could ride in the engine. He remembered that he was planning to go to Fort Yuma on a train, and it seemed like such a new adventure and exciting thing to do. For a moment, he was sorry that he had agreed to work for the Whitmans, but only for a moment because he remembered that by staying he would be near Mandy.

It took Tom several trips and most of the morning to get all the general store's merchandise from the depot to the store. As Tom arrived back from his final load, Mandy came running out of the side door with a big smile on her face and something hidden behind her back.

"Guess what I have, Tom!" she teased.

"What?" asked Tom as he wiped the sweat off his forehead.

"Guess! I'll give you three guesses," Mandy continued to tease.

"Ya gotta big cup of water fer my thirsty throat?" guessed Tom.

"No, but I'll get you a drink," said Mandy with a twinkle in her eyes. "Guess again!"

Tom thought for a moment, then took off his hat and ran his hand through his red hair. "Ah–, jus' tell me, Mandy," said Tom impatiently.

"Nope! Two more guesses," giggled Mandy.

"Is it food?" asked Tom.

"No, is that all you think about is something to eat or drink?" said Mandy and laughed. "One more guess!"

"Is it a letter?" guessed Tom.

"A letter?" asked Mandy somewhat solemn. "Who would you get a letter from?"

"My mother maybe, but prob'ly not 'cuz I don't think she knows where I am," answered Tom.

"Well, since you're a bad guesser, Tom Fleming, I'll show you! You made the front page of the newspaper!" said Mandy as she held the paper up for Tom to see.

Sure enough, there was the headline: "**YOUNG MAN BRINGS IN SNAKE EYES AND FREDRICK–DEAD! PUEBLO REJOICES!**" A long article went on to explain Tom's story and the reward and made it kind of sound as if he had dropped the reward money down the outhouse. The paper also showed pictures of Snake Eyes and Frederick, Tom and the sheriff, and Tom with his gooey wallet on a wire in front of the outhouse.

Tom started to swear, but realizing Mandy was near only said, "Oh, bother; doesn't that make me look like an idiot?"

"No! You're a hero!" exclaimed Mandy, as she giggled.

"Look at this here picture with me and the mucky wallet in front of the stinky outhouse!" exclaimed Tom.

"Oh, be a sport, Tom! It is just funny; it could happen to anyone! It **is** funny!" giggled Mandy some more as she took second and third looks at the picture. "Ha, ha, ha, ha, he, he, he, he," she laughed and then giggled some more.

"Very funny," smirked Tom, but he enjoyed seeing Mandy laugh so much.

Mandy and her mother fixed sandwiches for them at lunch. Mr. Whitman was able to sit at the table and eat with them.

"Feeling better, Sir?" asked Tom.

"Yes, thanks," replied Mr. Whitman. "How are you doing?"

Tom explained all he had done that morning, and Mr. Whitman approved. The two were able to talk easily with each other as Mr. Whitman explained his business and the work for the afternoon. Mandy sat at the table listening but had to get up often to wait on customers.

When Tom was helping to put the new order of merchandise in its places, he found himself catching peeks at Mandy. The girl stayed busy most of the time with customers. Tom looked at her each time he had a chance. Her long brown hair fell beautifully over her slender shoulders. The white bow in her hair matched her white straight teeth when she smiled, which she did often. The long brown dress flowed smoothly over her slim figure.

Tom hardly noticed the hard work as he moved boxes of materials, barrels of nails, bags of flour and other heavy supplies. His mind made a switch back to Jed because he suddenly realized that what was taking place was very much like what had happened to Jed when he had carried supplies to Mary's mission post and had worked hard for Mary and tried to catch peeks of her.

"I tell you, Tom," he remembered Jed saying..., "I could be tired and worn, and Mary would ask me to move something here or there and I would just forget I was tired. She might ask me to move this heavy keg or unload those heavy sacks and stack them here or there and I'd do it and all the time just kept stealing peeks at her and not even feel the heavy materials."

The week passed quickly and Tom got a bundle of work done for the Whitmans. Mr. Whitman was able to be up and about; and as he observed all that Tom had done and heard the good reports that Mandy and Mrs. Whitman made, Mr. Whitman praised Tom for his work, and expressed appreciation.

"And since business has been so good, Tom, I think I'll be able to pay you a little extra," said Mr. Whitman as he coughed.

"Well, I appreciate it, Sir, but ya don't have ta do that; seeing's you've been sick and all," replied Tom.

"Ah, but you are partly responsible for the well-being of my business this past week, Tom! You have done the work that I could not do and probably did more than I would of! I figure I'll soon be strong enough to work with you; and maybe before you have to go, you'll help me catch up with some much-needed maintenance such as oiling the floor and painting," explained Mr. Whitman as he coughed some more.

"Yes, Sir, I'll do whatever I can ta help ya all before I leave," Tom assured Mr. Whitman.

"Well, here is the pay for this first week. How about going to church with us tomorrow morning?" asked Mr. Whitman.

Tom really did not feel like going, but he knew that Mandy would be there and would be disappointed if he did not.

"Yes, Sir, I'll go. Drive ya in the wagon if ya want me ta," answered Tom.

"Normally we just walk, but since I'm still a little weak, might not be a bad idea. We have a covered buggy parked over at the livery that we can use if you'd like to get that for us," explained Mr. Whitman, with his voice sounding a little raspy. "Just use the same horse we use on the freight wagon; be by about 10:00, if you don't mind."

Before leaving for the evening, Tom purchased a nice set of clothes for church. Mr. Whitman said he would charge Tom only his cost and take it out of next week's pay.

When Tom walked into the hotel lobby and paid his bill for the week, the desk manager said, "I hate to say this, but some of our customers have been complaining about a bad odor and we can't find the source of it. Any chance that it's coming from your room?"

Tom felt his face turn red and mumbled something about dirty clothes and that he would take care of it. Once in his room he stood at the closet door and tried to think of what to do. He had closed the door tightly and stuffed rags and towels under the crack at the bottom of the door and left the windows open.

Maybe this whole thing would be so much better if I'd turn the money in, he thought. *Naw...I'll just hide it in a different place after dark.*

After the sunset, Tom opened the door of the closet and held his nose. He removed the carpetbag and crawled through his hotel window onto the roof. Quietly, in the dark, he searched for a place on the hotel roof to hide the bag. Finally, he decided to wedge the bag in the chimney coming from the hotel lobby, figuring that the smell would go up and not bother anybody.

The next morning as Tom went down to the lobby. Patrons gathered about talking about the odor. The hotel owner and desk clerk were discussing the problem.

"Smells like an old outhouse, Sir, but I don't think it's coming from ours. It's set plenty far back," explained the desk clerk. "Look, there's Tom Fleming now."

"Mr. Fleming, may we have a word with you?" asked the clerk. "We are still having a problem with that bad smell! Did you check your room?"

Quickly Tom searched for something to say.

"Ah..., ya-yes, I checked my room. I noticed the smell too and left my windows open, but I don't know what's causing the smell," he lied.

"Well, would you mind if we looked around too?" asked the owner. "I'm afraid we're gonna lose customers if we can't get rid of that smell!"

The three went back up to Tom's room. Tom felt a lump in his throat while they looked around his room.

"Well, I smell the smell strongly, but we can't seem to find the source in here," said the desk clerk.

The owner agreed, looking puzzled.

Tom went to the livery, then to the Whitman's, and drove them to church. He and Mandy sat in the front of the buggy while her parents sat in the back.

During the singing, Tom looked about. He was starting to notice some of the people he had seen and met at the store. The people sang with enthusiasm.

Pastor Jacobson gave the usual announcements, and the congregation rose for Scripture reading.

"Our passage this morning is Matthew 6:19-34," stated Pastor Joe.

The preacher reverently read a verse and then the people read a verse. Mandy shared her Bible with Tom and smiled radiantly at him.

The pastor read: "Lay not up for yourselves treasures on earth, where moth and rust doth corrupt, and where thieves break through and steal."

The people read: "But lay up for yourselves treasures in heaven, where neither moth nor rust doth corrupt, and where thieves do not break through nor steal."

Tom read with the people, too, but although his lips said the words, his mind was not thinking about the words, but rather how pretty and pleasant Mandy was.

When Pastor Joe started to preach, though, he got Tom's undivided attention.

"Money!" exclaimed the pastor loudly. "Oh, do we like this stuff!" he continued and held up a paper bill and smiled. "Money is very useful. Just yesterday, I took my bride down to Whitmans', laid some of the stuff on the counter and got what we needed. Useful! Money is not bad! No! Not money, but us! Money is good, but our wicked and selfish desires for more and more and more is very, very bad!

"People have killed for money! Now we would all agree **that** is bad. People have died for money! A number of people have worked themselves to death for money. People have cheated, lied, and stolen for money! All the Ten Commandments have been broken for the sake of money! The Holy Book says that the **love** of money is the root of all evil."

Tom listened closely and began to feel guilty about the money he had hidden but had not actually stolen himself. The pastor preached on and on forcefully about the evils of greed. The people were quiet, and the minister's interesting way of preaching would not allow anyone to go to sleep in the almost-full church building.

"So God says not to lay up treasures for yourself but to seek first the kingdom of God and then He will supply all your needs!" the pastor continued.

"Lastly, the Bible has a word to describe the money that is gained wrongly. The word is filthy! 'Filthy lucre' God's Word calls it. In other words, money that is gotten wrongly stinks!" exclaimed the pastor.

The pastor's eyes met Tom's eyes. The boy felt as if the pastor was preaching right at him. His face reddened, and sweat popped out on his forehead.

"It smells clear to high Heaven and God smells it and will not let the sinner go unpunished!" the pastor continued.

Tom squirmed in his seat. *"Does the preacher know about me?"* thought Tom.

"It stinks, stinks, stinks!" the pastor emphasized, "but there is hope because the merciful God of salvation forgives."

The rest of the message dealt with God's mercy and forgiveness, and people were invited to come forward and repent of their sins or be saved. Some responded.

"Why are you so quiet, Tom?" asked Mandy as Tom drove the Whitmans home. "Didn't you like the pastor's message?"

"Yes, I liked it fine," said Tom, but actually, it had made him miserable inside.

Tom had lunch with the Whitmans and then walked back to the hotel. In the lobby, he met the desk clerk. "Well, Mr. Fleming, the smell is leaving–almost gone–good news, huh? Sort of a ghost smell, though, since we never figured it out," said the desk clerk.

"Good!" replied Tom.

Tom went to his room with the money, the sermon, and the smell heavily on his mind. He realized that the odor had left because as the heat of the day warmed the building, the smell rose out of the chimney; however, when evening came and the building cooled, the cool air would fall down the chimney making the smell return. He had to move the money again or surely, it would be found. It needed to be moved before nightfall.

CHAPTER ELEVEN

Tom carefully crawled through his room's window again, hoping not to be seen. Since it was a quiet Sunday afternoon, he was able to retrieve the stinky bag of money to his room without anyone noticing. He stuffed the money and bag into his saddlebags.

Tom quietly walked to the livery to get his horse. The pinto had not been ridden for a week and seemed glad to see him. The nervous boy borrowed a small pointed shovel he found leaning against the wall and headed west out of town. Passing by the print shop, he spotted a wooden box that had contained some printing equipment. The box had been rejected, so Tom picked it up.

No one seemed to notice him on that quiet Sunday afternoon as Tom casually rode out of town. A mile down the road he saw the trail he had noticed when he had seen and heard Pastor Joe praying. Tom headed down the trail quietly until he again saw the pastor's horse tied alone. He realized that the pastor was probably praying again. He thought of the man and his sermon that morning and felt great guilt come over him for not turning in the money.

Tom turned the pinto around and headed further west looking for a place to bury the money. "I didn't steal the money," thought Tom aloud.

"*The Bible has a word to describe money that is gained wrongly. The word is filthy. 'Filthy lucre' God's word calls it–it stinks, stinks, stinks!*" Tom remembered what the pastor had said just that morning. He felt miserable. "It surely stinks," mumbled Tom. *Could it be that all this is somethin' God's tryin' ta tell me?*

Tom stopped the pinto, turned the horse around, and sat still in the saddle, thinking, not moving. He wanted to go back and turn in the money. After all, he would still get five hundred dollars. He thought about the total amount of three thousand five hundred dollars.

"It stinks, it stinks, and it stinks!" came the pastor's words to his mind. *"People have killed for it!"*

Tom did not move. His internal battle was very great. He hesitated. *Are you crazy?* he said to himself. *Give up three thousand dollars?* The guilty-feeling boy turned west and urged the pinto into a lope. The faster he went the more determined he was to get away from the guilt and keep the money.

Finally, he slowed and looked about for a place to bury the disquieting money. A rock outcropping among some trees seemed to be an excellent landmark, so he rode back a distance from the trail into the trees. At the base of a large pine, he dug a hole big enough for the box and money to fit into, covered it with dirt, and placed pine needles over it until it was imperceptible. Then, with the shovel, he marked the tree by knocking some bark off and scarring the trunk. He buried the carpetbag in a separate place.

A feeling of relief came over Tom as he rode back to town. He took a nap the rest of the afternoon until there was a knock on the door.

"Who's there?" asked Tom.

"Mandy!" came the feminine voice from the other side.

Tom opened the door and invited the girl to come inside the room.

"That would not be proper, Tom," explained Mandy. "I just came to invite you to take my parents and me to church tonight."

If she just knew how much of a problem the pastor's messages caused me, she wouldn't ask, thought Tom.

"I, ah, well–I'd rather just stay here and rest," said Tom; he wished he had not responded so hastily because he saw the disappointment in her eyes.

"Tom, please come with us. My dad still is not very strong yet, and I am not very good at hitching the horse to the buggy. You can come for supper!" pleaded Mandy.

"Okay, just for you, Mandy," Tom said quietly, smiling. He was actually glad to be with Mandy, at all costs.

"Maybe you can teach me to hitch up the wagon and buggy so that I could be more helpful if my father needs me to," stated Mandy.

"Sure!" replied Tom.

"Well, come along soon and we'll eat and then set off to get the buggy," said Mandy, very sweetly.

Tom enjoyed the home cooking and talking with Mr. Whitman while Mandy and her mother served them peach cobbler.

When the dessert was finished, Mandy went with Tom down to the livery to hitch the buggy. He carefully showed Mandy how the harness and straps fitted onto the horse. Mandy asked some questions, reached out, and tested the buckles. Mandy's nearness to Tom allowed him to notice her perfume. Even with the odor of the livery, Mandy smelled nice to him. She went around to the horse's head, patted the horse, and talked to her.

"Well, we had better go, Tom. Help me up into the seat like a proper gentleman," encouraged Mandy.

Tom took Mandy's hand and helped her balance herself as she took the first and biggest step up; then he stepped up and seated himself by her. They both looked at each other; they were close; they both had the urge to kiss, and they were alone. Tom leaned slightly toward Mandy and she toward him. Their eyes locked as he felt his heart start to pound and a tingly sensation go through his body. Mandy gently put her fingertips to Tom's lips.

"Tom, I want to kiss you, but I vowed to God that I wouldn't kiss like this until God gave me a husband. I'm sorry," she said pleasantly.

Tom wiggled the horse's reins, and the buggy rolled out of the livery. At first, he felt rejection, then anger and then he thought about it.

If Mandy isn't gonna kiss, 'cept her husband, that means he's gonna be one lucky guy and get one wonderful wife! Maybe someday I can be that one, thought Tom.

"Are you mad at me, Tom? I don't like you any less because we didn't kiss. Please don't be mad at me. I like you a lot," said Mandy so quietly she could barely be heard above the noise of the horse's hooves.

"No, I'm not mad, Mandy. I like ya a lot too, and I think that yer vow to God is a very good thing. I- I- I think that's what makes ya so special! I think that yer future husband's gonna be one lucky guy," explained Tom seriously.

They smiled at each other and rode quietly to pick up Mandy's parents. Many different thoughts ran through their heads. Tom's acceptance of Mandy's vow drew Mandy's heart closer to him than he would ever know. Mandy's vow actually made him realize what a prize she was and caused him to like her even more. He remembered the cattle drive and how some of the cowboys had talked about saloon women, they had met. He remembered seeing some saloon women when he was sneaking around in Red Rock, and he wondered about some he had seen in Pueblo. Mandy certainly wasn't about to be that type. Tom smiled to himself. He knew Mandy would make a wonderful wife. Some little voice inside Tom said, *And why?* The little voice answered the question: *Because she truly follows Jesus.*

****

The church service that evening started as usual with enthusiastic singing. Pastor Joe announced the Scripture, and the people stood and read from Joshua chapter seven. This time Tom read with understanding of the Biblical event, which he enjoyed until they came to the verse in which Achan confessed that he had hidden the wrongly obtained gold by burying it in the ground under his tent. Tom stopped reading and almost dropped his side of the Bible he was sharing with Mandy.

No! How could it be; another message on stolen money? thought Tom.

Pastor Joe did a splendid job of preaching. He was loud, then soft. He made the people laugh, then get solemn as he explained the sin of Achan.

"You see, he took the forbidden goods. God had said, 'No,' and Achan said, 'Why not?' When God says 'no,' we had better agree with him!" preached the pastor.

Pastor Jacobson got on his knees and pretended to be digging a hole. "Now, Honey, hand me the garment and the gold," he said while acting out Achan's sin. Then he changed his voice to a woman's higher voice: "But Achan, what good is it buried?" The pastor replied as Achan in a deeper voice, "For the future, dearest, for the future!"

Then Pastor Joe got up and pointed out to the audience as he pounded the pulpit and said, "It was for the future all right–a very short future which produced the judgment of God on Achan and his family–death!" Pastor Joe got louder: "The Bible says to be sure your sins will find you out! What should Achan have done? Obeyed God from the start! Why? Because God would have provided for them in all their needs!"

Pastor Joe continued loudly: "Would they have gone hungry? NO! Would they have lacked shelter? NO! Would they have gone unclothed? NO! A thousand times NO! NO! NO!" Many people said "Amen" as the pastor continued by saying quietly, "And we won't suffer these problems either as we obey God!"

The preacher finished by inviting anyone that needed to repent of sin to come forward or anyone with any need to come for prayer and counseling. Tom knew he had a need; he felt deep conviction, but the battle inside him raged strong. Tom's fingers turned colorless as he grasped the back of the scratched pew in front of him.

I didn't steal the money, thought Tom. *I only found it! God's speakin' to me; He must be! These messages are so much like my problem! Should I go forward? Yes! No! People're lookin'. Yes, go talk to the pastor. No! Just take the money back to the bank yerself!*

Tom did not go talk with the pastor. After the service was dismissed, Pastor Joe greeted people and talked politely to all. "Nice to see you again, Tom. I hear you are working for the Whitmans. That's good."

When Tom dropped off the Whitmans at their store, he asked if he might be a little late in the morning, explaining only that he had an errand to run.

Early the next morning, Tom went to the livery to saddle his horse and found Pastor Joe there. The pastor had already saddled his horse.

"Good morning, Tom. Beautiful morning! Where ya headed?" asked the pastor.

"Oh, I have a little ride ta take and a personal errand ta take care of," he answered.

"Going west? Ride a ways with me," the pastor said encouragingly.

"Okay," answered Tom, not really knowing what to say.

The two rode their horses slowly and talked. "Are you any relation to the Jacobsons that live down near Red Rock?" asked Tom.

"Yes," said the pastor. "How do you know them?"

"Well, my mother and ..." Tom hesitated; he did not want to call Frank Woods his stepfather; "... and I lived there fer awhile. My mother still does. I helped Mr. Jacobson and Howie and Frank drive cattle to Pueblo before!"

"Well, Frank and Howie are my nephews, and their dad, David, is my older brother," explained the pastor.

"Then Grandma Jacobson was yer mother?" asked Tom.

"Well, yes, but what do you know about Grandma?" asked Pastor Joe.

"Well, when I first went to Red Rock, there was a funeral fer her that I sort of went to with Frank Woods. She was really loved by a lot a people," explained Tom. "Were you there?"

"I couldn't make it in time from here. Too far. However, no matter, I will see her again in Heaven; I have no doubt of it. You knew Frank Woods?" asked Pastor Joe.

"Yes," answered Tom, not really wanting to converse about him. "He married my mother. But I don't wanna be called his son–step–or any other way."

"Why not?" asked the pastor.

"He beat me for somethin' I didn't do! I mean ta tell ya, he beat and beat and beat me 'til I said I did it and I didn't!" Tom's voice had risen, and he had stopped his horse to explain.

"Still bothers you a lot, doesn't it? How long ago did this happen?" asked the pastor in a caring tone.

"It happened when I was twelve years old," answered Tom.

"Tom, I used to pastor in Red Rock. I know Frank Woods well. He is a good man–not that beating you was good–he always did have a problem with temper flare-ups. I 'm sorry to hear he did that. Tell me more about what happened to you," said Pastor Joe.

"Ah...well, it's a long story and I have ta get on my way and get ta work at Whitman's, so maybe later, okay?" asked Tom.

"Sure, Tom. Here is all the further I'm going," Pastor Joe said as he turned his horse down the path to the place where Tom had seen him praying. "Have a real nice day!"

Tom loped his pinto on down the smooth road heading west until he came to the outcropping of rock. As he dismounted his pinto, he realized again that his horse was getting too small for him. He found the place where he had hidden the money and dug it up easily with his hands. He dusted off the saddlebags and then dug up the old carpetbag and dusted the dirt off it.

Strange, thought Tom; *I don't smell a bad stench!*

Tom rode back to town to the bank, arriving as Mr. Blackstone was just opening the door. "Good mornin', Mr. Blackstone!" said Tom, "May I speak with ya privately?"

"Sure, Tom, come on in!" the heavyset banker said with a friendly note in his voice, not noticing the carpetbag; "Come on back to my desk."

Tom walked with the banker and set the carpetbag down on the banker's large wooden desktop. The banker looked at the dirty bag with a recognizable sign of fear on his face.

"I found the stolen money, Sir!" exclaimed Tom. "I've brought it back!"

The banker relaxed, and Tom saw his features turn from fear to excitement. He reached out and opened the crusty bag.

"The stolen money! You found the money from the robbery I told you about! I thought for a moment you were holding me up–where did you find it?" the banker asked in quick statements, running out of breath.

Tom hesitated for a moment. "Well, it was stuffed under the seat in the outhouse where I dropped my wallet!"

"In the outhouse? You don't say! You would think it would stink! However, I do not smell a thing! Well, I will take care of the money, Tom, and I'll **gladly** give you the five hundred dollars I promised for the reward. Would you like the cash, or would you like me to deposit it in your account?" asked the smiling banker.

"Just put it in my account, Sir. Thanks," answered Tom. Tom took his pinto back to the livery and mentioned to the manager that he was going to sell his horse and might be getting a larger one. He walked over to the restaurant for breakfast and then went to the store.

"Good morning, Tom," Mrs. Whitman said as the youth walked into the store.

Mr. Whitman gave Tom jobs to do, and Mandy said "hi" very sweetly as she carried a bolt of material back to the rack she had taken it from while waiting on a customer. Tom wanted to tell Mandy what he had done because he wanted her to be proud of him and know that he was not a bad kind of person. Nevertheless, telling her would seem too proud, so he said nothing.

During lunchtime, while Tom was eating a sandwich Mrs. Whitman had prepared, Clem, the newspaper editor, showed up.

"Morning, Mrs. Whitman," he said politely. "I need to speak to Tom; he's done it again!"

"Done what again, Clem?" she asked.

"You'll see! You're not agonna believe it though!" answered Clem.

Tom just smiled at Clem.

"Tom, I want the whole story! Give me everything!" blurted out the reporter as he produced his pencil and note pad.

Tom thought for a moment. "Well, Sir, the last time ya got my story, ya made me look like a terrible idiot! Why should I tell ya anything?"

"Ah, Tom, it was all in fun. Everybody was really glad you brought in Snake Eyes and Fredrick!" explained Clem.

"Naw–ain't gonna tell ya nothin'," replied Tom, stubbornly.

"Well, I kinda think I know what happened anyways," replied Clem. "I'm gonna write the story, and I'll be more concerned about your feelings this time."

Clem left with the Whitmans still hanging around Tom seated at the lunch table.

"What did you do this time?" asked Mandy.

Tom smiled a big smile and said, "I found the bank's stolen money!"

"The stolen money?" the Whitmans all asked in unison.

Tom had to tell them about how he found the money and then returned it to the bank. He did not tell them all about the tremendous struggle he had been through with the money. Only he and God knew that.

After supper, Tom asked Mandy if she would like to go for a walk down to the little park by the courthouse. Mandy readily agreed, and soon the two were walking slowly down the boardwalk toward the park.

"That is really something; to think that you found the money! God seems to be blessing you," said Mandy in a distressed voice. "You know, Tom, I don't understand; my family and I have been praying for you to understand your need for Jesus, but God allows you to get all this money. People with a lot of money do not usually understand their need for Jesus. They think their money will bring them happiness."

Tom smiled, grinned big, kind of sputtered a laugh through his lips, and finally laughed aloud.

"Well, don't worry, Mandy; I think yer prayers are bein' heard by God," said Tom as he chuckled.

"Why do you think that?" asked Mandy seriously.

Tom told Mandy all the details of his struggles with the bag of money. Mandy laughed until tears came to her eyes as he told about the horrible smell in the hotel. Tom laughed and laughed too. He felt very relieved. He loved to make and hear Mandy laugh.

Tom went on to tell Mandy about the sermon in which the Pastor talked about filthy lucre and said, "It stinks, it stinks, it stinks!"

Mandy put her fingertips to her mouth and jumped up, "I remember that! And it was right when the stinky money was driving the people in the hotel insane?"

"Yes!" exclaimed Tom with a laugh. "But when I finally took it ta Mr. Blackstone, like I should've in the first place, the money didn't smell at all! Even Mr. Blackstone wondered why it had no awful smell since I found it under the seat of the outhouse!"

"My goodness!" exclaimed Mandy and laughed with joyful glee. "God **IS** working on you, Tom Fleming! God **IS** working on you!"

"There's more, Mandy! Do ya wanna hear it?" asked Tom.

Tom explained how he went out, dug a hole, and hid the money only to have the pastor preach about Achan digging a hole to hide the treasure under his tent.

"My, my, my, Tom; that is almost un-be-lieve-able!" exclaimed Mandy, drawing the syllables out slowly, but joyfully. "But with God, I can believe it!"

"We better be gettin' back; it's gettin' late, Mandy," said Tom, trying to be the perfect gentleman. "I enjoyed yer company. Thanks fer prayin' fer me."

The two walked back down the boardwalks to the store, Mandy's hand around Tom's arm. As they said good night, Mandy squeezed his hand and said very sweetly but seriously, "We are going to continue to pray for you, until you actually know Jesus."

****

On several more occasions that month, Tom and Mandy went for walks in the evenings. They really enjoyed being with each other and both started to dread Tom's going away soon.

One evening Tom told Mandy he wanted to tell her a secret but she had to promise to keep it to herself. Mandy said she would, as long as it wasn't something bad. Tom told Mandy about the map that Snake Eyes had given him moments before he died.

"Mandy, Snake Eyes prayed to God and said somethin' 'bout Jesus just before he died. Do ya suppose he went ta Heaven?" asked Tom seriously.

"No, I doubt it, Tom. He killed too many people!" replied Mandy.

"Well, what about forgiveness, Mandy? Can a person be forgiven of **some** sins and not of others?" asked Tom.

"Oh, w-well," stammered Mandy; "You're right. There is nothing for which Jesus did not die. The only sin that cannot be forgiven is rejecting Jesus and his payment for all sin when He died on the cross. So if Snake Eyes accepted Jesus before he died, he went to Heaven."

"Well, he said somethin' 'bout doin' somethin' good by givin' me the map," replied Tom.

"Well, that probably means that he was trying to please God with something he did rather than by believing in what Jesus did. So if that's the case, he didn't go to Heaven," explained Mandy sadly.

"I see," Tom said quietly.

"Look, Mandy, here's the map!" exclaimed Tom as he unfolded the yellow, sweat-stained treasure map.

Mandy studied the map "Gold? It's a treasure map leading to gold hidden someplace in Arizona Territory. It's not complete! Why would Snake Eyes have part of a gold treasure map? He probably stole it! Tom, I promised to keep your secret and I will, but maybe you should show this map to the sheriff because the gold probably was stolen if Snake Eyes had anything to do with it. If possible, the sheriff would help you find leads to find the gold, if it isn't illegal. He's a Christian; he'll help you!" exclaimed Mandy.

"Mandy, I know from firsthand experiences that everyone that says they're a Christian don't always do right! Just because the sheriff **says** he's a Christian doesn't mean he couldn't cheat me," stated Tom.

Tom told her about more of his experiences in Red Rock and about the people that appeared to be good Christians. He mentioned the doctor, schoolteacher, the sleepy church member, and told about the beatings Frank Woods gave him because Frank thought he had stolen the one hundred dollars the bank robber had given him.

Tom explained what a good friend Jed had become and how he now had to go to the prison to see him. "And ya know what, Mandy?" asked Tom, more making a statement than a question; "I think Jed got religion like you while he was in jail in Red Rock!"

"Well, Tom, I suppose you could say I 'got religion,' but knowing Jesus as Savior is more than getting religion. It is knowing Jesus paid for your sins. It's knowing Jesus is always with you and you can walk with him," replied Mandy.

"Well, anyway, Mandy, I'll talk ta the sheriff 'bout the map, just fer you. Then ya won't have ta keep a terrible secret," promised Tom.

When Tom showed the sheriff the map, the sheriff said he thought there was nothing to it but was probably a scheme Snake Eyes made up. "But," said the sheriff, "ya never know, there have been some Wells Fargo stages held up in which the gold was stolen off it and never recovered. You need the rest of the map. All you know from this part of it is that some mountain in the Arizona Territory that looks like that one on the map has gold on it—or in it. Find the rest of the map and maybe you could find some gold."

****

The month's work at Whitman's store was soon over, and Tom was especially sad about leaving Mandy. She was equally sad. The two had become very fond of each other; but more than that, they had grown to be really proper friends and were able to share innermost thoughts with each other.

Tom offered to give his pinto to Mandy, but she said she would not be able to afford the feed. Therefore, Tom decided to sell his beloved horse, knowing that the little animal was too small for his now-adult size. He also sold his pack mule and saddle.

Tom got his personal things together and bought larger saddlebags from the Whitmans. Mr. Whitman paid Tom as he said, plus he paid a little extra as he had hinted. Tom went to the bank and took out enough money to buy his train ticket and have extra cash with him.

The Whitmans took Tom to the railroad depot early Monday morning. Mandy had made Tom some cake and wrapped it in a cloth for him to take along. She also gave him five stamped and addressed envelopes with pencil and paper and asked him to write her until he came back. Mrs. Whitman gave him some jerky, beans, and biscuits to eat on the train. Tom was surprised to see Mrs. Whitman cry.

"I love you like a son, Tom. Come back and see us," said Mrs. Whitman kindly.

Mr. Whitman shook Tom's hand and said, "You're a hard worker. I appreciate your help. I cannot hire you fulltime, but I could always give you some work. God bless you, and don't forget the things I told you about traveling on the train."

Mandy stood at the bottom of the passenger car's newly painted black metal steps with her hands folded together in front of her. She had worn her best Sunday dress to see Tom leave. She looked very sad and had tears in her eyes.

The train started to move. Tom leaned down, took Mandy's hands in his and said to her, where only she could hear, "I'll be back, Mandy, and maybe someday I'll get ta be the first one ta kiss ya!"

Mandy's mouth opened wide; then a huge grin appeared on her face. The steam engine's whistle blew and the bell clanged and clanged as the train started to move forward. Tom hopped onto the bottom steps as the whole train rattled as each coupling between the cars took up the slack. "I'll be back! I Promise!"

The whistle blew again and black smoke billowed out of the engine blowing back over the train. Tom waved at the Whitmans until they were out of sight. In the last glimpse he saw of Mandy, she was bravely waving a tear-stained hankie while the wind and smoke blew her pretty long brown hair back from her face. Tom stared at Mandy until the little white dot that was she disappeared; then went inside the passenger coach, sat down on the wooden seat, and slid over to the window.

He unhappily felt like he was leaving his family behind.

I'll be back, Tom thought to himself. *Ya betcha I'll be back. I wanna be the first and last man ta kiss that wonderful girl!*

CHAPTER TWELVE

The train clicked and clattered down the track as Tom sat on the worn wooden seat with his bulky saddlebags beside him. He had strapped on his Remington .44 because of some of the things Mr. Whitman had told him about train rides.

The ride itself kept Tom occupied for a while. He watched out the open window as the land seemed to speed by swiftly. When the steam engine would climb up a steeper grade, it would belch out smoke, which would waft through the coach.

Soon the seat began to feel hard, and Tom stood up to walk down the aisle. Other passengers were getting restless and began to move around too. Returning to his seat, he realized he had carelessly left his saddlebags unattended with about half his money in them. Mr. Whitman had advised him to carry his money in more than one place while traveling so that if he were robbed, he would not lose all his money. Tom had placed some money in his boots, some in his wallet, and some in his saddlebags.

Tom sat thinking; he remembered Mr. Whitman giving him some other important advice before he had left.

"Tom, you might encounter good folks and bad folks on a train. Some people will look high-quality, smile at you, but rob you in a moment when your back is turned–so watch yourself–you can't always tell a person's character or intentions by the way they look," Mr. Whitman had said.

The first stop was at Bent's Fort, Colorado, where Tom would leave the Denver and Rio Grande Railroad and take the Santa

Fe south and west to California. Then he planned to take the Southern Pacific back towards the southeast to Fort Yuma in the Arizona Territory.

The train change was easily made because the side of the passenger cars had big white letters painted on them saying "Atchison, Topeka and Santa Fe."

The multitude of passengers on the Santa Fe had twenty minutes to get their lunch at the railroad station. Since it was crowded and people were impatient, Tom decided he would eat the food Mandy and Mrs. Whitman had sent along.

He found an empty seat and sat waiting for the train to start. A young boy came by selling newspapers, fruit, cigars, and guidebooks.

"Cigar, mister?" asked the newsboy, as he thrust a cigar into Tom's face.

Tom laughed. "Yeah, give me one with some matches," he told the boy as he paid him.

The newsboy hurried on, hollering out, "Newspapers, fruit, cigars, guide books; get your guide books before going any further west!"

A passenger who had bought a paper stood up and hollered at the boy, "Hey, Butch, this paper is old! Come back here!" But the train butch had gone out the door into another car. The unhappy passenger sat down swearing to himself and read the aged paper.

The train whistle blew loudly, and with no other warning, the cars started to move as some people rushed to get to a seat, while others rushed to jump onto their passenger car. Almost immediately, Tom's car became crowded as people pushed their way inside. A mixture of soldiers, cowboys, miners, immigrants, mountain men, and families with children all appeared at once it seemed. Tom realized he would not have the luxury of one to a seat going west on the Santa Fe.

A very big, broad-shouldered mountain man sat down by Tom. Tom put the saddlebags under his seat, figuring he would eat later.

"Smile?" asked the mountain man through a mouth with one tooth missing.

Tom smelled the stench of booze and body odor. The man stuck a whisky bottle out to him, and then Tom realized that when the man asked, "smile?" he wanted to know if Tom wanted a drink of his whiskey.

"Ah, ah–no thanks," Tom tried to say politely. The hefty man took a deep drink from his large bottle.

"Ahhh, good stuff!" he exclaimed loudly, then belched and took a plug of tobacco out and started chewing.

The train pulled out of Bent's Fort whistling and puffing while the conductor came around asking for tickets. Tom thought the man looked funny with a little cap on that said "CONDUCTOR." The mountain man was interesting to Tom. Working with cowboys herding cattle, and working with Jed trapping for furs, Tom had grown used to body odors, but this man's smell was still bothersome to Tom, and he was so large that the seat was crowded.

Presently the man decided to spit into a spittoon. Tom decided to light the cigar he was still holding. He puffed lightly at first. The big green-brown cigar made Tom's eyes water, but he liked the smell and realized that it helped to cover up the mountain man's strong odor. Tom inhaled a deeper breath and felt the hot burn in his throat. He coughed and looked at the mountain man through tear-filled eyes.

The mountain man smiled a knowing smile at Tom.

"First cigar, huh, kid? Let me shows ya how ta do it!" he said grinning and pulling out his own cigar. "First, ya bite the end off a little and soak the end of it in ya mouth a bit; that makes the smoke nice and cool, like this."

Tom noticed that the man had tobacco in his long black and gray beard. Tom soaked the cigar in his mouth a bit and puffed some more. He enjoyed it, and soon cigar smoke abounded everywhere as others lit their cigars. Most of the smoke drifted out the open windows.

When Tom's cigar was gone, he threw the stub out the window and watched the mountain man do the same. The man took another deep drink of his well-used bottle and began to talk to Tom as though he was an old friend. He offered him another "smile" and wondered why Tom would not take one with him.

"Well," explained Tom, "I've seen a lot of people do dumb and bad things because they drank, and I jus' don't wanna be like that. The only time I ever drank was when a doctor gave me some whiskey to help my pain."

"Oh, I sees," said the mountain man. "Well, how do ya know what it'll do to ya if'n ya don't try it? Ya might be missin' out. Ya don't have ta get drunk jus' 'cuz ya drink a little, ya knows. So here, give er a try, kid!"

Tom felt nervous because the man was very big. Tom felt very little and thus did not want to offend him. "Well, that's mighty nice of ya to offer mister, but not now–maybe some other time," Tom said trying to act thankful. The mountain man seemed happy with that and jabbered on about his trapping and shooting of wild animals. When Tom asked some questions about his traps and bait, the man grew more interested in talking to Tom, but kept drinking from his bottle. The bulky man's speech became labored; he yawned a deep yawn, belched, and fell asleep with his chin resting on his full-size barrel chest.

Tom took his saddlebags out and ate some delicious beans and biscuits Mrs. Whitman had made. He watched the man that crowded his seat making it hard to move his elbows. The sleeping man sat there slumped in his seat, wobbling significantly, as the train swayed along the tracks.

Tom took out the cloth, which was wrapped around the cake that Mandy had specially made for him. He sat looking at the cake in the cloth, thinking about Mandy. Finally, he opened the cloth, took out his pocketknife, and noticed a piece of paper. It was a note from Mandy.

"My Dearest Tom,

I hope you like this cake. I would like to make other things for you to eat. Please think about me as you eat it. I'm worried about you going on such a long trip. I know we haven't known each other very long, but I'm afraid you might not come back to me. Maybe I should not be so bold as to say this, but I love you! I miss you. Please come back to me.

I'm praying for you all the time while you're gone. I don't know if you understand, but I'm praying that God will help you see your need and what it means to accept Jesus into your heart. Thank you for helping us when Father was sick. You are so special.

All my love and prayers,

Mandy Whitman

P.S. Please write to me on the paper I gave you."

Tom read the note repeatedly. He could hear in his mind Mandy saying the words and imagined just how she would have said, "I love you" to him. It was the first actual time she had said, "I love you." Before this, it was always "I like you," or "you're so special." Now, seeing the words written out made Tom's heart pound hard and his head feel dreamy. He decided to eat the cake, write Mandy back, and say he loved her too.

The love-stricken boy folded the prized note neatly and put it in his hat next to his one-half treasure map. The cake was delicious, and he ate the whole thing.

It was difficult to maneuver the writing materials, but Tom managed to get the pencil and paper out and start writing a note using a saddlebag as a table on his lap. The mountain man continued to sleep, snore and wobble.

"Dear Mandy,

I'm on the railroad now heding towards Raton. Every thing is ok. Just ate yur mother's beans and biscuits fer lunch and the delishus cake you made me. Thank you Mandy. I was thriled to see you right "I love you", cuz I love you to verry verry much. I will come back to you–promis. I will bee back! You are the one that is special. You are most wellcom for whatever help I was to yer family. Thank you for praying for me. I would like to have the peace yer family has. I love you a lot yer so special to.

Yer Boy Friend, Tom Fleming"

While writing, Tom realized his need to improve his English. Mandy and Mrs. Whitman had helped him some. His language had changed a little.

When the train stopped at Raton, New Mexico, for water and wood for the engine, everyone got off again to eat at the station stop. Tom managed to buy his eats and mail his letter back to Mandy.

The train reloaded and continued on its way south along the foothills of the Rocky Mountains. The sun started to set in the mountains, and as the weary passengers began to get drowsy, they gradually began to slump against the passenger car and windows. Tom became drowsy and fell asleep against the wall. He soon awakened with a sore neck.

"A week of this?" grumbled Tom, as he readjusted to get more comfortable.

****

Passengers started waking up from their awkward sleeping positions, as the golden morning sun shown brightly through the coach's windows. Tom woke with a start and looked into the grizzly face of the smiling mountain man whose shoulder Tom had finally adjusted to, while sleeping.

"Oh!" exclaimed Tom with a raspy voice. "I'm sorry!"

"It's okay, kid," replied the mountain man. "You've been there most of the night. Didna have the heart to bother ya– you were sleepin' so well. Smile?"

Tom's cloudy mind found the situation funny, and so he laughed aloud. The smiling traveler laughed also. In fact, they both began chuckling and looking at each other, and for some strange reason they both bellowed and looked at each other until they were roaring with glee. Tom repeated the word "smile," pointed at the man, and giggled.

Drowsy passengers began looking at them and someone hollered, "Be quiet!"

The mountain man just hollered, "Ah shud up!" and Tom and the man continued cackling and wiping tears from their eyes until finally they snickered out.

There was something wonderfully strange about the event. The barrier Tom had felt toward the mountain man had dropped, and they became instant friends.

"Well, if ya ain't gonna have a drinkin' smile with me, ya can shore smile when ya laugh, kid," said the mountain man as he took another drink of his whiskey.

"Ahh–good stuff! Ya shore ya don't wan' a smile?" asked the mountain man again. "You jus' don't know what you're a missin', kid."

"Yeah, I'm sure," replied Tom. "What's yer name?"

"Hank. All my friends just call me Hank. My ma called me Henry, and a few of my enemies called me Hankie. Ya know, like hank-er-chief, ya knows like a bandanna. Something ya wipe sweat on or blow ya snought-filled snooter on. Well, that's funny all right, but I **always** gets the last laugh!"

Hank went on to tell Tom about how someone had called him "Hankie," so he smashed his face in, picked the individual up, and used his head to mop the barroom floor.

"You should've seen the looker on-ers. They all stood 'round with their mouths dropped open and they looked so funny faced that I got ta laughin' so hard I couldn't hold the guy up any more so I dropped 'im face first in a spittoon! It was full too! I never laughed so hard!"

As Hank told the story, he laughed over it again until tears came to his eyes. Tom laughed too. Passengers on the train were annoyed.

"Well, anyways, them folks never called me 'Hankie' again!" said Hank, slapping his knee, and laughing so loud it strained his voice.

****

The day went well. The train stopped at its usual stops for firewood, water, and food for the passengers; they picked up a fresh engineer just before dark.

Tom and Hank smoked cigars and talked the entire day about trapping and hunting. Tom told about his life and problems, and Hank listened very intently with an occasional laugh and knowing nod of the head, but shared very little about his own life.

"Hank, what do ya think about religion and God?" asked Tom after explaining the feelings he had about hypocritical church people.

"Well, Tom, ya have ta forgive people 'cuz we all make mistakes, 'cept fer a very few of us. As for God, I believe God he'ps those who he'ps themselves! In fact, I must believe in God a lot 'cuz I use His name a lot," said Hank with a little laugh, but Tom caught a slight glimpse of regret on Hank's face.

Darkness fell, and the conductor came through the coach and lit the wall lamps. People began to fall asleep in their now-accustomed miserable positions.

Hank drank more from his bottle and fell to sleep with his heavily bearded chin resting on his chest again.

Tom sat thinking about things for a while. He took Mandy's letter out of his hat, read it over a couple more times, and then sat thinking about Mandy and her family back in Pueblo. He wondered why he ever left his precious Mandy. Slowly, he drifted off to sleep.

Sometime during the night, the train slowed, came to a stop, backed up for a distance, and then stopped and went forward again. The extra movement woke a few people, including Hank. He stood and stuck his head out the window and looked around with certain alertness and knowing in his eyes. He had an uneasy feeling that something was wrong.

Shortly the train came to a halt again, this time quickly so that more people awoke.

"What's the matter? What's going on?" several people cried out loudly in the packed out coach.

More people woke and, finding that the night air had grown chilly, they shut their windows.

Hank stood up again, stuck his head out the window, and looked all around. He looked long and hard towards the engine that could not see since the night was so dark. Before Hank drew his head back in the window, the train shook and started backwards banging Hank's head a little on the windowsill.

"That's it!" exclaimed Hank while hitting his huge fist into an open hand. "I'm gonna do sompen' 'bout this!" He exclaimed again while looking down at Tom.

Hank took his bottle out and grinned big at Tom. "Smile?" he asked and laughed. When Tom refused, Hank took a gulp of the whiskey and then headed to the back door of the passenger car, bumping into many tired passengers as he went. Footsteps above told Tom that Hank was on top of the car! A moment later, Hank was smiling a big grin through the window at Tom. The upside down face of Hank startled Tom at first and then he laughed. Hank disappeared and Tom sat thinking about what was taking place.

Why was the train going so slow? Why had it stopped, backed up and started and stopped? wondered Tom.

The train came to a complete stop again. Tom began to think that maybe he should go see what was happening. He had heard about some of the possible troubles on the trains, and the thought crossed his mind that maybe someone was robbing the train.

Tom could feel his pistol in his holster and decided that he should set off and check on things. He left his seat and walked outside to the platform on the car. Since the train was not moving, he stepped quietly to the ground and began walking along the rocks of the railroad bed, finding it hard not to make a crunching noise with his boots. It was very dark, except for the dim light cast by the coaches. Tom stopped, waited, listened, and smelled the air. He could hear the steam engine ahead of him, reminding him of an animal resting and panting.

Tom moved off the rocks and walked quietly in the grass along the train bed. He noticed a dim figure on top of the train cars, jumping from car to car in a very sly fashion. Tom figured it was Hank, and so he continued walking quietly toward the engine. Finally, Tom came close enough to the engine that he could hear parts of an argument going on between the engineer and the fireman.

"Well, now, young fellah," the engineer was saying in a drunken manner, "I suppose ya think ya know better than me which way I oughta be goin'. I'll see ta it that ya don't have a job, soon as we git into the next station. Now leave me be and throw more wood into the fire!"

"Sir! Sir! Please! You've been drinking too much and we are not going ta make it to the safe siding for the eastbound train if we don't get moving right away!" pled the fireman.

Hank seemed to appear out of nowhere on top of the woodpile in the car behind the engine. "So, we've a drunken engineer, have we? Shame on you, sir! I shall have ta relieve you of ya duties so we can gets the show on the road!"

The engineer swore. "Who do ya think ya ar–?" The engineer tried to say, but was cut short by Hank who had jumped down in front of the man and then picked up the swearing engineer and carried him down the ladder to the ground below.

Tom was thinking quickly. He stepped out of the shadows and offered help. "Quick, let's put 'im in the first box car and lock the door!" suggested Tom.

Hank looked a little startled to see Tom, but only for a moment. "Right, Kid, good idea! Fireman, git that first car open!"

"Put me down," cried the drunken engineer while struggling rather weakly to no avail.

Hank and the fireman quickly had the engineer locked safely in the first box car. Hank scaled back up the engine, and Tom followed.

"Fire 'er up, fireman! Let's git movin'! Time's wastin'!" bellowed Hank who laughed as he released the break, shoved the Johnson bar forward, and pulled the throttle back as far as it would move.

"How much steam ya got?" Hank hollered at the fireman.

Tom watched Hank in amazement.

"One hundred eighty pounds!" exclaimed the fireman who stomped on the lever on the floor of the cab to open the fire box.

"Sand! Sand! Where's the sand?" cried Hank. "We need sand; the wheels is slippin'!"

The fireman stopped throwing wood into the firebox and reached over and showed Hank where the sand lever was.

"That's betta! We're haulin' now!" Hank hollered as the cab of the engine had gotten very noisy. "Yaaaa hooooo," hooted Hank. "Whoooop peeee! Look at us rolls along, boys!"

Tom looked out the left side of the engine. He could see only a little ahead of the huge engine since the train's light did not shine far into the darkness. It was all very exciting to Tom, and he loved it very much. The churning of the enormous wheels on the track, the engines pumping steam in and out, and the feel of a gigantic machine under him gave him a burst of excitement. Tom also let out a "Yaaa hooooo" scream that made Hank smile.

"See, Tommy Boy, I tole ya that God he'ps those that he'ps themselves!" hollered Hank, and let out a roar of laughter.

The engine puffed faster and faster down the track. If the length of the train hadn't restrained the speed, Hank would have pushed the speed too fast for the tracks. The fireman knew that the tracks could hold the speed and that they needed to make up time because of the coming eastbound train, so he encouraged Hank.

Tom helped throw wood into the noisy engine and watched out the window as the train seemed to fly down the tracks. The heat inside the engine's cab grew intense as Tom looked out of the window at the track ahead. The boy grew a little uneasy at the speed they were traveling, especially when they whizzed over the bridges.

Two hours passed with the engine going nearly full speed until the fireman said that they should stop fueling the engine and prepare to slow down for the siding that would be coming up shortly. Hank resisted at first but realized that the railroad worker probably knew what was best. He pulled the Johnson bar back and started a gradual slow down. A brakeman seemed to appear out of nowhere and threw a switch so the train could go into the proper siding.

"Well, where's the eastbound?" Hank growled at the fireman.

"Don't ya worry none; it'll be here," promised the railroad employee.

The approaching eastbound train could soon be seen. The headlight of the one-eyed, smoking, puffing, metal dragon was getting brighter and lighter, until finally the engineer on the approaching train blew the warning whistle at the westbound train. The fireman blew the whistle to indicate that everything was satisfactory, and shortly the eastbound train whisked by the left side of Tom's train. Tom felt as if he could have reached out and touched the black blur as it went by. For an instant Tom noticed that one of the passing cars had bright lights in it and that the people inside were sitting around tables as if they were playing cards. As fast as the train had come, it disappeared until only the sound of the engine panting like an animal at rest remained.

"Well, gentlemen, do ya think that the engineer is sober enough to git up here and do his job, or am I gonna have ta do it fir him all night?" asked Hank.

The three men went to the boxcar where the engineer was locked up to see if he had slept off the booze. When the door opened, the engineer stuck his head out and swore.

"What do ya think you're doin' lockin' me in here? I'm gonna report ya ta the authorities when we get ta our next stop!"

Hank laughed out loudly. "Ha, ha, ha, ya do, fella, and we will tell a story 'bout a drunken engineer. Now git up there and do ya job 'fore I lock ya up again! And no more funny business, since ya cain't hold ya booze!" Hank swore.

Hank helped the engineer as the man grunted, groaned, and sputtered but ascended the ladder to the cab of his engine. Tom and Hank started the stroll back to their passenger car.

"Hank, that other train that just passed us had a car that was all lit up this late at night with people sittin' around tables. What was it? What were those people doin'?" asked Tom.

"Well, some trains have special cars–some for eatin', gamblin', and some even have them fancy cars for sleepin'. In fact, lookie here at this car. I think its fer sleepin'," said Hank with a yawn.

"This car has beds in it?" asked Tom with amazement. "Why didn't we git one with beds in it?"

"Simple, Tom, we ain't payin' the extra money for it. It cost a lot more than those day cars we're tryin' to ride and sleep in. Boy, I wish I could lay down and sleep!" said Hank and yawned again.

"Next stop at a station–I'll git us one, Hank! I have the money," bragged Tom with a grin.

"Ya have that kind of money, kid?" asked Hank with amazement. "Where'd you git it?"

"I trapped furs in Colorado like I tole ya," explained Tom.

"Well, ya musta done mighty good ta wanna spend ya money like that!" stated Hank.

"I did," replied Tom with a chuckle.

Before they had walked back to their passenger car, the train started to roll. Hank jumped upon the first step and hollered for Tom to do the same. Tom did so with no trouble, and they both headed for their seats. Tom immediately realized that he had forgotten and left his valuable saddlebags on the floor under his seat; now they were gone.

"Hank, my saddlebags are gone, and the money!" exclaimed Tom.

Hank looked out the window, back down the side of the train.

"Yeah, I think I sees them, Tommie!" announced Hank as he pulled the emergency cord which put the train into a sudden stop.

People were dislodged from their seats, fell, and hurt their selves. Howls of protest, shouts of panic, and cries of "What is going on?" sounded.

"I'll tell ya what's goin' on!" bellowed Hank as he faced the whole car full of confused and angry people. "Someone in this very car is a lousy thief and has stolen my buddy's money from his saddlebags and then threw them out the window! Betcha! Tom, run back and see if ya kin git the saddlebags and bring 'em back here ta check on ya stuff."

While Tom ran to get the saddlebags, Hank bellowed out orders. "Turn those lanterns up bright! I want ta see the face of the rotten person that stole my buddy's money! Anybody wanta 'fess up and git this over the easy way?" shouted Hank. "You two blue coats, I expect ya'll help me shake everybody up 'til we finds the goods. At least see ta it that nobody leaves this here car!"

Hank's large frame and his growling voice made most of the people scared. It got very quiet. The two soldiers got up to help Hank, as the conductor opened the door.

"What's goin' on in this car?" he demanded to know.

Hank explained what had happened, and Tom showed up out of breath just then, carrying his saddlebags. Quickly Tom moved towards the lantern and looked inside the bags.

"They've stolen my money and my clothes!" exclaimed Tom as he tried to catch his breath.

"All right, people," shouted Hank from the front of the car. "We are now gonna find the guilty person. Tom, come up here!"

Hank straightened up, flexed his huge muscles, and belched. Rage showed on his face, and the shadows that were cast around him made him appear even larger, meaner, and more evil. The children began to cry in fright.

"Is this ya stuff, Tom?" asked Hank as he open the first bag he found under the first seat.

Tom looked, but it was not his. The soldiers and conductor were uneasy about what was going on but were actually afraid to go against the giant of a mountain man.

Hank continued going through people's things as Tom kept looking to see if the contents were his.

Abruptly Hank dived down the isle and hit the floor. A gunshot was heard, and a bullet hole appeared in the front of the car. Hank grabbed for the man with the pistol, and another shot went off as the mountain man grabbed the shooter's wrist. The bullet had gone through the roof and hurt no one. Only a brief moment passed until the gunman dropped the pistol as Hank squeezed the man's wrist until one could hear the bones breaking inside.

The man screamed with pain and begged for Hank to stop.

"First, where's the money; and the clothes?" Hank demanded to know.

"The money's in my pocket and the clothes in my bag," screamed the thief.

"Pull the money out wid the other hand and git the clothes before I rip ya head off!" ordered Hank roughly.

The man did as he was told and sat in his seat with his head bowed, holding his badly crushed wrist with his good hand.

"All right, conductor! Blue coats! Do ya duty before I do more than I ever should ta this loathsome piece a meat." That said, Hank spit on the man and picked up the pistol.

CHAPTER THIRTEEN

"Conductor, I want ta talk with ya," said Tom loudly. "Do ya have any room left in the sleepers?"

"Yes, as a matter of fact we do, but they cost more than these day cars. I doubt if ya have the money for it," answered the conductor.

The conductor found out that Tom **did** have the money, and for the rest of the night Hank and Tom slept peacefully in a pleasant soft bed behind a heavy curtain, which separated them from people sleeping in beds across the isle.

They both slept to their hearts' content. They slept after the sun came up and right through the station change when the train stopped for breakfast, water for the engine, a fresh engineer and fireman, and for the soldiers to turn over the thief and would-be murderer to the local authorities.

Hank finally woke first and stirred about. He soon discovered that the car they were on was for those people with money and therefore these passengers were served fancy foods and drinks. When the porter offered Hank a drink, he took the whole bottle and layback down sipping the booze as Tom woke up.

"Smile?" asked Hank as he grinned and laughed at Tom.

Tom laughed and asked, "Where'd ya get it?"

Hank explained the situation, and soon both were eating their late breakfast, sitting on their bed, which made up into a couch.

It came to Tom's mind that money was really nice to have and a person could live a lot better and enjoy life more if he had lots of money.

"I tole ya, Tom. I tole ya," said Hank softly, interrupting Tom's thoughts.

"Ya tole me what?" asked Tom.

"I tole ya that God he'ps those that he'ps themselves!" said Hank seriously. "Ya see, ifen I hadn't a done it fer ya last night, ya woulda lost all ya stuff and money. And ifen I hadn't taken care of the train and drunk engineer last night, we would all be a way back down the tracks yet," explained Hank.

"Thanks for helpin' me, Hank. Yep! I guess yer right. God helps those that help themselves! Boy, this car sure is somethin'! It's really nice," said Tom as he looked around. Tom noticed other people eating, drinking, and talking. The situation was so different from the day cars. The couch was upholstered, and the car was not crowded. The people were all white folks, most of whom were well dressed. Tom suddenly realized that he and Hank did not fit into the scene.

"Hank, do ya suppose we shouldn't be in here? I mean, look how these people is dressed!" exclaimed Tom.

"Ya paid ya money, didn't ya? Ain't gonna matter. We're here and we're gonna enjoy it," Hank said in a very determined voice, and swore. "Don't **ever** think somebody is better 'en ya 'cuz a their money or clothes. Remember, you're as good as any one, and besides, God he'ps those that he'ps themselves. You earned the money, you he'ped yourself, you deserve ta have it nice."

"Hank, how'd ya know that man was gonna shoot at ya last night? I didn't see nothin'!" explained Tom.

"I heard the click of his pistol as he pulled the lever back! Ya gotta be alert in this ole world, or it'll get cha. Ya beginnin' ta see what I means 'bout God he'ps those what he'ps themselves?" explained Hank.

Tom and Hank continued to chat as the train puffed down the track. Tom explained why he was going to the Arizona Territory, and Hank explained that he was going back into the mountains and would be getting off the train when it reached almost the top of the Rocky Mountains.

"Tom, ya sure ya got ya money by trappin'? I means, a fella kin make good money trappin'. But most trappers don't ride in these here cars. Did ya win some by gamblin'?" asked Hank.

Tom explained to Hank what had happened to him when he had come down out of the mountains and how Snake Eyes and Frederick had viciously attacked him and how he and the Indian boy had killed them. He also explained how he had received the reward money for the two criminals, and the reward money for the return of the stolen money.

Hank sat quiet–stunned.

"Yer the boy t'at killed Snake Eyes and Frederick? I heard t'at those two scoundrels were taken in dead, and I figered it must've been some-kind-of person that got 'um. Ya don't say! Those two did me wrong, once. Only people I know of t'at crossed me and got away with it! Well, let me shake the hand of the man t'at brought in Snake Eyes and Frederick! Smile? Ah, come on Tom, this calls fer ya to take a genuine drink!" stated Hank.

Tom grinned and said, "Well, maybe a little one."

Hank called for the porter to bring Tom a drink, and the two toasted to the death of Snake Eyes and Frederick.

The whiskey burned Tom's throat going down but gave Tom a warm, relaxed feeling.

"Wow, that had quite a kick, Hank," said Tom as he drew in a gasp of air.

"Hey, have another one, kid; it'll make ya feel real good!" laughed Hank.

Tom decided to have another drink, which soon made his head spin a bit but also made him very relaxed. He slid down in his seat and started talking about anything that crossed his mind. Much of what he had to say did not make any sense, and Hank thought it was very funny and laughed and laughed.

Tom babbled something about a treasure map that Snake Eyes had given him. Hank listened with interest and asked Tom questions about the map.

"Ya wanta see the map?" Tom asked with slurred speech. "I only got half of it. Some ole prospectin' Scotsman is supposed ta have the other. I got it ri' chere in my hat. See?"

Hank looked at the map carefully and with great interest and said, "Well, that there map don't tell the complete story. I guess ya'd better hang on ta it 'til ya find the ole prospector. If it's the Scotty that I knows, he'd treat ya fair, but he's gettin' older. I thinks that funny lookin' mountain may be in Arizona, though. Went through there one time. Too hot and dry fer me! Seems like I saw a mountain shaped like that. Kinda like a teapot or woman's upside down slipper. That's 'bout all I kin tell ya 'bout it, sorry."

"It's okay, Hank; I really don't worry 'bout it much. I jus' want ta see my friend in the pen, then I'm gonna go back 'n see the nicest, prettiest girl I ever met! I shouldn't be drinkin' like this. She's the kinda girl that goes ta church and loves Jesus and wouldn' like it if I drank!" exclaimed Tom, as the thought rather sobered him.

"Ah, forget 'er! Any woman that won't let a man take a little nip now 'n then is gotta be too hard ta live with! Believe me, I already been down that there road, and a woman can make ya life miserable!" Hank explained with a far-away look in his eye and drank some more.

"Well, Hank, jus' promise that ya won't ever tell 'er that I did this here drinkin' cuz it wouldn't be good for 'er to know," said Tom.

"Shore, I won't tell; ya might as well have another one now 'cuz ya already went and did it," chuckled Hank.

Somehow in Tom's confused mind that seemed right, and so he took another drink–and then another–and then another.

Tom decided to stand up and declare something, but he blacked out and fell back onto the couch.

Time passed, and the night came. The train started its climb into the steeper grades of the Rocky Mountains. But Tom slept on and on because of the alcohol.

Hank was alert to the fact that he would soon need to be getting off. He felt sorry that he had gotten his young friend drunk and would not be able to say good-bye to him. Hank covered the boy tenderly with the blanket. He wished he could write so that he could leave the boy a good-bye message. He wished to tell the boy that he was probably wrong and that it would probably be better not to drink and that a good woman was worth not drinking for, but he could not. The train would soon be coming to the spot where he would jump off, because there was no regular stop where he was going.

Hank looked down into the sleeping boy's youthful face. "Oh God, what have I done? I corrupted this kid!" A tear actually ran down the big man's cheek.

Hank looked out the window. It was time to leave.

"Good-bye, Tom, sorry. Hope ta sees ya again, soon!"

Hank paused briefly at the back door to say something to the conductor, and then he was gone into the night.

****

The sun shone brightly upon the people in the sleeping car. Tom awoke in a slow, dreamy way. He could not remember where he was. His leg ached because he had slept all night lying on his pistol. His head hurt as if it were going to explode.

He sat up and slowly began to remember the drinks that Hank had given him. *Hank? Where's Hank?* thought Tom groggily. Then he looked out the window and realized that he had slept a long time and that they had crossed over the mountains and that Hank had said that he wanted to get off before they went over the top. The sun hurt Tom's eyes, so he turned away from the window. He missed Hank and wished he could have said good-bye to him. The porter came and asked what he wanted for breakfast. Tom asked for water.

The ride continued uneventfully as the Santa Fe sped on into California. Tom enjoyed the comforts of the sleeping and eating car and often reminded himself about the advantages of having money. In fact, he wondered if he had done the right thing when he gave back the money he had found in Pueblo. Were all those things that happened to him and those sermons just coincidental? He thought about Mandy and even wrote her another letter, but did not say anything about his drinking or smoking. He knew that Mandy would be disappointed in him. Would she forgive him if she knew? Mandy had talked a lot about the forgiveness that her Jesus gave.

There was a long delay at the train depot where Tom had to change to the Southern Pacific to go southwest to Fort Yuma. This time when Tom sat waiting, he was very careful to keep an eye on his saddlebags.

The train finally arrived in Fort Yuma with all the usual noise, smoke, and excitement of the arrival. Townspeople came from all around to greet their guests or to receive their supplies from the train. Tom noticed that there was a marshal with a handcuffed prisoner getting off the train.

The town of Yuma had a wide, dusty, busy street that morning. Tom passed a man leaning against a worn post and asked where the livery was. He explained that he wanted to get a horse to ride out to the prison. The man said that he would not need a horse since the prison was not very far and pointed to a hill that the railroad tracks ran near.

"Right over there, fella! Why rent a horse ta go over there?"

Tom thanked the man and started the short walk following the dusty road as it led to the other side of the rocky hill and up to the prison. The scorching Arizona sun beat down as he walked the short distance up the hill to the prison gate. Tom swore aloud and mumbled to himself, "How in the world'll Jed ever be able ta take this horrible heat?"

Tom approached the large metal-latticed prison gate. A guard stepped out of a small guard shack next to the gate.

"I've come to see someone," announced Tom.

"Well, we have certain hours to visit and certain limitations," said the guard rather roughly.

"Well, what are ya hours?" asked Tom.

"Any time we decide to let ya!" exclaimed the guard with a laugh. "And ya ain't coming in wearin' no pistol like that! Who'd ya want ta see anyways?" asked the guard while rubbing his beard.

"Jed Thompson," replied Tom.

The guard looked Tom in the eyes and asked, "What's yer name?"

"Tom Fleming, what's yers?" asked Tom.

"Hartlee, just call me Hartlee," replied the guard. "Well, if you want to visit a guy like Jed, I guess we can work that out. Just hang on while I go get the Super."

Hartlee disappeared through the big iron latticed gate carrying his rifle and came back shortly with the superintendent.

"Hello, my name's Frank Ingalls. I am the superintendent here. Who are you, and what is your relationship to Jed?" asked the man.

Tom explained who he was and how he and Jed used to herd cattle and trap together and had become fine friends.

"Well, if I thought for one second you might be one of the bank robbers that Jed used to run with, I wouldn't let you visit him. However, I can see that you are too young to have been part of his bank robber pals. Check your gun and ammunition and any knives you have with Hartlee, then I'll take you in to see Jed," stated Superintendent Ingalls, rather flatly.

Tom gave his belt, pistol, and saddlebags to the guard and emptied his pockets of all their contents. Hartlee checked his person for any hidden materials. The superintendent led Tom into the prison.

"This here is what we call the bull pen," explained the superintendent. "It's where the men get their exercise and are allowed out of their cells during some parts of the day, if their behavior is good. Jed's been given a job in the blacksmith's shop. He is a good worker and is learning how to do the job very well. He has been a real help around here. He doesn't seem like the criminal type."

"Blacksmith shop?" questioned Tom. "You have a blacksmith shop here?"

"Oh yes, the inmates do all the work here; they even have to make their own clothes. The government has not given us enough money for this prison to run otherwise. There's Jed now. Hey, Jed, we got a visitor for you!" exclaimed the superintendent.

Jed looked up from the work on which he was concentrating. He was just about to bring a huge hammer down on a red-hot piece of iron.

"Tom! My goodness, ya come, Tom! I knowd ya would! Mr. Ingalls, kin I have some time ta visit my buddy here?" asked Jed excitedly.

"Yes, you may," answered Mr. Ingalls. "But you'll have to always have a guard with you."

The superintendent motioned for the already-present guard and told him to stay with Tom and Jed and allow them to have a good visit.

"My goodness, my goodness, Tom, ya look great!" exclaimed Jed with joy and delight written all over his face. "You've grown up and are a big man now. Look at those muscles. Boy, it's so good to see ya; I'm so thankful that ya come."

Jed took off his soiled apron and hung it on a large nail, revealing his entire prison clothes. The garments looked kind of like night clothes with black stripes painted across them.

"You look good too, Jed. I was afraid that maybe things'd be bad fer ya here, especially in this dreadful heat. How do ya stand it?" asked Tom while wiping the sweat off his own forehead.

"Well, it's terrible, all right, but we jus' drink lots of water, Tom. We drink lots of water," repeated Jed.

Tom and Jed began talking, and they both explained all that happened to them since they had last seen each other. Tom talked first and told Jed about everything that he could think of since they had parted. He talked about his winter alone trapping, his friendship with Hoga, about how Hoga shot Frederick, and how he shot Snake Eyes.

"Ya don't say, ya don't say! Ya actually brought in Snake Eyes and Frederick 'n ya weren't even tryin'," stated Jed with amazement. "Those guys were so bad that even outlaws hunted 'em!"

Tom told Jed about his stay in Pueblo, how he met Mandy, and even about the bank money he had found and returned. Jed roared laughing when he heard about the outhouse smell and all that happened with the sermons that had been preached and had made Tom feel so guilty.

"Sounds like the Lord's really workin' in yer heart! I hope ya'll listen afore it's too late," stated Jed seriously.

Tom even told Jed about the train ride and Hank but was ashamed to tell Jed how he had gotten drunk.

"Yeah, I've met men like that, Tom. They think they've the world by the reins and make it go the way they want it ta. But sooner or later they'll find out different. I was sorta like that myself for a while, but what'd it get me? Prison! Which actually is the best thing that ever happened to me!" exclaimed Jed.

"The best thing that ever happened to ya?" asked Tom with amazement.

"Why sure, Tom. Because that's what it took fer me ta see that Jesus **is** really the Creator and God, and that He died fer my sins and personally loves me. Now I have a relationship with God Himself here in prison! Somethin' most people don't have on the outside! Ya know what? Most men in here only think about one thing; it's always on their mind. Escapin'! And I don't even care ta leave here!" exclaimed Jed.

The inmate continued, "Ya see. I'm what ya call livin' fer the Lord now and not fer myself. So if the Lord wants me here, great! I'll be happy here. The superintendent's wife is teachin' me ta read and write; I can read the Bible some now! Mrs. Ingalls is a great lady. Here, look at this poem I wrote."

Jed pulled a sweaty, crumpled piece of paper out of his pocket and handed it to Tom. Tom took the paper, opened it up, and read aloud:

> *It really seems to me,*
> *How happy we all would be,*
> *If Jesus were in charge of us all,*
> *Instead of the Devil's alcohol!*

"That is real nice, Jed. I'm glad that yer happy, even in prison," stated Tom.

Tom, don' cha see? Cuz of Jesus we can triumph over our sinfulness, because we are always self-centered and caring only about ourselves. The greed is gone in my life and fer once I'm content. I'm payin' the price I should be fer what I done. Now I pray for others, and especially for you that ya'll come to know Jesus 'fore it's too late," explained Jed.

"What do you mean, too late?" asked Tom.

"Well, for shore I mean 'fore ya die, but also 'fore ya cause yerself a world of hurt–then wake up to yer need, like I done ta myself," explained Jed.

"Well, I appreciate yer prayers, Jed, and I know that there is somethin' to this Jesus thing, but I don't quite understand it all. Ya know, ole Snake Eyes even felt somethin' about God jus' before he died. He gave me a map as if ta make up for all his wrong doings. Here, look at this map," explained Tom.

Tom pulled the carefully folded map from his hat and handed it to Jed. Jed studied the map for a while. "Well, looks like ole Snake Eyes was tryin' to give you a hidden treasure map. It must be hidden on that mountain that looks like a teapot. You only have half of the map, though. Where's the rest of the map?" asked Jed.

"Some prospector Scotsman is suppose ta have it," replied Tom.

"I've seen a mountain like that before here in Arizona. Actually two of them. Jus' guessin' at the distance, I would say that one is 'bout a hundred and fifty miles from here and one is about a hundred miles from here.

"But ya got the same problem as ya had with the stolen bank money. It ain't yers, if it were stolen. That reminds me, I got a really big favor to ask of ya," stated Jed.

"Sure, Jed, anything I can do for ya, I will!" exclaimed Tom.

"Well, do ya remember back when we first met? I got yer help in findin' the grave of my brother, Ned?" asked Jed.

Tom nodded and listened with interest as he remembered very well that gloomy, scary night that they dug up the grave.

"I gotta ask ya forgiveness for this 'cuz I lied to ya. That saddlebag I put in the coffin wasn't jus' somethin' for Ned; it was two thousand dollars in stolen bank money I was hidin'! Will ya forgive me for lyin' ta ya?" asked Jed sincerely.

"Sure, I'll forgive ya, Jed. No big deal," replied Tom

"It sure **is** a big deal, Tom; ya see, I need ta clear my conscience. In case ya haven't noticed, I'm gettin' old and I want ta set my wrongs right. I guess it's 'cuz Jesus has been workin' in my heart.

So fer ya ta forgive me is a real big deal! That was not the only thing I needed yer help fer. Ya see, I tol' the judge that I'd tell them where the hidden money was–and I did–there in that grave in Red Rock. So they sent two federal marshals out ta get the money, but the grave they dug up didn't have any saddlebags in them, and they came back sayin' the money couldn't be found!" explained Jed.

Jed continued, "I need yer help, Tom. Do ya think ya could lead the marshals to the right grave? You were there; in fact, ya even had put them little rocks around it 'fore we dug it up–at least ya said ya did."

"Yea, I did, but I don't know fer sure that I could find the grave or not. Was it really your brother Ned in the grave?" asked Tom.

"Yes, it really was my poor brother, Ned. Would ya be willin' ta show federal marshals where the grave is, if you can? It's very important ta me, and since ya were willin' to return stolen money once, I believe I kin trust ya," concluded Jed.

"Yes, I'll do what I can for ya. I thought that I'd spend a week here in Fort Yuma and visit you everyday before I go back to Pueblo. If you make the arrangements, I'll show the marshals where the money is buried, if I can," said Tom.

During that week, Tom visited Jed every day and stayed as long as he could. Jed showed Tom around the prison with the ever-present guard near. The cell that Jed was locked in, with five other men at night, was only about nine feet by eight, with a high domed ceiling. Inside were two tiers of bunks made of steel about eighteen inches wide. There was no other furniture–no sink, no chairs, only a bucket to serve as a toilet for the men.

"Jed, how do ya stand bein' in here?" asked Tom while wiping the sweat from his face.

"Well, no doubt about it, it's hard, but I deserve it. I ain't got it as bad as others, though. See that hole and short tunnel in the rocks over there? That's a kind of dungeon we call the Snake Den.

Men that try to escape or won't cooperate are put in there fer days at a time. They see nothin' but a very small hole way up in the top of the mound. They get bread and water once a day. There's nothin' in there but rocks and their own filth," explained Jed.

"Wow, Jed, I hope you never get put in there," stated Tom.

"Well, notice these things, Tom, and ya make sure that yer never get put in prison for wrongs ya might be tempted to do! Look over there. See those men breakin' rocks out in the sun, and those men makin' adobe bricks? More men that won't cooperate or got rebellious with the guards. The other men ya see workin' are just doin' their jobs while in prison; the cleanin', the kitchen, and the blacksmith shop–just our jobs. But no pay. We seldom get any money. So ya think about it and don't be like me; earn yer livin' honestly," explained Jed.

****

During the last day, that Tom came to see Jed, the superintendent called the two into his office.

"Jed tells me that you saw him put some saddlebags in a grave in New Mexico, without knowing he was hiding bank money. Is that right?" asked the superintendent.

"Yes, sir, that's right. I showed Jed where the town of Red Rock had buried an outlaw, because he said it was his brother's grave. He wanted ta put somethin' in the coffin fer his brother. I figured that it'd make him feel better, so I went with him one night and saw him put some saddlebags in the coffin along with a blanket. I didn't know that it was stolen bank money," explained Tom.

"Son, do you think you could show the authorities where the grave is? Two federal marshals could not find it, along with the Red Rock Marshal and some townspeople. Do you think *you* could find it?" asked the superintendent.

"Well, if the marshals couldn't find it after checkin' with the town sheriff, I doubt if I can either. Prob'ly the rains and wind have erased all signs of it," stated Tom.

"That's what I thought, too," explained the superintendent. "But Jed here feels that it's important for someone to find it to help him make amends for his past, and I think that's a good idea too."

"Tom, it's really important ta me ta clear this up," stated Jed with a look of pleading on his face.

"Well, I'll try fer Jed's sake," stated Tom.

"Well then," said Mr. Ingalls, "I'll send a telegraphed message to Red Rock and let the marshal know you're coming. By the way, there's a letter here for you."

Tom gratefully took the letter from the superintendent and noticed that it was postmarked Pueblo, Colorado. He felt anxious to open the letter and hear from Mandy. He felt his heart pound a little when he smelled the perfume on the letter.

My dearest Tom,

It was so good to hear from you. Thanks for writing to me. I am so glad that you love me too. I pray for you every day and sometimes during the night. I think about you a lot. I really hope that this letter finds you in time.

My father is sick again. He tried to continue the work of the store but finally just could not keep going and is in bed again. The doctor cannot figure out why he gets these spells. He has been having trouble breathing. If you can come back soon and would like to work for my father, we could surely use you. My parents like you.

I really want you to come back for more than just working for us. I really miss you. I have even felt somewhat depressed since you left. I know Jesus doesn't want me to feel that way so He helps me through each day. I had to take the wagon to the train yesterday and pick up the goods for the store.

I have to go for now; write me soon as you can. Tell me where you are next, or I won't be able to write you. I love you very, very, very much.

Always your sweetheart,
Mandy

"Somethin' wrong?" Jed asked.

"Well, not really, jus' that Mandy's father is sick again and they could use my help in Pueblo," stated Tom sadly. "I'll go back ta Pueblo to help as soon as I try to find that stolen money in Red Rock."

CHAPTER FOURTEEN

Tom left Fort Yuma with a heavy heart. It had been so good to see Jed. It had been almost like going to see his father, since he had learned so much from him in the time he had spent with him before Jed had been arrested. Now Tom felt very bad for him. He knew he probably would not see him again in this life. Jed had a little cough, and although strong, he was aging. The work in the blacksmith shop was hard and hot, and the cells the men slept in were extremely hot in the summer and awfully cold and drafty in the winter since they had no doors except for the metal latticework that locked them.

Tom sat on the train thinking how strange it was that Jed still had a great amount of joy in this situation. His happiness reminded him of the smile that Mandy had. Tom realized that he himself did not have this joy or peace in his life. Jed had revealed so much to Tom about his inner self and past sins in a hope that Tom would not make the same mistakes.

Tom, I taught ya how ta play poker, and we spent many long hours playin' the game while waitin' out the winter storms, when we was trappin', but now I'm sorry that I taught ya about gamblin'. Yeah, we jus' played fer fun, but now ya knows how ta play the game. I'm 'fraid you'll get ta playin' poker in some saloon, which usually has the wrong kinda people hangin' 'round. Ya know what'll happen? You'll win! At least at first, 'cuz that's what hooks ya like bait fer a fish. That's the bait! Winnin' is bait. It'll hook ya into more playin', probably drinkin' and runnin' with the wrong kinda boys and probably even women. So Tom, please consider what I say. I kan't makes ya do right, but maybe ya'll remember what I'm sayin' when yer tempted and stay away from all that, thought Tom in recollection of what Jed had said.

The train whistle blew loudly, startling Tom out of his daydreaming. Tom decided to go to his bed on the sleeping car as he had once again paid the extra fair for the luxury. He reminded himself of the advantages of having money as he pulled back the clean sheets. He felt lonely but remembered that he would be able to see his mother when he arrived in Red Rock. He also thought about Frank Woods, and made a muscular fist.

Tom pulled out the precious letter Mandy had sent him in Yuma and read it over again. He thought about Mandy and tried to picture her happy, smiling face surrounded by the attractive long, brown hair.

I wish I had a picture of her, thought Tom as he slipped into sleep hoping that Mr. Whitman was getting better and that things were well for Mandy.

****

The next day Tom felt so restless he could hardly keep seated on the train. He wished he could do something, but he found absolutely nothing to do but eat and sleep, so he asked the black porter when he came around if there was anything to do on the train.

"Wells, suh, yous kin read these here ole papers, or I'll try ta gets ya a book, or ya could go ta the gamblin' car and plays poker, but I's won' rec-o-mend it," answered the man.

"Gamblin' car?" asked Tom, "There's a gamblin' car on this train?"

"Yes, suh, but I'll get ya a book," the man said and disappeared into the front of the car.

Presently he reappeared with a book and handed it to Tom. Tom took the black book and looked at the cover. "Holy Bible" he read aloud.

"Yes, suh, that's a fine book," said the porter and started to walk away.

"Porter, did ya know this was the Bible?" asked Tom.

The old man stood quiet and looked a little ashamed. "No suh, I kan't read," replied the porter in a quiet voice.

Tom leaned back in his chair. A tingle came over him. In a flash, his mind recollected the events that had happened to him in Pueblo, the ones that made him give back the money. Tom was afraid to open the Bible. He knew that he would most surely read a verse that said, "Thou shalt not gamble." He hesitated another moment and then opened the book to about the middle and looked at a verse and read it slowly.

"For ye shall go out with joy, and be led forth with peace: the mountains and the hills shall break forth before you into singing, and all the trees of the field shall clap their hands."

Huh? thought Tom. He actually felt surprised but relieved that the verse had nothing to do with gambling. *Wonder what kinda trees have hands on them that can clap?* thought Tom. He laughed aloud. He looked at another verse at random and another and felt glad that nothing was said about poker. Finally, he turned to the front chapter and read about the creation account until he tired of reading. The restless boy put the book down and strummed his fingers on the little table in front of him. The thought came to him that maybe he could just go watch a poker game and not get involved.

The train traveled down the noisy track a few more miles as he listened to the clickity clack, clickity clack, and then he slowly got up and walked to the back door. Outside in the air, the breeze felt good, and Tom stood watching the countryside for a moment and then walked into the gambling car.

The smell of cigars and liquor met Tom's nose as he sat down on a leather seat near a group of four men playing poker. All was quiet except for the clickity clack of the train and the ching of money tossed into the center of the gambling table. One man with a mustache was the most relaxed of the four men and snickered often. The other three men were not seemingly intimidated by this and continued to play with the bet. Finally, one man placed his cards faced down on the table and said, "I fold."

The man with the mustache sat up and leaned against the table on his elbows. Pulling the cigar from between his teeth, he said, "What's the matter, boy, too rich for your blood?" The man who folded sat back, crossed his arms, and laughed.

The man sitting between the mustached man and the quitter looked over his cards carefully and tossed two more gold coins into the kitty. The mustached man tossed two coins into the middle of the table and said, "I see yer two and raise ya two."

The man to his left threw in four coins and then a fifth. The mustached man jerked his head the other way in surprise.

"Oh, ya think yer still in this game, huh?" he said and cursed.

"Okay, you win! That's three coins too many for me. I've got hungry kids ta feed," said the man across from the highest bidder.

"It's just you and me, kid," said the mustached man. "What's yer bet?"

"You first, old friend; it's your call," said the man that was left.

The mustached man leaned back in his chair, took a couple of deep puffs from his old cigar, and smashed it into the nearly full ashtray. As the smoke slowly escaped from his lungs he said, "I see yer extra coin and raise ya, three."

The remaining challenger glanced through his cards one last time, laid them out face up, and matched the three previous coins.

The setting sun shone its golden rays through the open windows behind the mustached man, casting a shadow across his face. The tension was great as he lay down his cards exposing his three aces. He had beaten the final player who had three kings.

Men continued to come and go in the gambling car while Tom sat and watched the game as well as the countryside as it sped by. Nothing seemed so bad about what happened. No one got drunk or mad or shot anybody. Some men lost money; some men won money.

"What could be wrong with this?" thought Tom. He did notice that while many men came and went through the gambling coach, the mustached man did not leave, and he often won.

When the train arrived at Albuquerque, Tom got off since that was the closest point the train came to Red Rock. Tom debated whether to buy a horse or take the stage to his destination. If he took the stage, he knew that he would get tired of being bounced around in the dusty coach. If he bought a horse, he would later have to sell it or pay for it to ride the train also.

Tom decided to take the stage. He was delighted when asked by the driver if he wanted to ride "shotgun" up top since there was no help on this trip.

"Been some talk a Indians botherin' people again," said the driver. "So might be helpful, if ya want the job. Give ya a free ride!"

Tom accepted the job and was glad for it, especially since it was a free ride. During the trip the driver talked about everything under the sun, but at least it helped pass the slow miles. When the stage finally arrived at Red Rock, Tom was glad for the trip to be finished. He helped the women passengers down from the dusty coach and then helped the driver unload the luggage. Finally, he untied his saddlebags and said goodbye to the driver.

The anxious boy headed for the cafe where he hoped his mother still worked. His boots fell with a hollow sound on the old boardwalk as he walked toward the cafe. He was extremely impatient to see his mother since he had not seen her for over a year.

The dusty cow town had not changed much since Tom was there. The much-matured boy noticed only one new building before going into the familiar-looking cafe. His mother was busy wiping a table clean.

"Hi, Ma!" Tom spoke excitedly.

Ma Fleming Woods looked up and gasped.

"Tom, you're here; you're actually here! I prayed fer ya ta come, and now you're actually here! I almost don' believe it, but God does answer prayer!" exclaimed his mother.

Ma dropped her wiping cloth and gave her son a huge hug, while Tom gave his mother a kiss on the cheek.

"I've missed ya, Tom; been wonderin' and worryin' 'bout ya. Ya look so big an' strong, Tom–my, you've grown!" exclaimed the boy's mother with gladness in her voice.

"I've missed ya too, Ma. Sorry ta be such a terrible son to ya; I do think 'bout cha and care 'bout cha. I've wondered how ya were too," replied Tom quietly.

"Well, sit down here an' I'll get ya some supper. I have somethin' very important ta tell ya," said the lady with a bit of an anxious look in her eyes.

Tom ate the delicious supper that she brought him but did not get much time to chat with her because of the needs of other customers. Finally, Ma got a break and sat down to talk to Tom.

"Tom, somethin' very important happened yesterday. So important that I prayed God that ya'd come, and ya did!" stated Ma excitedly.

"What happened, Ma?" asked Tom.

"Well, Tom, Frank decided to build a new buildin' fer a better general store. It's all finished, and it's much bigger and better. He started to move the merchandise from the old store to the new store yesterday. When he moved the heavy cash register, he found the one hundred dollars that he accused ya of stealin'. It was underneath the register! He vaguely remembers thinkin' that he'd put it there for only a moment when he was interrupted by a customer while countin' money. Then when he got back ta finish the countin' much later, he had forgotten that he had temporarily hid the money there," told Ma very quickly.

For a moment, Tom just sat staring at his mother.

"I tol' ya that I didn't steal the money, Ma! I tol' ya but ya wouldn't believe me!" exclaimed Tom in a whispered voice.

"I'm sorry, Tom. I'm so very sorry. Please forgive me," said Ma with tears forming in her eyes.

"I forgive ya, Ma, but I can't forgive Frank, not after he lost his temper so bad and beat me almos' ta death," stated Tom coldly.

"Oh, Tom, that's why I prayed so hard fer ya ta come–so that things could be made right! Frank feels truly bad and says he wants ta ask yer forgiveness and wants ta make it up to ya. And look, the very next day, here you are! Please, Tom, let Frank ask yer forgiveness, and forgive him!" Ma said, and she reached over and held Tom's arm.

"Ma, I **can't**, an' **ain't gonna!** Why should I?" asked Tom.

"Because it's been a long time, an' wounds must heal or the bitterness will eat yer insides up. Frank has agonized over this fer years. Besides, it's the right an' Christian thing ta do," explained Ma.

"Christian thing ta do? Don't tell me 'bout the Christian thing ta do! I've seen the way Christians do things in this here town, and the Christian thing ta do is not what the Christians do here! Naw, Ma, I can't forgive him; he just beat me too bad. It was no Christian beatin' I got!" said Tom with a determined tone in his voice.

"Well, Christians do make mistakes an' need forgiveness; that's why Christ died fer everybody. Frank and I been tryin' ta live the Christian life better," explained Tom's mother with tenderness.

The words came out sweet to Tom's ears. They sounded like something Mandy would say. Tom and his mother sat looking at each other. Tom's mind went through the old struggle of right and wrong.

"Okay, Ma, I won't promise ya that I'll forgive him, but I'll listen ta what he has ta say," said Tom reluctantly.

Ma grinned and said, "Oh, thank you, thank you! I'm sure it'll work out. We can go over ta the new store before it gets too dark, or we can wait here till Frank comes over fer supper."

Tom chose to go over to the new store, but wanted to go alone. He was not so sure he would forgive Frank Woods but did not want to see his mother disappointed. While Tom was walking over to the new building, his mind began to think about the horrible beating that he had once experienced by this man who was not really his father. The usual feeling of anger and intense hatred came over him as he momentarily relived the unjust beating. He even reached down and checked his gun. He was determined that this man would never lay a hand on him again!

Tom found Frank, arranging goods on his new clean shelves. Frank looked up upon hearing Tom's boots on the wood floor. "Tom, I'm most glad ta see ya. You look good! Growd up a lot!" he exclaimed somewhat hesitantly.

"No thanks ta **you**; Ma said ya have somethin' ta say ta me," said Tom very coldly.

Frank cleared his throat; it was hard for him to talk, but he knew that he must apologize and ask for forgiveness. .

"Tom, I, ah, found the money that I thought ya stole. I had stuck it under the cash register for a moment, but then forgot about it. So now, I know that you did not steal the money and that I was very wrong. And, of course, I was very wrong for gettin' so mad at ya and beatin' ya the way I did. Will you forgive me?" asked Frank slowly, and stepped closer to Tom.

"Why should I? You only believe me and feel that cha did wrong cuz ya found yer money!" Anger flooded Tom's mind and his face turned red to match his hair.

"If it wasn't for Ma, I'd, well, I'd–in fact I jist might anyways!" hollered Tom as he hurled his right fist squarely into Frank's face.

Frank did nothing except to step back and put his hand to the bruised cheek. He maintained his composure. "I'm sorry that ya won't forgive me, Tom. I guess I have it comin'," said Frank calmly. "The only reason that ya should forgive me is because there was someone else that was falsely accused and then beaten and yet forgave His accusers."

"Oh yeah? Who?" asked Tom loudly.

"Jesus," replied Frank softly.

Tom was taken back. He knew that Frank was saying things like Mandy and that Tom was wrong. He stood thinking for a moment and then backed out of the new store. In a maze of thought, he walked down the street to the boarding house and paid for a room.

During the restless night, he relived the event with Frank. He had often thought of what he might do if he ever came face to face with the man, and hitting him was one of the things he had thought would bring him delight; but now he did not feel good.

If only he'd put up a fight, then it would've been good. But now Frank comes out with that Jesus stuff like Mandy and Ma, thought Tom.

****

The next morning Tom went to the sheriff's office to talk to him about recovering the bank's stolen money.

"Well, Tom Fleming, ya did show up ta help find the money yore outlaw friend Jed hid. Ya look good. Growd up a lot! Still carryin' the gun, I see. Not necessarily bad, but could cause ya some trouble. But I've heard good things 'bout ya, so I guess ya carry yore gun with care. I'm glad," stated the sheriff with a smile. "Why don't we go over ta Clara's first and get us some of those delicious biscuits and gravy and coffee?" declared the sheriff.

Tom noticed that the sheriff limped more than before as they walked to the cafe.

"Good mornin', Liz! Lookie here who I drug in fer breakfast! Bet cha know him. He's gonna help me find the buried money the bank robber hid. Boy! This is gonna be somethin'!" exclaimed the sheriff with obvious excitement in his voice.

Tom's mother looked at him with a sad face, so that he had a hard time looking her in the eyes. He knew that forgiving Frank was an important thing to her, and now she was sad because of what he had done. The sheriff did not seem to notice and went on talking about how Jed had made such a change and had become a Christian while sitting in his jail, and now Tom was here to show them exactly which grave had the money.

The two sat down at a colorful red-and-white-plaid covered table, and Ma brought the coffee for each of them without saying anything.

"Just bring us those delicious biscuits and gravy and maybe a little sausage on the side," ordered the sheriff. He noticed that no one else was talking.

"Somethin' wrong here?" asked the sheriff.

"It's personal, Sheriff. Don't worry 'bout it," stated Mrs. Woods.

"Oh, uh, yeah, okay," said the sheriff as he noticed Tom's mother's sad face and Tom's downcast eyes.

Frank Woods walked in as the two were served their breakfast, and the sheriff invited him to eat with them.

"Wow! Where'd ya get that shiner? Who hit you, Frank? Musta carried quite a wallop!" exclaimed the sheriff.

Frank did not say anything. He just looked at the sheriff somewhat sadly. The sheriff pondered the situation as he took his first bite of breakfast and then began to wonder if Tom had something to do with it. The three ate their breakfast in silence, and Tom never looked at Frank. He hurriedly finished and got up.

"I'm gonna walk out ta the graveyard, Sheriff, and see what I think. Meet ya out there; bring a pick and shovel if ya want, but I doubt I could do any better than you," stated Tom.

"Now wait a minute, boy; let me finish my breakfast and I'll get us a couple of horses from the livery and we'll go out together," ordered the sheriff.

Tom did not say anything but walked out toward the livery.

The sheriff sat and told Frank and Ma about Tom's involvement in the hiding of the money. They were both very amazed at that which their young son had been involved.

"Yeah, he's quite a fella," said the sheriff.

"He's goin' through a struggle with himself right now," stated Tom's mother.

Tom and the old sheriff rode the short distance to the graveyard with picks and shovels tied to their mounts. Tom did not say much but just let the sheriff chatter. The events of the night before had happened so fast Tom needed to think about it, so he really did not listen to what the sheriff was saying. He felt that the sooner he left Red Rock again, the better it would be for all.

"Right here is where we thought we buried Jed's brother. How fir off do ya reckon we were?" asked the sheriff.

Lost in his thoughts, Tom did not reply.

"Tom! I said, right here is where we thought we buried Jed's brother. How fer off do you reckon we was?" asked the sheriff loudly.

Tom looked around and studied the cemetery. He knew right away that they had dug on the wrong side of the graveyard.

"Well, let me think 'bout it, Sheriff," stated Tom.

Tom walked around acting as if he were inspecting the location. A little smile came to his face. *They were so far off I can't believe it. I can go right ta the grave, if I wanna. Do I wanna? I could leave things the way they are and pretend I can't find the grave and then come back some night and dig up the money fer myself. Why not?* thought Tom. But Tom reasoned in his mind that for Jed, his true friend, he would set the stolen money straight. He was somewhat grieved, though, at having to give up the idea of keeping the money for himself.

"Sheriff, yer so far off, it makes me wonder how ya ever find yer way to the outhouse, even if it stinks so bad the skunks stay away from it!" Tom said and laughed with glee." Don't ya keep records or anything 'bout this sorta thing?" he asked, making fun of the sheriff.

"Well, ya ain't showed me where it's at yet. So quit being such a smart one and get on with it," replied the sheriff.

Tom pointed to the other side of the desert cemetery and rode on toward the east side. In doing so, they passed Grandma Jacobson's grave. A white, well-painted picket fence was around the grave. Fresh flowers were on it.

"Wish I could have known her," Tom said sadly.

"Yeah, she was an angel of a person all right–the kind of woman that somehow made ya want ta do right. Well, I don't go in for much of this religious stuff, but I suppose that whatever Grandma Jacobson had was the right stuff," said the sheriff as he sat in his saddle with his hat off.

Enormous guilt flooded Tom's feelings. He somehow knew that he had done wrong by not forgiving Frank.

I'll help find this money and then just go away. Things'll be okay," thought Tom.

He led the sheriff to Ned's grave without any problem. The ground was a little eroded and sunken, but the rocks were still there, just the way Jed and Tom had put them back that moonlit night they had opened the grave.

"That's it right there. I've no doubt 'bout it!" exclaimed Tom.

The aging sheriff started in digging with the pick, but stopped shortly. "My, it shore is hot already! I need a drink of water and a break," he declared.

Tom dug the hard ground for a while and then shoveled the dirt out. It **was** a dreadfully hot day, and the morning sun was already beating down hard. Once the hard packed topsoil was dug loose, the dirt began to come up easier and Tom began to make faster headway. The sheriff took a short turn while Tom rested and reflected on the night he and Jed had come here. *What a different scene it is now,* Tom remembered with a momentary chill running up his back as he pondered the events of that night.

I wonder what the coffin and body'll look like now?

Tom relieved the sheriff and began with the pick again. As he dug, he thought about Grandma Jacobson and the fact that she was the mother of the preacher in Pueblo. It dawned on Tom that it was the preaching of that man that had influenced Mandy and her parents to be such good Christians. Tom realized that meant that Grandma Jacobson had touched Mandy through the son she had raised, and thus she actually touched his life through Mandy. Tom mused on the continuation of a person's life through those they touch, until his pick suddenly hit a hollow spot.

"Reckon I'm at the coffin, Sheriff," stated Tom.

"Probably not much wood left by now, Tom," stated the sheriff.

"Want me to get down there and see what I think?" asked the sheriff.

"Naw, I can handle it," replied Tom.

Carefully Tom dug the dirt away from the coffin. The wood was there, but was beginning to rot away. Finally, he quit using the shovel and used his gloved hand to wipe the dirt off what was left of the lid. When he tried to open the lid, the wood crumbled in his hands, so he broke it back until he could see inside.

It was a gruesome sight. There was nothing left of the body but the skeleton. Insects or rats had gotten into the box and had cleaned the flesh and eaten most of the blanket Jed had placed inside the box. The leather saddlebag looked shrunk and darkened, but seemed intact. When Tom picked the bag up, however, it crumbled, and the money inside spilled out covering the skeleton. The old sheriff and boy just stared at the unusual scene, speechless.

Finally, the sheriff said slowly and quietly from above, "I, a, well, I think there's a lesson in this somewhere."

Carefully Tom gathered the money and handed it up to the sheriff who put it into a superior saddlebag. Tom was careful not to touch the skeleton; he felt somewhat sick to his stomach. The boy was on his knees picking up the money as his gun caught on the edge of the remaining coffin. He remembered that the gun had belonged to the dead man.

Finally, the job was over and the two went back to Red Rock. After dousing their heads and drinking lots of water from the tank near the sheriff's office, the officer invited Tom to go with him to the bank to return the money.

The banker was so overwhelmingly thankful when he heard all that Tom had done to recover the stolen money that he gave him two hundred dollars. The sheriff told Tom that he would telegraph a message to Mr. Ingalls at the prison in Fort Yuma so that Jed would know that the money was returned to the bank. Tom was pleased for Jed's sake.

****

Tom was tired from the work of digging up the grave and burying it again, so he went back to the boarding house and lay down to rest for a while. He was restless and could not nap well. He thought about how he had not forgiven Frank Woods and the reaction that Frank had given him. He wished he could talk to Mandy about it, but he was ashamed of himself. He was not sure he wanted Mandy to know what he had done. He wondered how Mandy's pa was doing and if he should hurry to Pueblo to help out at the store.

Finally, Tom got up, poured water from the pottery pitcher to wash his sweaty face, and then walked over to the telegraph office.

Sending a telegraph message to Pueblo for Mandy was easy. He simply asked the girl if her pa was still sick or if he was getting better.

Tom received a reply in two hours.

"Daddy is better than he has ever been–Love you–Mandy."

Tom was glad to get the message and felt happy to read the "love you" from Mandy. Because he thought all was well there, the pressure to go to Pueblo lessened in his mind somewhat.

While returning from the telegraph office, Tom ran into Howie Jacobson.

"Well, son of a gun. Ifen its not Tom!" exclaimed Howie. "How ya doin' cowpoke?"

Tom, equally glad to see Howie, replied, "Oh, I'm okay Howie. Boy! Just lookie at ya! Yer so tall and skinny; I always knew ya'd turn out to be a real slim guy. Ya look great! How's yer pa and things on the ranch?"

"Things are good, 'bout the same, gettin' ready for the final roundup this year before drivin' the bevies to Pueblo again. Interested in helpin' out?" asked Howie.

Tom thought for a moment. He wanted to go to Pueblo, but he would really enjoy the roundup; and now since Mandy's pa was well, maybe he could do the roundup and then go to Pueblo.

"How come ya still go clear to Pueblo? Can't ya find a place ta load them on the train that's closer?" asked Tom.

"Yes, but my pa says that it still costs him less because we'd have to go over the mountain and worry with Indians. Also, the railroads are chargin' way too much," explained Howie.

Soon Tom was at the Jacobson ranch riding a ranch horse, feeling right at home, and loving it. He was a little out of practice when it came to roping the calves for branding, but after a few days he started doing well again. In the evenings, the cowboys lay around the bunkhouse playing cards, telling jokes and stories, and bragging. Occasionally some would go into town, drink, and gamble. But most of them did not have the money to do much.

Tom entered into the poker games with the cowboys. He never told any of the men how much money he had. When the story of the recovery of the stolen money became known, he had been forced to tell all ranch hands all about the event. They looked at him as some kind of a boy wonder and minor hero. Most of them told Tom that he was crazy for revealing the whereabouts of the money instead of just keeping it for himself.

Usually the cowboys gambled only pennies. Tom soon found that he was good at taking the other cowboys' pennies away from them, and he loved doing it.

Tom went into town on several evenings to visit his Mother. He told her all about Mandy and things that had happened to him while he was trapping and while he was in Pueblo.

"Yes, Tom, we heard 'bout the outlaws you killed and 'bout how you lost your money down the outhouse. In fact, I have a newspaper clippin' of it! Wanta see it?" asked Tom's mother.

"No, I don't, I've already seen it–made me look very stupid, Ma," replied Tom. "How'd ya get a clipping of it anyhow?"

"Oh, mothers have ways," she said with a smile. "I'm just so thankful that God protected ya, Tom. Now if you could just make things right with Frank."

****

The roundup soon ended, and Tom decided to go on the trail drive. He rode to Red Rock to say his goodbyes to his mother. She pled for him to make things right with Frank.

"Ma, I think I'll jus' let things be the way they are fer now. Maybe, someday, Ma; maybe, someday," he said and gave his mother a hug and then headed out the door.

His mother wiped her hands on her apron and waved goodbye as Tom waved and rode off toward Jacobson's ranch at a gallop. She knew that there was no way to keep him with her any longer. Her lips moved as she prayed, "Dear God, keep my boy safe and turn his heart to the Lord Jesus."

Just then, Ma remembered that she had a letter that came to the general delivery for Tom, and the postmaster had given it to her to give to Tom. The letter had come from Pueblo, and Ma guessed it was from Mandy. Ma had approved of the things that Tom had told her about Mandy.

"Too bad, too bad. Maybe I can send it back to Pueblo," she said aloud.

****

The cattle drive was everything Tom had remembered it to be–except that he was bigger and more durable now–and the crew of cowboys was adequate for the job.

The time went slowly for Tom. He tired of the job, wishing that he had not taken it.

"Jus' think, I could've been in Pueblo with Mandy now," said Tom to himself one night as he tried to get comfortable in his blankets on the hard ground.

"What ya say?" asked Howie.

"Ah, nothin," said Tom.

"No, it weren't 'nothin'!' I heard ya say somethin' 'bout a girl named Mandy," replied Howie.

Tom lay in his blankets on the ground by Howie and started telling him everything about Mandy. He really enjoyed telling of his getting to know her and what she meant to him and what a wonderful person she is. Tom went on and on until he heard Howie snoring.

The next morning, Tom asked Howie if he remembered anything he told him about Mandy.

"Uh, well, ya said her name was Mandy and she lives in Pueblo," answered Howie.

"Is that all? I tol' ya 'bout her fer half the night, and ya only know that she lives in Pueblo?" asked Tom.

"Half the night! Boy, ya got it bad, Tom. Real bad!" exclaimed Howie.

"What do ya mean by that?" asked Tom.

Howie grinned big and started to say something but just shook his head as he put his chaps on and walked over to the cook's wagon and put in his bedroll.

From then on, it seemed that Mandy was constantly on Tom's mind, and he wished that he had written Mandy a letter and mailed it from Red Rock.

Finally, the cattle drive came to Pueblo, and Tom kept looking over his shoulder hoping that Mandy would show up sometime as he helped prod and poke the resistant animals into the smelly boxcars.

"Well, why should she?" reasoned Tom when the girl did not appear. "She didn't know when I was coming. I should've written her from Red Rock."

It was late afternoon when the cowboys finally finished the loading and drew their pay from Mr. Jacobson. Tom hurried toward the general store to see Mandy as soon as possible. Then he realized that he was very dirty and stinky and decided to go to the hotel and get a room and a bath before going to see her.

The bath felt so good that Tom lingered in the tub even though other cowboys were hollering for him to hurry up so they could get their turn. By the time Tom had washed his rather worn out clothes and waited for them to dry, it was getting late. He hoped that the Whitmans were not gone to bed yet.

Tom walked the short distance to the Whitmans' general store but saw no light either in the store or in the back where they lived. He guessed that he was too late and should wait until tomorrow.

Tom lay in his hotel bed and thought about Mandy and how it would be to sneak up on her and holler "boo!" and see her turn around and see her pretty face and the gladness she would express in seeing him. Maybe he would fall over the stove again just to let her know that he still fell for her. As he thought about bringing her flowers...the young romantic cowboy went off to sleep.

The morning sun shone in Tom's hotel window and woke him with a start. "Oh, brother, I must of overslept," he said out loud to himself as he dressed and looked in the mirror. "Wow! That's quite a beard yer getting there, Tom, but ya'd look better without it."

Even though Tom was eager to see Mandy, he decided to take time to eat a quick breakfast, then go to the barbershop for a haircut and shave. He wanted to look presentable.

The barber remembered Tom and greeted him with a smile.

"Been a while, Tom! What ya been up to?" asked the barber.

Tom told the barber about his visit to Fort Yuma and the cattle drive, while the barber cut his red hair and shaved his face.

The barber was quiet until he had finished the shave.

"Tom, did ya jus' get in town taday?" asked the barber.

"Late yesterday afternoon, after we finished loadin' the cattle on the train," answered Tom.

"Well, I guess ya haven't heard, and I hate being the one to tell ya, you having worked for the Whitmans and all. George Whitman died–probably about when you began the trail drive! Mandy and her mother are planning on moving back east this week," stated the barber rather sadly.

Tom paid the barber and asked him some details of the event and left to go directly to the store. He walked a little slowly turning the news over in his mind. Mandy had said that her dad had never been better, and now he is dead. Tom felt remorse for not coming sooner. He would need to help Mandy and her mother run the store. He was going to miss Mr. Whitman; he had become a real friend of Tom's.

Tom heard the train whistle as he arrived at the store. *Maybe Mandy is at the depot pickin' up supplies fer the store,* thought Tom. *Too hard of work for her; I'll have ta do it from now on.*

Tom entered the store expecting to see Mandy or Mrs. Whitman, but an older woman that he remembered seeing at Mandy's church was behind the counter.

"Where's Mandy?" asked Tom anxiously.

"You're Tom, aren't you? asked the lady.

"Yes! Where's Mandy?" answered Tom.

"I thought I would recognize you. Mandy asked me to give you this letter, in case you came by. She and her mother just left for the train. They are moving back east," explained the lady and handed the letter to him.

Tom grabbed the letter and ran out the door. He could still hear the steam engine as it began to leave town; the whistle sounded again. Tom ran as swift as he could for the train. He reached the depot to see that the train had gained speed and was on its way. He put an even greater burst of energy into his run as he sped past the crowd of people at the depot. He hardly noticed them, but thought he heard his name called.

The people stopped and turned to watch Tom trying to catch the train. He began to catch up with the train every so slowly, his boots making dust along the side of the tracks. The train began to move a little faster, and for a moment, the train and Tom were going the same speed as he ran even with the caboose. The people anxiously watched and cheered for him. Some of them knew why Tom wanted to catch that train so badly.

Straining with his entire strength, Tom made the final effort to cross over the cinders onto the tracks. The crowd grew quiet; the people seemed to hold their breath as he reached for the black metal rail on the steps of the caboose. His fingertips momentarily touched the black railing when his pointed boot stumbled on a larger than usual cinder. He went plummeting head first onto the railroad tracks. His body rolled several times and came to rest sprawled face down upon the railroad crossties. His head began to bleed.

There was a moment of disbelief as the crowd became quiet. Then, as they saw that Tom did not move, they charged out to help him.

CHAPTER FIFTEEN

Two lengthy days later Tom woke. He was in the humble home of Pastor Jacobson. His head throbbed, and so he gradually put his hand to it and found it bandaged. Mrs. Jacobson came in and greeted him.

"Well, Tom Fleming, you finally decided to wake up. That is good; you were beginning to worry us. I'll get you some food and call the pastor," she said quietly.

For a while, Tom could not remember what had happened. Then between throbs of pain, he remembered his train chase. Tears rolled from his eyes at the thought of missing his beloved Mandy.

The town doctor came in, and Mrs. Jacobson gave Tom a drink of cool water. It was the first he had had for two days, and the liquid tasted great. The doctor declared that Tom looked satisfactory and that his head should quit hurting shortly. The pastor came in, talked quietly with Tom, and prayed for him. He told Tom to take as long as he liked getting well and that he was welcome to stay until he healed.

"The letter?" Tom managed to squeak the words out of his chapped lips.

"Oh, yeah," replied the Pastor, "Got two for you; one from your mother and one from Mandy." I know you can't wait to read them, but perhaps you should rest a bit more.

Tom could not wait, and tried to sit up and see to read; but when the pastor slowly opened the curtain to let light in, it hurt Tom's eyes. The pastor offered to read the letters to him.

"Ok, please do. Read the oldest one first," said Tom.

Pastor Joe opened the somewhat wrinkled letter from Tom's mother first and found a letter from Mandy inside along with a note from his mother.

"Dear Son,

I hope this letter finds you well at the end of the cattle drive. I didn't remember to give you this letter from Mandy in time before you left so am sending it to Jacobson's brother who lives in Pueblo. He is a pastor so he will get it to you, I'm sure. We are all ok, and praying for you. Please change yer mind bout Frank, he really is sorry for his wrong. I wish we'd had more time to spend together. I love you, Mother"

Pastor Joe paused. "I'll read Mandy's old letter first; that way you'll get more understanding of what has been happening to Mandy and her family," he said sadly.

"I wish I had gotten the letter sooner," mumbled Tom.

"My dearest Tom,

I received your telegram only hours after my daddy died. When you asked me how he was, I told you that he is better than he has ever been, because that is true, he is now with Jesus in Heaven.

I probably should not have said only that, though. I did not mean to deceive you. I really miss my daddy. My heart really hurts. He was so good to my mother and me. We know that he is in Heaven though and much better off than ever.

We are not sure what to do now. If you could come and help with the store for a time, we would really appreciate it. You were such an enormous help when you were here before and besides, I miss you and I know you care for us. I love you and will continue to pray for you.

Mandy

P.S. Please come soon."

Tom's eyes teared up, and in anger, he hit the bed with his fist. "Why didn't I get that letter?" he exclaimed.

Pastor Joe said, "Yeah, that's too terrible, Tom. Do you want me to read the last letter now? You should rest."

"Yes! exclaimed Tom.

"My dearest Tom,

I guess you did not get my letter or else I know you would have come to me. My daddy died three months ago and Mother decided that she and I could not run the store without Daddy. I was hoping you would come before we have to leave Pueblo. I will leave this letter with the new owners of the store, as I know you will go there.

Mother is not sure where we are going back east. We have several relatives that we might stay with, including her parents. I will write a letter and send it care of the new storeowners as soon as I know.

I am sorry I missed you. I wanted to stay until you came back but Mother insisted we leave.

I still love you a lot even though it seems we have not seen each other in a long time. I guess love never ends.

I will always be praying for you, Mandy Whitman"

Tom lay motionless on the bed, trying to hold back the tears and anger. He felt bad, his head throbbed; and now he felt anger, despair, and depression all at once.

"That Mandy is quite a girl. I didn't realize that you two were so concerned for each other, although I suspected something," said the Pastor.

"Why didn't God let me get that letter?" asked Tom.

"I don't know why, but I know that He had a reason for it, and He knows best," answered Pastor Joe.

"Well, then, if God had anything to do with it, He ain't fair! Ahh… it's just bad luck, Pastor Joe, bad luck! God didn't have anything to do with it! Just bad luck," stated Tom in a moaning sort of voice.

"Well, you rest now and we'll talk about it later," replied the pastor kindly.

Mrs. Jacobson attended to Tom's needs, and in two days, the doctor came and removed the stitches from the middle of Tom's head.

Tom was soon up and about and wished to go back to the hotel. He thanked the Jacobsons and tried to pay them, but they would not take any money. He also paid the doctor who advised him to take it easy for a few days.

Tom did not know what to do with himself. He was restless. It seemed as if everything depended on getting a letter from Mandy. He rested and healed for a few lazy days and went to the store every day to ask the new owners if a letter had come for him.

Tom went to church on Sunday but had a hard time listening, even to Pastor Joe. Monday came and no letter came. Tom began to wonder if he would ever hear from Mandy again.

The west side of town had a drinking and gambling establishment called "Trail's End" which Tom began patronizing. He usually ran into some cowboys he knew and started playing poker with them. Most of the time Tom did well and made money. He felt he could tell what other players had for hands by studying their faces. Sometimes Tom lost, though.

Two weeks passed and Tom did not get a letter from Mandy. It depressed him. He knew he should be doing something like getting a job. In his mind, he reasoned that he was going to go to Mandy as soon as he knew where to go. Tom prepared for a trip by buying new clothes from the new storeowners.

One night after Tom had played several rounds of poker, an old looking man walked into Trail's End. The man went to the bar and ordered a drink. He stood with his back to the bar, looking the people over in the room. Shortly, he asked the bartender something, then came over to Tom's poker table, and asked to enter the next game.

Several rounds of poker were played as the men got to know each other. Finally, the strange old man asked Tom if he could talk to him privately.

Feeling rather surprised and uncomfortable about a stranger wanting to talk to him, Tom asked him what he wanted.

"Well, me boy, a friend of yours and mine did send me, his name being Hank," replied the man with an obvious Scottish accent.

Tom immediately remembered his mountain man friend and excused himself from the poker game so that he and the old Scotsman could go to a private table in the corner. A kerosene lamp flickered over the table, apparently about to go out.

"Barkeep, bring us a pitcher of beer!" hollered the stranger.

"How is it you know Hank?" asked Tom.

"Well, me and him 'ave been friends fer many many a year, Chap," explained the stranger as he pulled out a pipe and prepared to fill it with tobacco from a little brown leather pouch.

"Ole Hank and me go way back–ta forty nine when we tried to make it big in Califor-ne-ya. He saved me life once, he did. We did a lot of prospecting together. Hank sort of tired of it and went to trapping and I stuck with looking for gold," continued the Scotsman as he stopped to light his crusty pipe.

The flickering lamp cast shadows across the man's long, gray, bearded face as he exhaled the smoke from his lungs with delight.

"How's Hank doin'?" asked Tom.

"Not so good, laddie, not so good. I stopped by his mountain hideaway to see him and he's not good. A terrible cough he has, and he's drinkin' way too much–almost always," the Scotsman spoke softly and sadly, shaking his head. "Ole father time is startin' ta takes his tol' on us."

"Well, why'd ya come ta see me?" asked Tom, but he was beginning to suspect he knew the answer.

"Well, lad, our friend tole me that he met ye and that ye be havin' the high honor of havin' killed ole Snake Eyes and also Fredrick and that ye now possess one half of the map that was once me own. Ye be seeing, I once had the whole thing; got it from the owner of a very rich mine in Arizona, but before I was smart enough to memorize it, I lost too much to ole Snake Eyes in a poker game and he settled on half the map until I came up with the money to pay him. The miserable snake! I think he cheated anyway! Good riddance!"

"So ya think I have the other half now?" asked Tom cautiously.

"I be knowin' ye do lad; Hank said so! We are buddies to the soul. He wouldna' be lyin' ta me!" replied the man with a big almost wicked grin that showed through the hairy gray beard.

"So yer the Scotsman that Snake Eyes mentioned ta me. Then ya called yerself Scotty?" asked Tom.

"Aye that I do, young Laddie. Scotty."

The two sat looking at each other for an extended moment. The pieces all fit. It all added up to Tom. He believed that this was the man whom Snake Eyes had whispered of, moments before Snake Eyes died.

"So ya say the map is of a rich gold find in Arizona?" asked Tom.

"Aye, laddie, I already be seein' some chunks of ore come from it. Very heavy! I got somethin' fer ye ta be thinkin' 'bout. Here tis," replied Scotty. "I'll give ye twenty percent of all the wealth I be gettin' from the mine, and ye wont even be 'avin' ta pick up a pick or shovel, or ye can come help and we'll be splittin' fifty–fifty," answered the old Scotsman.

Tom took another sip of the warm beer.

"If I was ta go with ya, when do ya want ta leave?" asked Tom.

"Well, soon as possible; no sense in stayin' in Colorado when winter is comin'. Not me!" explained Scotty.

Tom's mind was thinking it over. The actual lure of the gold interested him. He had experienced a little of how nice it was to have luxuries that only money could buy. He had also seen how hard most men labor for money for just necessities. Not getting a letter from Mandy distressed him intensely. He took a cavernous drink of the beer.

"Well, I'm interested," said Tom. "But give me 'til tomorrow night. Meet me here and I'll have yer answer."

After a restless night, Tom rose and went to breakfast. He was not sure what to do. More than anything else, he wanted to go see Mandy, but how could he? He did not know where she was. The mail that day still did not contain a letter from Mandy.

That night Tom met Scotty as planned and showed him his portion of the map. Scotty produced his also, and under the still-flickering lantern, the two could see that the torn pages fit together flawlessly.

Scotty studied the map with his nose almost touching the paper.

"I say, Barkeep! Will ya be bringin' a pitcher and some kerosene fer this here lantern?" hollered Scotty.

The beer was delivered, and the barkeeper brought a full, clean, glass lamp to hang above the table. He removed the grimy, flickering lamp.

"Aye, that be much better, Sir, much better, thank ye," said Scotty. "Let me be seein'," mumbled the old Scotsman as he reexamined the pieced-together map in the better light.

Tom studied the map too, and tried not to shadow it as Scotty studied it for a lengthy time with his nose almost touching the map.

"Ah, aye, oh, ahoy, I thought so," mumbled Scotty as his mind fitted the details together, slowly.

"I be thinkin' that we can find it. It's somewhat south of Fort McDowell and some east. Desolate country! Little rain! We'll be 'aving ta buy some proper mules ta get us into it—maybe horses. No water there much, unless we get rain," said the old prospector.

"Well, what did ye decide, Laddie? Ye be comin' with me, or will ye settle fer only twenty percent?" asked Scotty.

"Who's gonna provide the outfittin'?" asked Tom.

"We'll each be providin' our own," answered Scotty.

"Okay, Scotty, I'll go!" answered Tom.

The two sat and talked for several hours, Scotty mostly explaining about gold mining and Tom asking questions. It became apparent to Tom that Scotty was glad to have a young man come with him. Scotty started calling him "helper." Tom figured the man was on the square about the whole thing, and he began to get excited about the unusual quest.

The old man and young man departed from Pueblo on the train the next day. No letter had come from Mandy: Tom had a funny feeling, as if he was deserting Mandy by leaving Pueblo.

They followed the same route Tom had taken before to go to Fort Yuma, but this time Tom and the Scotsman planned to get off on the mountain pass the same way as Hank.

"Now Tom, me boy, when ye jump, jump the direction the train is travelin' and start them legs runnin' for all ye got. That a ways ye can be a gettin' ye very self off the train with no injuries. I'll be goin' first. Ye watch and see how I do it!" explained Scotty.

Scotty figured the time came when the train slowed as it went up a steep switchback toward the top of the mountains in the dead of night.

The old man stepped to the lowest step, sort of swung his left boot to the rhythm of the train, and then hollered, "Here goes!" He jumped and hit the ground running but somersaulted and fell.

Tom was disturbed by the man's fall. He was afraid the Scotsman was hurt, and for a moment, his remembrance of his own accident haunted him. He knew if he did not jump soon, they would be separated because the train would accelerate and he would never be able to get off to find the Scotsman.

Tom hollered, "Here goes!" jumped, and ran. He felt his boots hit dirt and grab, and he was able to come to a balanced stop with no harm.

Tom heard another, "Here goes!" and heard the thud and roll of a human body near him as the train finished rumbling past him.

"Well, I'll be!" and Scotty swore.

"Scotty?" asked Tom.

"Ye be calling, Laddie?" answered Scotty.

"How'd ya get here? I thought ya already jumped!" exclaimed Tom.

"That's right! That is right! I did, but I didna' be seein' ye jump, so I got back on and jumped off here closer ta ye," replied Scotty.

"But I thought ya got hurt!" exclaimed Tom. "Are ya all right?"

"Well, I be admittin' that I didna' make too good of a landin', because the ole legs ain't what they used ta be ye know," replied Scotty.

Tom began to understand the old man in a different way. At first, he was afraid that the old fellow was fragile, but now he knew that he must be incredibly tough to endure all that tumbling.

Tom began to laugh at the half-moonlit spectacle, partly in relief that the man was not hurt.

"Tain't funny, young un. No one can help gettin' old, and it ain't nice to be a laughin' at your elders!" exclaimed Scotty.

Tom laughed some more.

"Now ya be a stoppin' that jus' now or I'm gonna 'ave ta give ye a whippin', Sonny," said Scotty.

Tom knew the old man was upset with him and tried to stop laughing but could not. He tried to bury his mouth in his hand but only ended up making sputtering, air-leaking noises, which just served to make Tom snicker the more.

The old prospector began to feel anger. "What are the young people coming ta? I try to help ye and almost get meself killed, I did, and all ye kin do is hoot is it? Well, I won't be takin' it," growled Scotty.

With that said, Scotty lunged for Tom and had him on the ground. Tom's saddlebags, which he had on his shoulder, went flying. The old man quickly had Tom pinned to the ground and was twisting Tom's arm.

At first, Tom resisted, but that caused him more pain, so he got serious and quit laughing.

"Ye be seein', Laddie, it's not a nice thing ta be a doin' ta laugh at ye elders. Now be sayin' ye won't be laughin' at this old prospector!" hollered the Scotsman loudly.

Tom started to laugh again because Scotty had released the pressure a little, but Scotty twisted his arm again until Tom thought it might break.

"Say ye won't be a laughin'!" commanded Scotty.

"I won't be laughin'!" exclaimed Tom in pain.

The old man released Tom and got up. Tom sat up and rubbed his arm, but a chuckle, which he tried to subdue with his hand, came to his throat.

"Psssst, ha, fip," came the sound.

"All-right then!" Scotty exclaimed. "I see ye kin not be a keepin' your word! I'm through with ye then!"

Scotty took off along the railroad track. He felt that his personal honor had been violated. Tom could not believe what was happening. He picked up his saddlebags and took off running after Scotty.

"Scotty! No! Wait! Ya don't understand! I didn't mean nothin' by it!" exclaimed Tom as he worked hard to catch up in the dim light of the moon.

The chase went on for quite some time until Tom ran out of breath and tired and sat down. Tom could hear Scotty continue up the mountain through the brush toward the pine trees. He realized that without Scotty he was lost, so he got up and continued the chase after the old man.

The sun came up and shone through the pines as the two came into a beautiful valley. Down into the valley and to a western ridge, Scotty led until they came to Hank's cabin.

"Ahoy!" hollered Scotty.

Hank was thrilled to see the two. Scotty was indeed an old friend "to the soul," and Tom a new friend. The joyous, boisterous greetings were soon saddened, though, as Hank stumbled back to his bunk, coughing.

"Sorry boys, I'm not gonna be much of a host today. Kinda under the weather fer a change. Hardly been sick in my life, but now I'm a little ill," said Hank mournfully.

"Aye, ye be sick! 'Tis that bottle, Hank! Ifen ye don't be cuttin' the bottle out, I'll be a buryin' ye body soon!" exclaimed Scotty.

"Would ya do it for me, Scotty? Would ya bury me? I'd like ta be buried down by the stream, underneath the trees," stated Hank quietly and seriously between coughs.

"Of course I would, Hank, but I'd rather be a havin' ye around for a spell yet," replied Scotty.

The three buddies talked at length, and Hank began to feel sleepy. He told Scotty and Tom to make themselves at home and help themselves to whatever they needed.

Tom found some pelts and made himself a place to sleep. After eating several pieces of jerky, he was soon in a deep sleep, his tiredness caused from chasing Scotty most of the night and day.

When morning came, Scotty awakened Tom.

"Well, Laddie, are ye gonna be comin' with me ta get the gold without laughin' at an ole man or shall I be leavin' the sleepy baby boy with Hank?" asked Scotty with a smirk on his face.

Tom got up. He still felt very tired, and his muscles felt extremely sore. Hank was preparing flapjacks for his friends. His huge body seemed too much for him to move about, but he was feeling a little better.

After breakfast, Scotty had Hank study the complete map, and they agreed to the location of the gold being about where Scotty had thought.

"Now before we be a goin', Hank, I want ta ask ye what ye be thinkin' of this here young'un. He done laughed at this ole man when I had a tumble gettin' off the train! I don't be takin' a fancy ta be laughed at or lied ta," said Scotty.

Hank slightly laughed. "Well, he's okay, Scotty. Don't worry none 'bout Tom. What happened anyways?"

"I didn't mean nothin' by it, Hank. It's just that Scotty was tellin' me how to get off the train when it's still movin' and he decided to show me how. Only he fell! I was truly startled and afraid he got hurt. I hesitated to get off but finally did okay. Then, in the dark, Scotty jumps off again, falls, and rolls again! I didn't even know he got back on the train! When I find out he's okay, the whole thing struck me funny, so I laughed and he got all mad. I didn't mean nothin' by it!" explained Tom.

Hank grinned and burped loudly. "You mean Scotty got off twice but only got on once?" asked Hank mischievously.

"No, ye big goat! How could I've been gettin' on once and off twice?" asked Scotty starting to get upset. Hank laughed and put his thumbs between his grimy suspenders and dirty shirt.

"Well, Scotty, I could see why that mighta been funny to Tommie Boy. Of course, ya got on twice, but it surprised Tom and of course, ya fell, so it musta been quite a sight. Wish I coulda seen it myself!" Hank laughed some more and then coughed.

"Enough!" cried Scotty. "I danna see why everybody has ta have their laughs at me expense! I'm goin' fer the gold! So, Tom, ye can come be me helper, if ye be mindin' your manners. And, Mr. Funny–Guy Hank, ye could come too; but no, ye be wantin' ta stay up here in the cold and drink and kill charmin' little animals all winter."

"Ya got it right, Scotty. I wish ya luck; my days of chasin' my shadow are over! I make more on the furs," answered Hank.

After a short goodbye, in which Hank promised to drink less, Tom and Scotty turned south again toward New Mexico. They bought horses as soon as they came to a trading post and they continued further south into New Mexico Territory until they came to a small mining town called Kelly. Scotty said he wanted to rest a while and do a little gambling. That evening Scotty took Tom to a busy saloon that was more of a casino than a saloon. It was soon obvious to Tom that the men that were there were of the violent criminal type. He felt uneasy and checked his pistol, but noticed that Scotty quickly got himself involved in a card game.

Tom decided to join a poker game but did not want to play against Scotty, so he found a group of men at a large round table and asked to play.

Soon the men were deep into poker and were friendly to Tom calling him "Red." Tom did not like the nickname but said nothing. He had been called that often before. It turned out to be a lucrative evening for Tom, so that he finally quit around midnight with eighty dollars more than he started with.

The men told Tom that he had beginners' luck and invited him to come back tomorrow evening and give them a chance to get their money back.

Tom found out that Scotty loved gambling and poker, and he was more than willing to stay another day to "rest."

That evening when Tom and Scotty went to the casino saloon, they both readily got involved in poker games.

Tom played with the same group of men, except for one different player the men called Sye. Sye was dressed better than the other men who looked like cowboys and miners. Sye was dressed in a black suit.

"Well, Red, how's your luck gonna be tonight? Think ya can do it two nights in a row?" asked one of the players. "We'll see," said Tom with a smile as he sat down.

The men seemed more serious tonight than last night as they sat looking at their cards. Tom noticed that the new player had an injured right hand from some occasion in the past. This made it difficult for him to hold cards with that hand. The poker game went on and on into the night with several pitchers of beer being consumed by the men and Tom. Tom continued to do well, but he began to sense a tension in the other players. He figured it was because they had lost money. One man said he had had enough, that this just was not his night, and left.

As the time got later and later, other men began to drift out until just the two tables where Scotty and Tom played were left. In his next hand, Tom drew four aces and laid them down when the betting stopped. Sye laid down his cards with his good hand, which had an ace in it. Tom took a double look and sucked in his breath.

"Wait!" Tom exclaimed. "Look! There's five aces on the table!"

The men sat quietly looking at each other. Everyone knew that someone had tried to cheat.

"So we do; now we know how you're winning!" exclaimed Sye and began to rise to his feet slowly.

"Not so!" exclaimed Tom. He looked Sye in the eyes, recognizing him. He was the man, who on Tom's first train ride, had stolen his saddlebags and gotten his hand crushed by Hank.

The men all got up; Tom got up too. They pressed slowly toward Tom. As the youth reached for his pistol, he realized that his holster had been robbed sometime that evening. He remembered that there had been a barmaid hanging around the table standing behind him occasionally that evening. He had been set up! Someone grabbed Tom from behind.

Scotty saw what was happening and came to Tom's aid. "Now ye lookie here; me helper is no cheater! Take ye hands off him..."

Someone stopped Scotty by hitting him on the head with a whiskey bottle. Tom began to fight. He kicked the table up into Sye and stomped on the foot of the man who held his arms. The man released him, and Tom swung at the two men who came at him. One man fell down, but the other got a punch into Tom's face, knocking him down. Before Tom could get up, someone kicked him in the ribs, knocking the air out of him. Tom grabbed the man's boot, pulled him down, and punched him in the face.

Another man punched Tom in the head knocking him back. The man punched him repeatedly. Tom's mind raced. He needed help but remembered that this little town had no sheriff.

"Okay, boys, save some for me!" hollered Sye.

Two men held Tom up as Sye punched Tom's face repeatedly with his good fist.

"Remember me, Red? Yer mountain man buddy is the one that ruined my hand!"

Sye punched Tom's bloody, swollen face repeatedly. Tom knew he was going into unconsciousness.

Oh, God, help me! Tom cried out in his heart, as everything grew purple then black.

Tom's head fell forward as he lost consciousness. Nevertheless, Sye was not finished with him yet. He held up Tom's right hand and hammered at it with the butt of his pistol, only he missed and hit his wrist. Then he punched him some more.

"Okay, boys, finish him!" commanded Sye.

A man pulled his weapon out to shoot Tom.

"No, wait; that's too good for him," said Sye.

The men threw Tom to the floor and kicked him. Tom threw up and blood came from his mouth. One man jumped on Tom's legs and arms. Then suddenly, almost strangely, everyone stopped. They stood looking down at the badly beaten bloody body. They knew Tom was dead. Some felt remorse. One man mentioned that he was just a lad.

"What should we do with him?" one of Sye's men asked.

Sye discussed it quietly with two of his men. They picked Tom up, put him into the back of a wagon, and headed out of town.

Scotty awoke with blood running down into his silver beard just in time to see them carry Tom's bloody, limp body away. "Wait!" he hollered as he got up and stumbled toward the open door. Someone tripped him; he fell and became unconscious again.

CHAPTER SIXTEEN

The elderly woman woke with a start and sat up. "What?" she whispered into the dark. "The sun isn't up yet. Why did I wake up?"

She lay back down. Her heart was racing as if she had wakened from a nightmare, but she could not remember any dream. "Lord, what is it? Are you trying to tell me something?" she prayed.

The aged lady got up and tried to light the lamp, but it refused to light. She looked out the wood frame window to see the stars shining brightly and noticed the moon had already set.

"Something's going on!" she exclaimed as she stumbled around in the dark trying to pull her clothes on. She could not locate them in the dark, and she stumbled and fell, bruising her hip.

"As if I don't have enough aches already," she whispered and then chuckled. "What's the matter, Lord? What do you need me for? Must be something. Satan doesn't want me to do it. Lord, drive away the powers of darkness in Jesus name! Allow me to be your servant. Thank you, Jesus," she prayed aloud.

The mature lady found the lamp and matches again, and this time she was able to easily light the lamp.

"Ah! See! Thank you, Father! I know it's you..." she talked to God as if he were bodily there.

The woman dressed and opened the door of her small gray wooden shack she called home. She peered into the darkness of the very early morning and said, "Anybody there?" but all was quiet and still, so she turned to making some breakfast. She somehow knew she was going to need an extra heavy breakfast.

After eating a hearty breakfast, she opened her much worn Bible to read from where she had left off the night before. The passage was Luke 10, and it contained the story Jesus told of the Good Samaritan. She read the story twice.

"Lord," she prayed, "Is this it? Am I to help someone who is hurt today? Okay, Lord, I'll try again, but you know I'm getting old and weak. But whatever you want, Father, just give me the strength!"

The lady finished cleaning her breakfast dishes, expecting a knock on her door at any time. *It will probably be some of my Indian friends who come for help, and they will bring a sick or injured person that the witch doctor couldn't help,* she thought.

She checked her stock of homemade remedies, bandages, splints, salve, and homemade teas. She reminded herself that she still had plenty of plump chickens she could cook. She thought of what all she might need and felt somewhat prepared to help someone in her old-fashioned way.

The sun began to rise, and the old lady went out on her rickety porch and pulled her favorite chair to the east side to watch the sun rise. She had left the chair on the west side the night before to see the sun set.

She sat watching the beautiful sunrise. Just above the distant mountains she could see red and yellow color showing with a faint hint of purple and then blue. It was very pretty to her, but the feeling that someone needed her troubled her mind.

"Lord Jesus," she prayed, "am I just imagining this? Why do I have this anxious feeling? What are you prompting me to do? I'm ready, Lord; here I am. Send me!"

Her eyes continued to watch as the glorious morning sun completely showed itself over the not so distant mountains. She continued to pray and felt more compelled to do something.

"Maybe I'm done in this life and you're taking me home today, Jesus," she prayed aloud with old arms outstretched, and she stood up looking at the morning sky. She grinned, "Okay, Lord, take me home now; I love you!"

She stood like that for a minute but dropped her arms in disappointment and sat back in her chair. She watched the sky and the birds circling nearby and continued to pray silently with her lips moving. Her eyes closed, but her lips kept moving in prayer for a while until suddenly her eyes opened wide, almost as in fright.

The elderly lady scurried inside her shack and put several items in a bag, grabbed a jug of water and her walking stick, and started off at a brisk pace towards the birds. She struggled to keep up the brisk pace but continued through brush, cactus, and dry creek beds until she found what the buzzards were circling. She stopped abruptly, out of breath, but what she saw astounded her the more. Quickly she chased away a redheaded buzzard that had already landed. "He's not yours, yet!" she hollered at the buzzard.

"Have you sent me here to bury the dead, Lord?" she prayed as she drew closer to the body.

The body was an awful sight to see. It lay twisted on the ground. Its face was bloody, battered, and swollen. Its shirt was hanging by one armhole revealing bad bruises on its chest and side. The body's right arm was broken so badly that it was at a right angle to the rest of the arm, as was its left leg, which bent back under the body. The body had no hat, boots, or personal belongings. Wagon tracks near the body revealed that someone had chosen just to dump the body in the desert rather than to bury it.

"Oh my dear God, help us! Could this poor boy still be alive?" prayed the lady still trying to get her breath.

She bent down closer and looked at the battered face. His eyes were swollen shut, one side of his jaw was broken with a tooth missing, and his bloody mouth hung open with his enlarged tongue hanging slightly out.

"Just a young boy, but he's dead!" she spoke aloud as she stood up but still kept looking down at the body. Tears rolled down her wrinkled cheeks. "Just a boy! Just a young boy that got himself in trouble with someone. Look at that young face! Maybe, just maybe..." she mumbled as she reached down slowly and touched his bloody face very tenderly.

Carefully she pressed her ear to the boy's battered chest and listened for a heartbeat. Her eyes opened wide. She thought she heard a heartbeat but was not sure. She decided to work on the body as if he was alive. *Why else would God have prompted me to come here?* she thought. Tenderly she straightened out the legs and arms and put a few drops of life giving water on his tongue. Carefully she washed his face and put a few more drops of water on his tongue. Then she put some salve on his eyes and the bloody bruises on his face, and put a few more drops of water on his tongue and watched it run into his mouth. As she worked, she prayed and prayed, "Oh God please let him live long enough for me to tell him about Jesus."

As if God was answering, she saw the boy pull his swollen tongue back into his mouth. The Good Samaritan grinned, poured just a sip of water into his mouth, and examined inside his mouth with her finger. She pulled out pieces of the broken tooth and examined the broken jaw. She decided to tie a large bandanna around his jaw to the top of his head to hold his jaw shut. The missing tooth in the side of the jaw served to allow a place to put a little water in from time to time.

The experienced woman felt carefully of the bones in the boy's arm and put them in place as carefully as she could and wrapped his arm with homemade bandages.

She prayed aloud while she worked. "Lord, I don't know what to do; help me! I can't possibly move him back to my home where I could help him most. Please help me or send help!"

The tender hands examined the broken thighbone and placed it in a position as best as they could, then wrapped the broken thigh. The birds above continued to circle overhead as the sun, now high in the sky, beat down on both of them. The chill of the morning had left.

The hands of mercy reached out to Tom's broken nose and tenderly tried to form it back into its normal shape. The fall day warmed up; the thoughtful old lady knew that the boy must have shade, so she dug four small holes with a stick and placed tree branches into the holes. Then she spread her petticoat across them to shade the boy's head and upper body.

She kept giving drops of water to him and rejoiced when she saw his throat swallow. The afternoon wore on until the sun began to set. The boy moaned a few times, encouraging the lady as she bathed his white freckled face and ate some jerky for herself.

"Lord, the night's coming, and you have sent us no help. I know you know what you're doing, Lord, but I don't know what I'm doing. Please help me!" prayed the tired old lady.

Looking about, she saw there was plenty of wood for a fire, so she gathered a large supply for the coming night. Her body had grown very fatigued.

The chill of the night came on early as the sun disappeared with a glorious, bright red color mixed with shades of velvety purple crossing the sky, but slowly fading into darkness as night came. The full moon came up in the east, and coyotes could be heard laughing in the near distance.

The wise old woman made her fire big and sat praying as long as she could. Finally, she pulled the unconscious boy's shirt around him as best she could and lay down against his body, hoping to help keep him warm.

She slept but woke to look up and see ghastly yellow eyes looking at her as the fire flickered dimly.

"Shoo! Get out of here!" she hollered as she sat up. The animals ran away into the shadows and watched her as she built the fire bigger. As the fire got brighter, the animals moved further away. The relieved lady realized that she would need more firewood, so she searched as far out as she dared for wood. She found plenty, but some wood was still green, causing the fire to smoke. She lay back down next to the boy, the fire warming them both.

The sun rose again waking the tired aged lady. She sat up, feeling sore from having slept on the inflexible ground. She remembered the night and the animals. "Thank you, Lord, for protecting us through the night," she prayed, then tenderly felt of the boy's chest. She smiled. His heart had a much stronger beat, and she could now hear him labor at breathing. Occasionally he would moan.

"Father," she prayed, "please send me help, and send it right away!"

"Miss Mary!" called a voice from behind her.

She turned to see her Indian friend and her convert to Christianity. "Oh, Gray Fox, you're an answer to my prayers!" she exclaimed.

"I felt need to come yesterday, Miss Mary. Not find you at house but saw smoke. Is he alive? How come he here?" asked Gray Fox.

"He's alive! I don't know why he's here. Just another young cowboy that got himself in trouble. God sent me to him. He was almost dead. He is a little better; his heart beats stronger," she explained.

The Indian bent over the boy and slowly examined the wounds.

"Young boy, big fight, much kick, hurt inside," said Gray Fox.

"Yes, I know, Gray Fox. I thought he was dead when I first saw him. I think God is going to give him a chance to hear about

His Son, and He is going to use us," explained Mary with a tired but obvious smile of delight on her wrinkled face.

"You here all night, Miss Mary? Bad! Need move boy to house!" said Gray Fox.

"Yes, Gray Fox, how can we move him? He has a badly broken arm, leg, and jaw," explained Mary.

"Miss Mary put sticks on broken bones; Gray Fox carries!" said Gray Fox.

"Okay! First run back to my house and get the splints and fill this water jug, and hurry!" commanded the old missionary.

Gray Fox ran amazingly swiftly and was back in a very short time.

When the splints were tightly in place, Gray Fox lifted the boy with difficulty and started walking towards the shack. Miss Mary followed behind at a slower pace.

Gray Fox stumbled with the heavy boy and almost fell.

"Careful, Gray Fox!" exclaimed Mary as she struggled to catch up. "Won't do any good to hurt him more than the poor child is already hurt."

"Big boy, heavy boy," mumbled Gray Fox as he breathed hard.

Finally, Gray Fox made it to Mary's shack, and with much effort and strain, he laid the injured boy on Mary's bed that had a colorful but worn quilt.

Without pausing to catch her breath, Mary began to work over the boy, doing all she knew to help him. She was rewarded with an occasional groan from the young redheaded cowboy.

After all was done that was possible, Mary sat in her rocking chair by the bed. Gray Fox gathered firewood for the old missionary, fed her chickens, and gathered the eggs. Mary slept.

✳✳

Mary woke with a start. The sun was setting, and she realized she should have been tending the boy. Her fears eased as she saw Gray Fox dripping chicken broth through the gap in the boy's teeth.

"You are such a blessing sent by God, Gray Fox," she said.

Through the night, the two took turns watching the badly hurt boy. They carefully reset the splints, wrapping them with cloth that is more comfortable. Mary prayed for God to give the boy another chance, and she read the Bible aloud and talked to the boy as if he could hear her.

"Now, just rest, young fella. Old Mary is here to watch over you. You're going to be all right. God will heal you," she said many times.

CHAPTER SEVENTEEN

Something ... pain ... clouds ... confusion ... blurriness ... met the young boy as he moaned, opened his eyes, moaned, and tried to speak. Mary jumped up. "Praise God!" she exclaimed, "Now just lie still, young man. You've been hurt quite badly. You have broken bones and need to lie still," she said tenderly but commandingly.

Mary gave the young man water through his missing tooth gap. He readily swallowed, as Mary explained that he had a broken jaw and should not try to talk. The boy turned his head, looked around the shack, and saw Gray Fox grinning at him.

"This is Gray Fox. He helped to save your life; he carried you here," explained Mary.

The boy groaned and appeared to fall asleep. In the hours that followed, Gray Fox and Mary continued to tend the boy, but his groaning got louder because he apparently fell into mental confusion as a fever rose in his body.

"The devil is out to get him!" exclaimed Mary as the two tried to hold him still.

Mary prayed, "Oh Heavenly Father, drive the evil one from here in Jesus' name. Touch this boy and bring healing to his battered body and soul!"

Through that second night Gray Fox and Mary sat with the boy, giving him water and chicken broth, and wiping his forehead as he moaned and thrashed about. Finally, the boy settled down and fell into a quiet, peaceful calm, and slept.

The sun was coming up as Mary covered the boy with her ragged quilt. Gray Fox tended the chores. Mary sat back in her rocking chair and let herself relax a little. She woke to see Gray Fox watching over the boy, who was now awake but quiet.

"Hi! You're looking better. What is your name?" asked Mary.

Through closed teeth, with a painful expression, the boy managed to say "Tah-mmm."

"Tom," repeated Mary. "Well, you're looking much better, Tom. We know you have a broken left leg and right arm and jaw. With God helping me, I tried to set the bones in place as best as I could. Can you move your right leg and left arm okay?"

Tom moved them and made the motion of writing with his left hand.

Mary found a modest piece of paper and a pencil for Tom to write. He managed to write the letters "r i b s." Mary felt that Tom had internal injuries but did not know what or how bad.

"Tom, we will try to wrap your ribs a little; maybe that will help," she explained.

However, the pain Tom experienced when he tried to lift up kept them from wrapping him.

Tom slept off and on as the days started to slip by. He began to show signs of healing and sipped a lot of chicken broth as if he were hungry. Gray Fox had to go back to his people but promised to return soon.

Tom and Mary began to communicate. Tom writing a few left-handed words on a slip of paper, and Mary talking. Mary talked to the young boy about God.

"You know, Tom, Christ died for the sins of all of us. All people are sinful and have fallen short of being what God requires to go to Heaven. God, the Creator of the entire universe, actually came down to earth and took on a human body. He was born as a baby boy; Jesus. He lived a perfect life; He never sinned, and He was obedient to His parents. He was so loving to everyone and healed many people and even raised some dead people.

Nevertheless, what did mankind do to Him? They crucified Him, which was a terrible but wonderful thing! Terrible because He must have suffered horrible pain, but wonderful because He paid the price for all our sins before a holy heavenly Father, a price that we could never pay ourselves!

He carried our sins to the cross so that we could have new life in this world and in Heaven. However, Jesus didn't stay dead. After three days, He rose up from the dead! All that keeps us from this new life is our not accepting this wonderful thing Jesus did for us all. Do you understand, Tom?" asked Mary.

Tom understood perfectly clear. What Mary had just said was not new to him; he had heard the story more than once at church and especially at Mandy's church when Pastor Jacobson preached.

Tom shook his head slightly to indicate yes.

"Do you want Jesus to be your Savior, to come into your inner self, or heart, and save you?" asked Mary.

Tom again shook his head *yes*.

"Then pray this prayer in your mind to God and He will save you," said Mary.

"I'll pray out loud, and if you believe all of it, then squeeze my hand and I will know that you believe and that the prayer is yours and not just mine, okay?" asked Mary.

Tom nodded his head *yes*.

"Dear God, I know that I'm a sinner and don't deserve anything from you, but now I know that Jesus died for my sins and rose again. I understand what Jesus did for me and want Him to come into my heart and save me and make me a new creature. Thank you. This I pray in Jesus' name, amen." Mary prayed aloud, and Tom squeezed Mary's hand hard all the way through the prayer.

The faint peek of a smile crossed Tom's tender face, and tears watered up in his eyes as he felt joy and peace inside. *Why was I so stubborn as to not accept Jesus sooner?* he thought.

"Now you just lie still and rest, Tom, and think about what Jesus has done for you," said Miss Mary.

Tom slept more peacefully and continued healing as the days crept by. Each day Miss Mary would clean his body, feed him broth through the missing tooth hole, and change his bandages. Then she would sit by his bed, read the Bible to him, and pray.

Tom listened closely and found the Bible accounts extremely interesting. They made more sense to him as Miss Mary explained their meaning.

Tom had a lot he wanted to ask Miss Mary, but his jaw was so painful he could not talk yet. Therefore, he waited and listened closely to the Bible readings and prayers of his spiritual mother.

In December, the weather turned bitterly cold, and the hefty supply of firewood that Gray Fox had prepared for Miss Mary quickly vanished. Tom was beginning to feel his strength come back, but he was not ready yet to get up and around, much less chop firewood. His left leg was still very sore and swollen. His right arm had healed so that he could move it cautiously, and finally Miss Mary took the bandages off Tom's tender jaw so he could talk.

Not talking for over a month had been difficult for Tom and not eating solid food was still difficult. He had lost a lot of weight.

"Miss Mary," Tom whispered carefully as he sat up and tried to talk. "Miss Mary," he repeated, "thank you fer savin' my life and my soul. I think I'm gonna be able to talk."

"You're very welcome, Tom, but it's really God that you want to thank. He is the one who is healing your body, and He is the one that saves the soul. Eventually you'll be able to see that God works through His children. God often answers His people's prayers through other people; you'll see. In fact, you've already seen God send help when Gray Fox came," explained Miss Mary.

That night Tom carefully and slowly ate some tender pieces of chicken and some peaches. His jaw was sore, but he knew it was healing. Miss Mary prayed for help for the much-needed firewood.

The next morning Gray Fox showed up with some fresh venison.

"Gray Fox sees young man is much better! How do you call yourself?" asked Gray Fox.

Tom put out his right hand, and Gray Fox shook it carefully. "My name is Tom, Tom Fleming. I already know much about you. You also know Jesus, and God uses you to answer Miss Mary's prayers!" whispered Tom.

Gray Fox laughed. "Yes, it good to help God answer Miss Mary's prayers. You need firewood today? Up on road to Kelly a large wagon carry too much firewood; broke apart. The man got smaller wagon and carried much he could. He told Gray Fox he have rest. I got wagon and started take the wood home, but God told me to bring here! Cold in here! You pray for firewood, huh, Miss Mary!"

Miss Mary only grinned and said, "Praise be to God! And thank you, Gray Fox, for listening to God."

Soon the old shack warmed to the fire Gray Fox kindled, and Miss Mary made hot oatmeal on her wood stove. Gray Fox helped Tom get to the table and mentioned making a crutch for the boy. Miss Mary asked Gray Fox to pray for the breakfast.

"Tom trusted Christ as His Savior, Gray Fox!" exclaimed Mary with twinkles in her eyes and a smile on her face.

"That good, Tom! You now my brother in Christ! Welcome!" exclaimed Gray Fox.

"I have a lot to learn about Jesus," whispered Tom as he rubbed his sore jaw.

"We all learn more about the way of Jesus. His way good. His way give peace inside. Man way give no peace, only big troubles. You stay, make well, learn much from Miss Mary," said Gray Fox forcefully.

Gray Fox stacked the firewood while Miss Mary cut the venison into strips to dry by the fire. Before leaving, Gray Fox made a crutch for Tom to use.

In the days that followed, Tom got his voice back and was able to ask Miss Mary many questions. "Miss Mary, do you believe that everything is a part of God's plan, or are some things jus' good or bad luck?" asked Tom.

Miss Mary sat smiling and thinking for a minute. "If you're asking, 'Is God in control of everything?' the Bible says He is," answered Miss Mary.

"But if God controls everything, why do things that are awful happen, like my Pa dyin'?" asked Tom.

"Why was it bad for your pa to die, Tom? Do you think he was not a Christian?" asked Miss Mary.

"He was loved and needed by Ma and me," explained Tom. "I believe he was a Christian."

"Well, Tom, it was only you and your mother that saw it as bad. Your pa saw the presence of God! He has no more pain, sorrow or the problems of this sinful world! He's with God, he is in Heaven, and it is wonderful for Him! Would you transport him back from that if you could?" explained Miss Mary.

Tom thought about that and said he was pleased that his pa was with Jesus.

"When Ma and I went west, we were in a stagecoach holdup, and I got shot! Why? That was really terrible!" exclaimed Tom.

"Yes, that was dreadful, but God didn't cause it; man did. God didn't shoot you or hold up the stagecoach; a man did. Yes, God could have prevented it, but in His all-knowing, He allows man to make choices; and yet God's Word says, "All things work together for good for those that love God..." We won't always understand everything, sometimes not ever, but God lets us understand sometimes."

Tom told Mary about his life and the move to Red Rock because of the holdup. He told about how the stagecoach robber gave him $100 and how he got beat by his stepfather when the man thought he had stolen the money.

He told her about his running away and meeting the very outlaw who gave him the money and who became his best friend.

Suddenly a thought pierced through Tom's mind like an arrow. It was such a breathtaking thought he could hardly speak.

"Miss Mary... I... a... you are Mary!" exclaimed Tom.

Miss Mary stared at Tom with a greatly amused look on her face.

"Why, I am Mary. I was Miss Mary when you met me, and my name is still Mary and if God allows it, I will be Mary tomorrow," she said with a chuckle.

"You're the lady Jed Thompson talked about! Mary, a missionary in New Mexico, which he used to make mule train trips to!" exclaimed Tom with much excitement.

"Jed Thompson? You know Jed?" asked Miss Mary excitedly.

Tom told her all about his friendship with Jed and how they herded cattle and trapped together until finally Jed was caught. He told Miss Mary about how Jed met Jesus in the Red Rock Jail while remembering what Mary had told him years before about Jesus. He told her how Jed had talked about her as if she was an angel, and how Jed wanted to marry her but Miss Mary would not let him because he was not a Christian. He also told her about the buried money and recovery and how Jed was doing in the prison at Fort Yuma.

Miss Mary started to cry softly.

"Miss Mary, what's wrong? Why are you cryin'?" asked Tom. "Is it because Jed's in prison?"

"Just joy; just joy, Tom." God has answered my prayers for that man. You see, I've prayed for years for him to come to know Jesus, and I prayed recently to hear about him. I haven't heard about him in years! I loved him, too. I wanted to marry him, but God forbids marriage to an unbeliever. It was really hard for me to obey God in that. My heart used to flip flop when he looked at me," Miss Mary said with a bit of a chuckle and a bit of a sigh in her voice.

"I'm so glad he's come to know my Jesus, Tom. God is so very, very good!" exclaimed Mary.

In the days that followed, Tom regained his strength. Soon he was able to get around without the crutch, but he limped a little. Miss Mary had done an excellent job setting the bones. Miss Mary also sewed and patched his clothes but could find only a pair of worn out boots that were too loose for him.

Tom began to help Miss Mary with the chores and made some badly needed repairs on Miss Mary's house after he finally found some rusty nails and a hammer in an old shed.

In the afternoons, Miss Mary and Tom studied the Bible. Tom learned to pray by listening to Miss Mary. They often had lengthy discussions about the Bible, sometimes going on long into the night.

"There are three things that cause bad things to happen, Tom. First, there is us. The Bible calls us "flesh." We do bad things because God allows us choices. If we choose to do certain things that are dumb or bad, we, and sometimes the people around us, suffer the results. However, if God interfered with those choices, then we wouldn't truly be free to honor Him by making right choices. Don't blame God for bad things people do. God also gave people the ability to do wise and good things," explained Miss Mary.

"The flesh tends to do bad or sinful things. We all inherited this sinful nature from our first parents, Adam and Eve. We can do good things in Christ, but we will continually have to fight the old nature. We can win, though, if we walk close to Jesus," Miss Mary continued.

"The second thing that causes bad things is the world system. All around the world, people with this sin nature are trying to live without God. They think in terms of man's ideas instead of God's. Some believe that they can be good enough to deserve to go to Heaven. Some call evil good and good evil. Some live for the moment, only for physical pleasures. They eat, drink, and are merry.

"Another cause of bad things is Satan and his fallen angels. The Bible says they go about trying to destroy people. They use the flesh and the world system to work against humanity. Satan is terrible and the father of lies and deception. He makes activities that are bad look good and those that are good look bad! He is the great enemy of God and all Christians."

Tom told Miss Mary about Mandy. "I think I feel about her just like Jed felt about you. She was so pretty and sweet. She had trusted in Jesus before me and took me to church in Pueblo where God was tryin' to get me to be saved then, but I was fightin' His will," Tom explained.

Tom told Mary about the money he had recovered from the outhouse and how God used Pastor Joe to preach sermons that would convict him of hiding the money. When Tom told her in detail about the stinky money and the sermons, Miss Mary laughed until she cried.

"God certainly was working on you, Tom Fleming," she said while wiping tears from her eyes on her colorful apron.

"Miss Mary, Mandy was so special and loved Jesus so much that she wouldn't let me kiss her. She said that she'd promised God that she'd save her first kiss fer her husband," explained Tom.

"She is really a jewel of gold; if I were you I wouldn't let her slip away. She sounds like the type worth fighting for!" said Miss Mary firmly.

"She's very pretty, too," said Tom with a faraway look in his eye. "But now I don't know what happened ta her; she was gonna write after she moved away from Pueblo when her pa died, but I never heard from her."

"If it were me, Tom, I'd go after her! God can help you find her!" said Miss Mary unwavering. "A faithful girl like that may be hard to find. She would be worth dieing for!"

The time came in January when Tom realized that he was well and should think about leaving, but somehow he did not really want to leave the old missionary. He had grown fond of her, and he had shared his inner feelings with her; she had caused him to grow in his Christian faith. He felt enormous debt to her for saving his life and all that she had done.

Miss Mary encouraged Tom to do what he thought was best, but she was happy to have him stay as long as he liked, especially if he wanted to study the Bible more.

Tom decided to stay longer, and he studied the Bible with Miss Mary every afternoon. In the mornings, he would chop firewood, work on the house, help with the chickens, and fix the chicken pens.

While Tom stayed with his new friend, Indian people would often come for medical help. They would ask the missionary to pray for them, or ask her what God's book said about something.

In June, Tom began talking to Miss Mary again about leaving. "Miss Mary, how can I leave? I don't have a horse, and these boots are just so large for me I couldn't ever walk the twenty miles to Kelly! But once I get there I could wire fer some money from my bank account in Pueblo," explained Tom.

"Do you have a need, Tom? Do you really feel that you need a horse and some better boots? What does the Bible say about God supplying our needs and why we don't have some of the things we need?" asked Miss Mary.

"We have not because we ask not," replied Tom quietly.

They prayed for Tom. They prayed for God to show him what to do next. They prayed for a horse for him and for boots. After a week, God had sent nothing for Tom.

"Miss Mary, God didn't help me by sendin' me any boots or horse. Why?" asked Tom.

"God answers prayers in four ways, Tom. Sometimes he says 'no,' sometimes he says 'yes,' and sometimes he says 'wait,'" explained Miss Mary.

"Yes, no, and wait. That's only three! What's the fourth way, Miss Mary?" asked Tom."

"Do it differently!" replied Mary.

"Do it differently?" asked Tom puzzled.

"Yes, sometimes God gives us our needs, but in a different way than we think," explained Miss Mary. "Its going to be so pleasurable seeing what God is going to do!"

That week while working on Miss Mary's leaky roof, Tom looked up and saw dust in the distant desert. He knew that there were probably some animals causing the dust. The idea came to him that there were wild horse out here. He asked Miss Mary about it.

Miss Mary grinned, "This could be God's answer, Tom. We used to have wild horses running out here, but they have either all been caught or moved elsewhere."

Miss Mary gave Tom some rope, and he set out in his overly large boots to see if wild horses caused the dust. He still had a limp in his left leg.

Tom saw that wild horses caused the dust. He quietly followed and watched them and lay in wait for them to run by him. He remembered his time with Hoga and was thankful for what his Indian friends had taught him about being still.

Toward evening, the horses moved near the bushes that Tom was hiding behind. Tom jumped up and lassoed a large red-brown horse. He turned the rope around the base of the bush. The horse jerked the bush right out of the ground and almost jerked the rope out of Tom's hand, but he held on. As the horse reared and jerked, Tom held on tightly, but finally the horse began to drag him. The large boots came off the boy's feet. Tom let go, got up, and cursed, using God's name. The horse ran off, dragging the rope from its neck.

Tom stepped lightly back to the old boots, trying not to hurt his feet. Then he walked back to Miss Mary's shack and told her what had happened. Miss Mary brushed off Tom and sympathized with him.

"Miss Mary, I cursed God! I feel really awful about it!"

"It's good that you do, Tom. That shows that the Holy Spirit is at work in your heart. You must confess your sin to God; He will forgive you," encouraged Mary.

"Remember you told me about the hypocrites in Red Rock and about Frank Woods, and what a hard time you were having forgiving them? Well, you're in their shoes now. Just as God will forgive you for cursing, He will forgive those people, too," explained Miss Mary.

She continued, "Christians still fight the flesh and sometimes fail. That doesn't mean they aren't believers; it just means they need to walk closer to Christ by confessing their sins and being in the Bible."

"And Frank Woods..." Miss Mary continued with a pause, "You **have** to forgive him; not only for his sake, but also for your mother's and your own sake. If we don't forgive others, bitterness develops inside us that will cause us much hurt. The reason to pardon others is because Christ has forgiven us."

"I think I understand, Miss Mary, and I'm ready to be forgiven and to give forgiveness," said Tom quietly.

Tom prayed and told God what he had done and asked God to help him do better, and that if it were God's will that he would be able to catch the horse.

Early the next morning there was a knock on the door. Gray Fox was standing there. "I was on way to Kelly to sell moccasins. Wild horses run by. You try catch horse, Tom? I saw rope," asked Gray Fox.

"Yeah, but he jerked me right outa my boots and so I let go of 'im," explained Tom.

"Boots no good; you buy moccasins from me. Feel good, run fast," explained Gray Fox.

Tom turned and looked at Miss Mary.

Miss Mary smiled at Tom. "Do it another way," she said softly.

"But Miss Mary, I prayed for boots, not moccasins!" said Tom.

"You **want** boots. Your **need** is foot protection," answered Miss Mary.

Tom paused and thought for a moment and then grinned. "Gray Fox, I don't have any money to buy the moccasins," Tom said.

"Gray Fox thinks you help Gray Fox catch a horse for Gray Fox and for Tom and that will pay. Okay?" asked Gray Fox.

Tom looked at Miss Mary.

"I told you that God uses other people to help answer their prayers. You help Gray Fox catch a horse for him and it will also answer a prayer for Gray Fox," explained Miss Mary.

That afternoon, wearing amazingly comfortable Indian moccasins, Tom lassoed two horses after Gray Fox chased them toward Tom's hiding place. One was the red-brown, so Miss Mary's rope was recovered.

Gray Fox and Tom worked together the rest of that week to break the horses Indian style, without a saddle. That proved to be a week of building friendships for both of them.

Early Monday morning of the next week, Tom sat on the horse, looking down at Miss Mary standing on her porch.

"Well, look what God gave you, Tom Fleming! A nice looking grand horse and Indian boots!" exclaimed Miss Mary with delight.

"God's given me more than that, Miss Mary. He gave me life when I shoulda died, and He gave me eternal life when I don't deserve it. He also gave me yer love, Miss Mary. Thanks again for all ya did for me," said Tom.

"Don't forget to mail my letter to Jed. And go see your Mother," said Miss Mary.

"Ok, I will," said Tom hesitating to leave.

"Where will you go? What is God going to have you do?"

"I'm gonna hunt fer a certain girl until I find her and ask her if I can kiss her!" exclaimed Tom as he gave the saddleless horse a light kick. He went a little way, stopped, and looked back at the sad, yet happy, old missionary standing on the porch of her fixed-up old shack. She had been praying that someone would come and do the repairs.

"Good-bye, I love you," said the Christian cowboy; "I'm off to kiss a very special girl!"

ABOUT THE AUTHOR

Rich Mann grew up in the desert mountains of Arizona where he learned to enjoy and appreciate the beauty and adventure of the wilderness that surrounded his small home town of Ray. Frequent hikes into the mountains and "up the creek" became demanding treks that were sometimes harsh, but enjoyable. He learned a little of the value of the spirit of the western  pioneers who, a century earlier, had faced survival in the same desert area.

Rich trusted in Christ as his Savior while a youngster living in that small mining town. Around his freshmen year of high school, Rich realized the need to follow Christ completely and shun the evils of the world. He went to a Bible college, in Phoenix, AZ, now called Arizona Christian University. There he earned his BS in elementary education in 1973. Since college, Rich's career has been spent mostly teaching young people in Christian Schools.

The author resides in Phoenix with his wife, Kathy, where they enjoy their four children and ten grandchildren.